A CORPSE ON THE
BEACH

IZZY PALMER BOOK THREE

Copyright

This is a work of fiction. Names, characters, places, and incidents are either the product of the author's imagination or are used fictitiously. Any resemblance to actual persons, living or dead, events, or locales is entirely coincidental.

Copyright © 2020 by Benedict Brown

All rights reserved. No part of this book may be reproduced or used in any manner without written permission of the copyright owner except for the use of quotations in a book review.

First edition June 2020

Cover design by info@amapopico.com

To my wife Marion,
my daughter Amelie
and my accomplice Lucy.

Welcome Note

Welcome back, everybody, to another Izzy Palmer mystery. This is just a quick note about language in this book (not the rude kind.) The story is set in my adopted country and so there are a few references to Spanish words and phrases.

Most are very simple to understand in context, but I don't like it when writers use foreign languages without any explanation so, if you need it, everything is translated on the very last page of this book.

There are also several international characters who speak in a non-standard manner so, if you think you've found a typo, let's say that's the reason!

Thanks for reading and I hope you enjoy **"A Corpse on the Beach"**.

Prologue

The sun beat down in endless waves. I could feel my skin turning redder by the minute, but after the wettest September since British records began, I needed this. Lying on those Spanish sands, with no one else around, had recharged me after the strangest year of my life.

The cove where I was sitting was cut off from the main tourist areas and was only accessible through the grounds of the hotel. I'd woken up early to make the most of the solitude and couldn't help feeling a little proud of myself. It's not often that I'm first at something but I'd beaten every last guest to the beach. There were a few gulls around, running away from the water like children whenever the tide came near, but they didn't bother me and I didn't bother them.

I leaned back and listened to the sound of the sea. It had been years since I'd heard it. As a child, our regular daytrips down to the pebbly beaches of the south coast of England had been my greatest reward for good grades at school and inspired my choice of university. And now here I was; not at work, not at home, but on a distant beach at the beginning of October, just in time for an Indian summer.

It was only nine in the morning but, like some fancy goose in a fancy restaurant, I already felt as if I'd been cooked twice over. I had my copy of "Death on the Nile" with me, ready to be enjoyed, but I couldn't stop watching the tide rolling in and back out again. There was something hypnotic about the gentle swaying and switching. It was as if the waves were a puzzle that could only be solved if I concentrated hard enough.

It's curious to think what would have happened if I'd simply opened my book and got lost in Christie's elegant mystery that morning. My life is not the only one that would have been immeasurably different.

Even when I noticed it there, sticking up out of the sand, I could have stayed right where I was. I could so easily have taken it for some insignificant piece of sea-junk, carried across the Atlantic from who knows where; a hunk of polystyrene perhaps or maybe an old hubcap. But then, leaving things alone has never been my strong suit and I got to my feet. I thrilled in the feeling of warm sand beneath my toes as I padded between the foamy patches of sea spray on my way to investigate.

I couldn't make sense of what I was seeing at first. It was as if someone was playing a practical joke and, at any moment, she would jump out of the sand to scare me. But there she was, a pretty face looking straight at me; her lips Hollywood red, her eyes deep brown and her life extinguished.

For a moment, I thought I recognised her but then the tide washed in again and her features transformed. The look on her face was oddly serene and her long, dark hair splayed out in the water like seaweed. My heart stung a little as I noticed a slender wound on her forehead. I wished for a moment that it was just a game; that children had buried her in the sand to take a photo and would help her back out when it was done.

But if wishes were horses…

I think I'd known what I was about to find even before I got there. After three murder investigations in the space of six months, I'd come to expect dead bodies to pop up wherever I went. Perhaps if it had just been a foot poking out, she wouldn't have caught my eye, but that strange, half-moon shape rising above the surface had reeled me in.

Even after everything I'd seen, chancing upon a body like that made me stagger back to my towel in a daze. I stood there for a moment, staring at the red hardback book that I'd had since I was a child. I half wanted to reach down and open it. I had this ridiculous urge to skip to the end as if it could tell me who had killed the poor girl. Of course, I knew that real life doesn't work like that so I pulled out my phone and called the police.

Chapter One

There's something about corridors that I've never liked.
Does anyone actively like corridors then?
Perhaps it's the memory of sitting outside my headmistress's office in secondary school after she found out that I'd shared an intimate picture of Gary Flint. In my defence, he'd told Martin Thompson that I kissed like a giraffe, which annoyed me massively as, not only was it a really lazy insult – I'm tall, I know that – but I actually think giraffes would be pretty good kissers. They have huge tongues.

I remember sitting out in the hall, trying to work out if I'd be in less trouble if I told our appropriately named head Mrs Raven that the frankly unimpressive photo I'd shown to every girl in the sixth-form was a fake. I had a similar dilemma to deal with now.

"Miss Palmer?" The clerk emerged from the narrow entrance and held the door open for me.

"Miss Palmer is my mother," I said, wishing I could keep my mouth shut once in a while. "Well, actually her maiden name was Gibbs, but after she got divorced from my dad she kept her-"

"They're waiting for you." He was a very beige sort of person and did not appear to be charmed by my no doubt adorable chattering.

Ever since the date was fixed, I'd been dreading this moment. I walked through the door, up a few steps and emerged in the courtroom to be led over to the witness stand. Everyone was there waiting. It felt like I was the conductor and the orchestra couldn't start without me.

David was over in his little booth but I couldn't look at him just yet. I scanned the courtroom for friendly faces and found the Izzy Palmer fan club in the back row. There was Dean, Mrs Dominski from the newsagents, Ramesh, three quarters of my parents and obviously Mum's hairdresser too.

"Go, Izzy!" Fernando from Penge shouted.

He received an immediate glare from the judge. "Any more outbursts like that and I will clear the public gallery."

I've never understood why British judges and barristers wear long curly wigs. Presumably it's not a health and safety issue, like hairnets in a kebab shop. I wonder if there are rules about exactly what kind of wig it has to be, or whether they could get away with something a bit more modern these days. At the very least, it would be good to have some highlights to liven up the grey.

The prosecution rose and my interrogation began. "Miss Palmer, I'd like you to take us through the events of that fateful day in your own words."

"I had a curry pasty for breakfast."

Everyone in the courtroom laughed at that.

Even the prosecuting barrister failed to keep a straight face. "Perhaps you could skip to the moment you arrived at work."

"Oh, okay." It's fair to say I was a little on edge. "I went up in the lift with my colleague Suzie. She doesn't speak much and I felt very awkward. I do this thing whenever I'm with quiet people where I chat and chat and chat." I was doing it right then. "It's pretty embarrassing and, to be honest, I-"

"Miss Palmer, what I'd really like to know about is the moment you walked into Mr Thomas's office and what you saw there."

The courtroom fell silent and I dared a glance at David in the dock. If giving evidence against your boyfriend in a murder trial counts as a date, this would be our fourth. He looked calm – far more prepared for this than I was – and he smiled across at me supportively.

"The first thing I noticed was that Bob Thomas wasn't in his own chair. He was in front of his desk, not behind it and that struck me as odd." I was trying to get the whole thing out without stopping. "I knew that he was dead. There was something about the position of his body. It was slumped forward uncomfortably and I doubted that he was just asleep." I could no longer remember if what I was saying was actually true. "Oh, and the knife sticking out of his back, of course. That was a bit of a clue as well."

"You said you found it strange that he would not be in his own chair." David's enemy for the duration of the trial had a nasty glimmer in his eyes whenever he addressed me. "What exactly did that imply to you?"

I hesitated, then said the wrong thing anyway. "I thought that whoever had killed him must have held some power over Bob."

Izzy, are you listening to yourself?

"So, his boss for example?" The barrister smugly replied.

"No. I mean… No, that didn't enter my mind. It could have been anyone."

The bloke in the wig did not look happy with me. "I see. Please continue."

This was getting tricky. I didn't want to lie, but I didn't want to make David's life any more difficult than it had to be. Yes, he was a murderer, but he'd killed Bob for a very good reason. I sought out my mum's face in the crowd and could tell from her wincing expression that my performance wasn't up to standard.

"I had some work to give Bob so I decided to go in a bit further."

"You thought Mr Thomas was dead and yet you still wanted to give him the work he'd asked you for?"

Oops, he's got you there.

"Yes, but I'd never seen a dead body before and…" My words faded out. I could no longer remember what had compelled me to walk into a room with a corpse inside.

"Let's move on." The barrister shuffled some papers and looked up at me with a patronising smile. "How would you characterise your relationship with Mr David Hughes before the murder?"

"I didn't think he knew my name." My precarious balancing act wasn't going too well but at least I'd got a few more laughs from the gallery.

"But then, over the course of the next few weeks, the two of you started a romantic relationship, isn't that right?"

"You make it sound so sordid. I don't think-"

"A yes or no answer will suffice, Miss Palmer."

I didn't like this guy. "Yes."

"And would you say it's normal behaviour for a man to murder a colleague and start in on an affair with a younger member of staff mere days after the killing?"

The defence did not like that line of questioning. The slightly weary old man who was representing David lurched to his feet to object. "Leading question. Your honour, Miss Palmer is not on trial."

The judge deliberated silently for a moment. "Rephrase the question, Mr Barton. And can we please rein in the emotive language?"

"Very good, Your Honour." Nasty Mr Barton turned back my way. "Why was it that the two of you got together?"

11

I wasn't sure what had just happened but I answered anyway. "I think that people fall in love for all sorts of crazy reasons."

Izzy, get it together. You sound like you're quoting a pop song.

"I see." The barrister changed topic. "From what I hear, you're something of a murder mystery fan." I didn't think this required a response. "Was that what attracted you to the defendant?"

"I don't understand what you mean."

I could tell he was building up to another snide comment. I put my hands together in front of me and awaited the inevitable insinuation.

"Did it give you a thrill to be involved with a killer?"

The defence barrister was having none of it. "Your Honour, I must object to my learned friend's treatment of the witness." It suddenly occurred to me that he was the spitting image of my mum's uncle Bill.

The prosecution, meanwhile, looked like the villain from a Bond movie. "The question goes to the defendant's thinking at the time of the murder, Your Honour."

The judge wasn't impressed. "Mr Barton, I've given you one warning already." She looked down her nose disapprovingly at the slick young prosecutor in a way that only people with glasses can.

"Of course, Your Honour. It won't happen again."

The look of feigned innocence on his face right then told me he knew exactly what he was doing. He'd been pinging between topics and pushing the limits of what he was allowed to ask, solely to unnerve me. It had worked until now, but the fact he'd tried to manipulate me into giving the worst possible account of David's behaviour somehow gave me confidence. If my testimony was going to do anything but outright condemn him, I needed to find a way to shift the focus. I steeled myself for his next question.

"I believe you were the one who ultimately revealed the defendant's guilt."

"With a little help from my friends, yes." I looked at Mum once more, but the barometer of her face had not budged a millimetre.

"What was it that told you he was the killer?" Barton was too smooth for his own good and his question had given me a lifeline.

"There were five people who had access to the Porter & Porter server room from where the surveillance footage was removed. Each of them had their reasons for wanting rid of Bob Thomas." I checked the gallery to make sure Bob's wife wasn't there before continuing. "He was a very unpopular man and made working at P&P a nightmare for many of my colleagues. But the fact is that David Hughes was the only one who cared. The only one of us who was good and brave enough to put a stop to the terrible things that Bob took such pleasure from."

Go, Izzy, you've got him on the ropes. Forget about being a detective, you should become a lawyer.

There was some quietly impressed murmuring from the public and Mum gave me the half-smile I'd been hoping for. Mr Barton turned over the paper in front of him and searched for his next point of attack.

It was a long morning and I felt drained by the end of it. For every moment like this one, where I could support my favourite murderer, the prosecution managed three more in their favour. It was a strange sensation to be up there and sometimes felt like I was trying to erase the work I'd done to find Bob's killer in the first place. I never lied to protect David, but I wouldn't let them represent him as a monster either.

As the young barrister's argument developed, he accused me of being a murder junky, a busybody, a tramp and a co-conspirator, all in the roundabout, borderline polite way that is characteristic of British High Court trials. I was happy when lunch was finally called and I could have a break.

"You were amazing up there, Iz," Danny told me, when we convened in a café across the road from the court. He was looking at me in his usual excitable way, which had been a feature of our limited interactions over the last couple of months.

Ramesh was next to comment. "What I don't understand is why they have to have a trial if David admits he's the killer."

Everyone was there, huddled together around a table for four.

"Keep up, darling," my mother replied for me. "He's claiming diminished responsibility in the hope of getting a lesser sentence." I don't know why she was being so smug, I'd had to explain the exact same thing to her a month earlier. "He hopes to show the court that Bob's crimes and bullying had a psychological impact that drove him over the edge."

"It's like watching the telly," Dad put in as he emptied a bottle of ketchup into his bacon bap. "Only far longer and occasionally quite tedious. Could you pass the brown sauce, please?"

13

There was a moment of quiet munching as we tucked into the greasy plates of deliciousness that had been served up by the rather sleepy old woman, who appeared to be the only person working in the packed café.

I felt sorry for my techy millionaire mate, Dean, who was sandwiched between the exuberant Fernando and Mrs Dominski. Danny was sitting next to them and I was once more glad that he had adopted a more patient strategy than after his first attempt to woo me. Either way, I was still too hung up on David to even consider the previously unlikely possibility of us dating.

As we ate, small conversations broke out to dissect that morning's events and I chatted with Ramesh. "I think I need another holiday. The last one didn't cut it."

"I have days to use up before the end of the year if you fancy going somewhere together. Patricia and I were supposed to be heading to the Greek islands for a bit of sun but, since she got her new job, I've hardly seen her."

"Anywhere that isn't waterlogged and preferably free of corpses would be great."

"Oh come on, Iz." He smiled his big goofy smile. "You like the corpses."

"Thanks, Ramesh." I shot him a sarcastic look. "You make me sound like a psychopath."

"Tell you what, my uncle's just bought a hotel in Spain. I saw him at my grandad's funeral and he said we can go whenever we like. He showed me photos and it's pretty swanky."

I thought for a minute about whether Ramesh's idea of a swanky hotel would match up with my own. I didn't have any other offers of a holiday though, so I said, "Sounds perfect. Let's get through the trial first though."

After lunch, we managed to shed a couple of the less integral members of my mother's crime solving squad and sadly Dean had to leave early too.

"I'm sorry, but we're launching a new range of tracking devices this week and I should really get back." He wasn't apologising to me. He and mum had become firm friends since the investigation at Vomeris Hall. "It was lovely to see you, Rosie."

He went around shaking hands with everyone in turn. Dean was a shell of his former self – actually, wait, what's the opposite of a shell? He was suddenly friendly, polite and able to look people in the eyes. I kind of missed the nerdy weirdo I'd become friends with.

"Any luck on the dating front?" my mother enquired, before he could escape.

"Not for the moment." His gaze dropped to the ground and I caught a glimpse of the old Dean. "I think I'm going to take it slow from now on."

"Darling," my mother made this one word last about fifteen seconds. "You mustn't give up. The right person is out there waiting for you. What's your next step going to be?"

I could see that Dean wasn't comfortable with my mother's interrogation techniques so I helped him slip away. "Thanks so much for being here. I really appreciate your support."

"Come along then, Izzy my love." My father threaded his arm through mine to escort me back to court. "Let's get this over with."

Despite looking like my mum's sweet old uncle, the defence barrister's grilling that afternoon was just as hostile as the prosecution's had been. I thought he'd be on my side but he was quick to plant the idea in the jury's mind that I was a meddler who had interfered in the investigation for my own ends.

As long as it helped David, I didn't really mind, but it was not an experience I want to repeat. I kept catching his parents' eyes and feeling guilty for building the case against their son.

That evening, alone in my bedroom with only my faded James Blunt poster for company, I had a bit of a cry and wished David was there with me. Five seconds later, my phone rang.

"Hello, Izzy."

"David!" It still gave me a thrill when he used one of his limited calls to talk to me. My tears somehow dried on hearing his voice – such is the power of love. "I'm so sorry about today. Everything I said came out wrong."

"Don't worry about it, mate."

Mate? Why is he calling us mate?

It was hard to know how to reply. "Are you feeling alright?"

For a few seconds, all I could hear down the line was the faint murmur of people talking in the background. "Well, if my girlfriend giving evidence goes that badly, what do you think the rest of the trial will be like?"

It was my turn to drop into silence. I'd never heard him sound so negative. We'd spoken just a couple of days earlier and he thought his chances were good. But that was before I messed everything up.

"Izzy, I don't want you coming to the trial anymore," he said and my heart split in two. "It's not your fault, but today nearly killed me. My solicitor says we could be there for another week and I don't think I can bear seeing you suffer day after day."

One thought jumped out in my mind and it was all I could think to say. "But I love you, David." It was a line straight out of a soap opera.

His breathing had become short and noisy and his resonant voice dropped lower. "It's not about that. It's not about you and me. I just can't have you there. Consider it a favour if you like. For my sake, you have to let me do it alone."

I'd like to say I instantly respected where he was coming from and promised to stay away, but there was a lot more sobbing and insecurity to get through first. And when the conversation reached its conclusion, the last thing I said was, "You don't deserve to go to prison, David. It's not right."

"I love you, Izzy Palmer. I should have said it before." There was another painful hush. "Thank you so much for trying but I have to do this on my own now." And then he hung up before I could start crying again.

I lasted about five minutes on my own and then went back to my mobile and dialled someone who's always there for me when I need him.

"Ra, can you ring your uncle and find out when we can go to Spain? I really have to get away for a while."

Chapter Two

Two days later, at a ridiculous hour of the morning, we drove in Ramesh's car onto a Eurotunnel train headed for France. I should have known right then that this holiday was not going to go well. We could have flown straight to Santander but, with his girlfriend working long hours, Ramesh couldn't leave his cats Elton John and Kiki Dee on their own. So there they were, crammed into the back of his little white Ford, staring angrily at us through the bars of their cat carriers.

"It's not my fault, Iz," my best friend claimed. "Elton hasn't forgiven me for putting them in a cattery when I went to Edinburgh last month. If I'd stuck him on a plane, he'd never have spoken to me again."

The tomcat let out a screeching howl to which Kiki quickly joined in. It was like a feline cover version of "Don't Go Breaking My Heart" except that it lasted all thirty-five minutes of the channel crossing.

I said nothing but my face told Ramesh everything he needed to know.

Sadly for me (and the big, fluffy tortoiseshell cats in the back) my friend is a uniquely terrible driver. I don't quite understand how he has a licence as he doesn't appear to know how to steer or change gears. He executed the thousand mile journey almost exclusively in second, with the motor revving like the engine on a transatlantic cruise liner. He went slowly on motorways, fast on country roads and seemed determined to go round each roundabout we came to at least three times. It gave me a greater appreciation for my mother's idiosyncratic driving skills.

By the time we got past Paris, Ramesh had capitulated and allowed Kiki and Elton to break their imprisonment and wander free across the luggage which was piled up in the back of his car. An hour later, I could take it no more and insisted that we stop for a break from the symphony of engine torture, catty wailing and Ramesh's attempts to sing along to French chansons on the radio – without knowing more than three words of French, one of which was fromage.

"It's not my fault I studied Spanish at school."

We were eating ham-and-cheese-filled croissants beside the motorway. "Yes, but nobody made you sing along."

He looked at me like I was being thoroughly unreasonable. "If the song is catchy, I can't help it. It's practically a medical condition."

"In that case, I'll choose what we listen to from now on and it's going to be Japanese industrial noise music from here to Santander."

Back in the car, I fired up the app on my phone and searched for the least singalong-able option I knew. Sadly, within ten minutes, Ramesh had found a way through the walls of radio static and endless bass and was imitating the high-frequency beeps and scratches, in a French accent.

Fun fact, I once dated a guy who was really into Japanese industrial noise music. And yes, I did pretend to like it too. And no, the relationship did not last long.

Urggggghhhh, Nigel. Shudder.

Oddly, that cacophonous noise helped to calm the cats down. Kiki came to sit on my lap in the passenger seat and Elton curled up in a ball on a stack of Ramesh's Heat magazines and fell fast asleep. I lasted it out for about three tracks before I decided that French radio was the lesser evil.

"Bonjour, croissant fromage," Ramesh was soon chanting once more, to the tune of an old Céline Dion song. "Croissant fromage, bonjour."

Around Bordeaux, Ramesh got tired of singing and decided to discuss his current favourite topic. "Izzy, I've come up with a name for your new company. 'IP PI' Detective Agency. What do you reckon? IP, for your initials and PI, like a private eye."

I thought about it for a minute. "Nice try, but I don't want to start the name of my company with, 'I pee pee…'"

"Hmmm, good point." He quickly brightened up again and landed upon another idea. "What about Miss Palmer Investigates? You know, like Miss Marple."

"Not bad." I'd definitely heard worse suggestions, most of which were from my mother.

"Have you ever noticed that Palmer and Marple are anagrams?"

He turned from the road to look at me and I got very scared that we were about to hurtle into oncoming traffic so I pointed at the approaching truck in panicked fear.

"Yes, I have noticed that," I said, once disaster had been averted and I could breathe again. "When I was a teenager I thought it was a sign I'd be a real detective one day."

We were overtaken by an old lady on a bicycle, but Ramesh kept smiling. "I bet it was!" He reached forward to turn the radio up, again forgetting to focus on the task at hand. "Oooh, I like this one."

He sang along to a Gallic rap song and I put my fingers back in my ears. Finally, after about twelve hours, we crossed the border into Spain and I no longer had to listen to those made up French lyrics.

"Buenos días, Buenos días, queso… croissant," he crooned instead.

"I thought you said you studied Spanish at school?"

With his eyes on the road for once, he looked put out. "I did, Isobel. That doesn't mean I'm any good at it. How do you say croissant in Spanish anyway?"

I may not have mentioned before, but there are a few areas where I excel. Aside from detective work, I play a mean accordion, bowl a 280 average and speak Spanish to a C1 level. I learnt it at school but didn't get really good until university when I spent every summer taking courses and teaching English in a few different places on the Mediterranean coast. I still didn't know how to say croissant though.

"I'd go with, ensaïmada. They're Spanish and a bit like croissants. Except that they're sweeter and covered in powdered sugar." We were driving past the exit for San Sebastian and Ramesh suddenly wrenched the steering wheel to send us towards the off ramp. The cars he cut in front of expressed their disapproval with lengthy honks.

"What the hell are you doing?" I asked as I grabbed hold of Kiki to stop her flying across the car.

"It's your fault. You've given me a hankering for ensaïmadas."

The unexpected pit stop turned into a lengthy break in the journey as first we had to find a bakery, and then we had to look through three more as none of them sold ensaïmadas. By the time we'd found our tasty treat, we were hungry enough for dinner.

We parked the car and searched out an incredibly busy bar on the seafront, which sold tiny morsels of deliciousness stacked on top of crusty bread.

"This is the best pincho de tortilla I've eaten in my whole life," Ramesh declared as we sat looking across the golden sands and over to the pretty island within the bay of San Sebastian. Countless boats bobbed up and down in the water and, on the far hilltop, a gigantic statue of Jesus smiled down at his dad's creation. The sun was dropping behind the headland, but the air was still toasty. It finally felt like we were on holiday.

I let out a sigh of contentment then felt guilty for not thinking about David in the last five minutes.

"Listen, Izzy, I know I'm not the easiest person to travel with." Ramesh sounded genuinely sorry. "I'm really excited about being on holiday with you though."

I tossed a scrap of jamón to the floor for Kiki and Elton to fight over. "Me too, Ra. Thanks for bringing me."

Chapter Three

It was already dark by the time we finished dinner and we didn't reach the hotel until late.

"Hello?" came the reply, when we finally pulled up to the grand gate of The Cova Negra Hotel and Spa and Ramesh pushed the buzzer to be let in.

"Uncle? Is that you?"

"Who is this?" The man spoke with a thick Indian accent, characteristic of the older members of Ramesh's family and, I had to assume, Indian people in general.

"It's me, Uncle. It's Ramesh." He waited for any sign of recognition. "Mum told you I was coming."

"Ramu? But I thought that was next October. I haven't prepared for your stay. You'll just have to come back then."

I looked at Ramesh, he looked at me. We both wanted to cry.

The intercom crackled and then burst into life. "I got you there, my boy." Mechanised laughter boomed out of the little speaker.

The gate clicked open as if pushed by some invisible hand and Ramesh crept the car forward. I don't know what I was expecting when he'd first mentioned his uncle's hotel, but this wasn't it. A huge blue and white, four-storey building stood large at the end of the stately drive. I could see the glow of an outdoor swimming pool, reflecting off the side of the hotel and pretty gardens stretched across the grounds.

We pulled up beyond an illuminated fountain with a statue of a young boy holding a porpoise as its centrepiece. A short man in a neat black suit and matching tie descended the stairs at the entrance as Kiki jumped from my lap and out of the window.

"Don't worry about her," Ramesh said. "She'll turn up in a couple of days once she's got the measure of the place."

"Ramu!" The man exhaled and pulled my friend from the car with great joy. "Little Ramu, you're all grown up. I haven't seen you since your grandfather's funeral."

"That was about three weeks ago, uncle."

The little man laughed. "I know but you've got awfully big since then."

I got out of the car and Ramesh made the introductions. "Izzy, this is my Uncle Kabir."

"It's a pleasure to have you here, Izzy." He opened his arms and spun around on the spot, as if he was just as impressed by the place as I was. "What do you think of my new venture? Not bad, eh?"

His great, noisy laugh exploded out to us once more. He was a very round man with chubby cheeks and dyed black hair. His hefty paunch was supported by two short legs and he had a manner of constant busyness even when he was standing completely still.

"It's amazing, uncle." Ramesh's eyes, were possibly wider than mine right then. "I thought you were just going to buy a little B&B somewhere. This place is a palace."

"Well, you only retire once." He spoke in a self-deprecating manner, like it was really no big deal. "Now let's get you inside and I'll show you to your rooms. We're practically closed at the moment, Izzy, so you can have your pick."

Ramesh grabbed Elton and, suddenly full of energy, we ran up the steps.

Uncle Kabir explained the situation as we entered the foyer. "We did the full summer season but I've taken the hotel off all the apps and websites until spring next year so that I can concentrate on stamping my own identity on the place. The only people here are a few existing bookings I couldn't cancel. I have extra waiting staff who come in to help and a cook working, but most of the hotel is shut down."

We'll have to have a word with the cook about her lemon meringue pie.

There's more to life than dessert you know.

How dare you!

The entrance hall was dominated by an obscenely large crystal chandelier. It was so big that it looked like it would bring the ceiling down at any moment. The rich red carpet beneath my feet was thick and springy and every ornament, fixture and frame in the room was painted gold.

Kabir popped behind the gilded reception desk and unhooked two keys. "Izzy, you will be in The Presidential Suite."

"Wow, did a president stay here then?"

"That's right!" I loved this guy, he was even more enthusiastic than

Ramesh. "The president of the North Cantabrian Agricultural Society has stayed here for their annual meeting the last five years running."

Hmmm. Slightly disappointing.

Kabir turned to his nephew. "And, Ramesh, you will be in one of the staff bedrooms, next to mine. Your mother told me to keep a close eye on you and I like to keep her happy."

"Uncle! How is that fair?"

I felt genuinely sorry for my unfortunate friend, but that didn't stop me launching myself up the sweeping staircase, in search of The Presidential Suite. Unsurprisingly, Elton the cat decided to join me.

"Third floor, Izzy," Kabir shouted after us. "I'll have somebody send up your bags once my lazy nephew unloads them from the car."

I broke into a sprint and made it to the top level of the hotel in no time. My room was the first door I came to. Elton seemed almost as excited as I was and I fumbled with the key card to open the door.

"Oh my giddy goat." The space in front of me was like something from the golden days of Hollywood. It made my room at Vomeris Hall look like my room at home. The colour scheme was hideous, all pinks, peaches and purples, but that didn't detract from the luxury on display all around me. "Elton," I said to the cat who was already getting comfortable on a plush pink sofa, "I'm never leaving this place. They'll have to drag my cold, dead body out when I'm ninety-five."

I ran inside, planning to belly-flop onto the bed, when I realised I still hadn't reached the bedroom. Two great double doors divided the space into a living room – complete with a feature-wall television and walk-in mini bar – and sleeping area. On opening those doors, I beheld a sight which I'd never imagined possible.

"A six-poster bed!" I couldn't quite believe my eyes. "Now that is swanky."

I was about to check out the bathroom when I decided it was all too overwhelming and that I needed a sit down first. My suite had three balconies to choose from and each one gave a view over the gardens towards the cliffs and beaches of the Cantabrian coast. It was past midnight but a warm breeze still swirled about.

On the patio beneath me, I caught my first sight of the other guests. There were tables set out across the elegant terrace. On the far left, in line with the path which led down to the sea, a woman dressed in a full-length silk gown was smoking a cocktail cigarette.

"Everything goes downhill. What's good one year is rarely good the next and I've been coming here for a decade." She couldn't have been more than fifty, but spoke with the weariness of a woman far older.

A man directly beneath where I was standing called back to her. "Oh, I know that. I don't have a problem with them doing the place up. I just can't stand how creepy it is here without anyone else around."

He was a little younger than her and was dressed for a day on the beach. He sported the kind of vest that old men wear under their shirts, paired with lurid green shorts that stopped high above the knees. Every trace of skin he had on show was bright pink.

If you work really hard, you'll look like that by this time tomorrow, Iz!

They were sitting half a building away from one another and were practically shouting to be heard over the sound of the crashing waves. Two children were trying to kick one another nearby and, from the look of their clothes, I assumed the man was their father.

"It could be worse," the woman stated. "Three years ago this place was infested with Belgians. Now, I'm no racist, but if there's one group of people I can't stand it's Belgians. Are they French? Are they Dutch? I wish they'd make up their minds."

Just then, she caught sight of me and tipped her head back to get a better view. "Oh look, a newbie. You're not Belgian, are you?"

For a moment, I didn't know how to respond. "Urmmm, no. But my dad's cousin has a timeshare in Brussels."

The man swivelled in his chair to look up at me. "Oh good, another Brit. We were just saying how we're normally outnumbered in these parts."

The woman picked up an empty cocktail glass from her table and raised it in my direction. "I'm Delilah Shaw," she said in a manner which suggested I should already know her name. "Why don't you come down to the bar and we'll get Kabir to mix us a round of Manhattans?"

The drink was tempting, the company not so much.

"I think I'm going to call it a night," I told her. "It's been a long day; we drove all the way from London."

She did not reply, but raised one eyebrow to suggest she didn't agree with my decision.

"No doubt we'll see you over breakfast." The comprehensively ruddy man had already turned away before finishing his sentence.

I was tempted to linger to hear what else this odd pair might have to say when there was a desperate knock on the door and I went to see who it was.

"Izzy, I'm about to drop these," a voice said from behind a pile of walking luggage. "Take one, would you?"

I removed a bag from the pile to reveal Ramesh's face. He staggered into the room with my remaining cases and dumped them down on the sofa, sending Elton screeching into the bedroom.

"Why do you have so much stuff with you anyway?" He was particularly pouty having lugged my possessions up from the car.

I figured I'd use his sort of logic back on him. "I've got so much stuff with me because I'm really bad at packing. You should think yourself lucky I didn't take the extra case with the kettlebells I bought several years ago and keep promising myself I'll use. I was this close to bringing them."

Having caught his breath and stretched out his back, my travelling companion had a chance to take in the suite I'd been given. "I can't believe Uncle put you in here. My room would fit in your wardrobe."

"Sorry, Ramesh. But do you mean the wardrobe/dressing room with its rotating electronic shoe racks and mirrored ceiling, or the Napoleon the third antique beside my six-poster bed?" I would probably have been more sympathetic if I hadn't had Edith Piaf's seminal "La Vie en Fromage" stuck in my head.

"You have a six-poster bed?" He sounded just as impressed as I'd been. "Is that even a thing?"

"It is now."

A cheeky look crossed his face. "Izzy… Can we jump up and down on it?"

I didn't answer, but ran into the bedroom to get the best spot on the humungous mattress. Fifteen minutes later, we finally got tired of acting like children. I'd also got tired of being awake.

"I think I'd better go to sleep before I crash out unconscious and split my head open on some valuable piece of furniture. You can sleep in one of the spare rooms if you like?"

Ramesh looked disappointed as he climbed down from the bed. "No, it's fine. I don't want Uncle to tell my mum on me. I'll go back to the single mattress on the floor of my plain white room with a toilet in the corner."

"Hey, at least it's en suite." This did not cheer him up. "Sorry mate. You can come up here whenever you like."

His face had fallen a few millimetres further. "Come on, Elton John. Daddy's going home now." He put his hands out and attempted a big smile but Elton stayed right where he was, licking his fur from buttock to foot, pretending that he hadn't heard.

"Night, Ramesh. I'll see you in the morning."

He turned and shuffled out of the door without another word. Alone once more, I took a peek over the balcony but the other guests had retreated into the bar. Muffled voices and the occasional clink of a glass floated across the deserted terrace.

Still in my London 2012 Olympics T-shirt from the journey, I peeled my jeans off and climbed into my colossal six-poster. Elton came to stretch out beside me. He was the first man I'd shared a bed with in months and, ten seconds later, I was fast asleep.

Chapter Four

Breakfast the next morning was served on the patio.

I'd been planning to get up early to make the most of the day, but failed to emerge from my room until ten o'clock. When I got downstairs to the dining room, I was surprised to see Ramesh in a crisp white shirt and black bowtie, serving hot drinks.

"Save me, Izzy," he mouthed as he bussed a tray full of empties back towards the kitchen.

"Don't worry about the boy," his uncle told me. "A bit of hard work will do him good." He was standing by the French windows onto the patio, welcoming each new table of diners. Now, Izzy, what can he get you? Tea, coffee, hot chocolate, herbal infusion?"

Ooh, tough one.

"I think I'll go with some hot chocolate please, Kabir."

He pointed me to an empty table beside the glamorous yet trashy Delilah Shaw and disappeared back into the dining room.

Dressed in a loose-fitting, gauzy beach dress, she looked at me in the haughty manner I'd already come to expect from her. "That's the wonderful thing about Indians, they're very good at taking commands."

For someone who claims she's not a racist, she makes an awful lot of racist remarks.

I wanted to deliver some really smart retort to shut her up but nothing came to mind. I smiled submissively and then felt bad about it.

While I waited for Ramesh to appear with my drink, I took in the world around me. The terrace was raised above the level of the formal gardens and tennis court which occupied most of the space between the hotel and the cliffs. Further along the coast, large towns were visible with the typical, towering white buildings of Spanish coastal resorts, but The Cova Negra was a perfectly isolated enclave, for those who could afford it.

The British man I'd spoken to from my window the night before was there with his family. His sneezy wife and rowdy children looked equally sunburnt and he was struggling to play peacemaker between them. The contrast with the adjacent table could not have been more dramatic. A man of about fifty with slicked-back, silver hair, wearing fine clothes like he'd just stepped off a yacht, was talking to his three perfectly behaved daughters. In immaculate black and white dresses with red ribbons in their hair, the girls looked identical. They had very dark features and, from the faint notes I could hear of their father's sermon, I guessed that they were Italian.

On the other side of the patio, an old Spanish couple were enjoying their silence together. Neither made eye contact as they covered their toast with pureed tomatoes and olive oil. The woman wore a bright floral dress and the man was kitted out for a tennis match. There was something very unusual about them and I struggled to pull my eyes away. If it hadn't been for a sudden outburst back at the Italians' table, I could have watched them all morning.

The girls' mother had appeared and did not look happy. Italian is not so similar to Spanish that I could understand more than a few words. I know that she was complaining that they would be late, but the only other thing I caught was a brief phrase in the middle of so much Latin flair.

Ramesh would have transcribed it as something like this, "Bongiorno lasagne Next Phase cannelloni Donatello." When she said those two English words, heads around the patio began to turn.

A moment later, the sunburnt Brit came to speak to them, presumably happy to escape from his own squabbling family.

"Mr Romanelli? Just thought I'd introduce myself. Ian Dennison's the name. Sorry to intrude, but I'm a great admirer."

Mrs Romanelli looked shell-shocked and cast her eyes to the table as if she needed permission to speak to him. Her husband was similarly taken aback by the intrusion but soon found his words. "Nice to meet you, Ian," he replied with a thick, almost musical accent. "We are all looking forward to tomorrow."

I was unable to hear the rest of the conversation as Ramesh had returned with my hot chocolate.

"Iz, you've got to help me." I could tell from his frazzled expression that he'd been up since the dawn. "I swear my uncle only allowed us to come here so that he could use me as cheap labour."

"That's terrible. It sounds more like slave labour." I took a sip from my drink. It was delicious. "You've got to stand up for yourself."

At that moment, Kabir came to check on his new employee's

performance. "Have you told Izzy about the continental buffet breakfast?"

"No, uncle, I was just-"

"So get to it." Kabir was clearly a hard-nosed businessman. "And don't call me uncle in front of the guests. They don't need to know our family history."

Ramesh peered between me and his boss and when it was clear his uncle was not leaving until he'd performed the task, he launched into his spiel. "Good morning, Madam. Here at The Cova Negra Hotel and Spa, our guests are entitled to a full continental breakfast. Cooked options are available on request. Do you have any special dietary requirements?"

"None whatsoever. Just keep the hot chocolates coming." I honestly felt terrible for Ramesh's situation, but who else would serve me breakfast if he didn't? And besides, it was only fair. I kept having traumatic flashbacks to the twenty different near misses we'd had on our journey.

Ramesh hurried away, but not before attracting the approving glance of Delilah Shaw, who clicked her tongue appreciatively the moment his back was turned, like a lecherous hen.

"That's another great thing about Indians," she said with a leer. "The young ones come in pretty packages."

For the first time in my life, someone had made me feel cheap and seedy just for being a woman. I wanted to run upstairs and have another shower.

I took my plate back into the dining room and filled it with seven types of pastry and a selection of cold cuts. I was pacing myself. Tomorrow I'd sample the English breakfast. By the time I'd got back to the patio, most of the other guests were preparing to leave. Fifteen minutes later, the only person remaining was a bloke about my age, sitting on his own beside the garden wall.

He had a smiley face and a well-trimmed beard. His hair was dark, his skin late-summer brown and he sat very upright, like he was waiting for a job interview. Our chairs were pointed directly at one another and I felt self-conscious as I stuffed mini pain au chocolat after mini pain au chocolat into my mouth.

In Spain they're known as mini-napolatinas.

Thanks a lot. Where was that kind of knowledge when I needed to translate *croissant* yesterday?

It was becoming a bit silly that I hadn't said anything to my breakfast companion. But, instead of waving hello and starting in on a conversation, I decided to be British and swivelled my chair away. I was relieved when he finally left and I could gorge myself in peace.

"So, Izzy, what have you got planned for today?" Kabir asked as he cleared the last few plates which Ramesh had left behind.

"I thought we might head down to the beach." I smiled back at him. Despite his slave-driving tendencies, I couldn't help but like the cheerful little man. He reminded me of an Anglo-Indian Poirot.

"You're very kind to think of me, Izzy." He tilted his head appreciatively. "But I'm afraid I am too busy for sunbathing today."

I laughed at his joke. "I meant Ramesh, but you're welcome to join us too."

"I'm sorry, but your friend will also be busy. I lost my best chambermaid yesterday and somebody has to make up the rooms." Kabir glanced across to his nephew who was polishing silverware by the breakfast buffet. "It'll do that boy good to experience some proper work instead of all this playing about on computers that he normally gets up to."

Ramesh must have caught what his uncle said as there was a clattering of falling cutlery and Kabir rushed off to chastise him.

I took my time getting changed before indulging in a leisurely stroll around the gardens. The old Spanish couple, whose names I soon learnt were Sagrario and Celestino, were busy shouting insults at one another in thick Andalusian accents over a tennis net, but the rest of the grounds were free of people. I wandered along a curling path past more fountains and flower beds until it led me down to the beach. I was not the first to arrive.

It seemed like everyone from the hotel was already there, laid out on beach towels and hotel loungers. The handsome Italian father and his daughters were splashing about in the sea, and there were two young German women, playing volleyball nearby. The cove was small, with little more than a spit of sand when the tide was in, and was enclosed by imposing cliffs. The land stretched out into the water on either side to prevent uninvited members of the public from having access to this exclusive spot. I spread my towel out near the rocks and got to work coating myself in factor fifty from forehead to toenail.

I've always loved people-watching and the beach is one of the best places to do it. I spent that morning creating imagined personas for each of my fellow guests. Ian Dennison and his perfectly British family became undercover Interpol agents on the search for the two young, suntanned Germans – who didn't let the ball touch the water for the first half an hour I was there. The Germans themselves were an up-and-coming synth pop duo who were using their burgeoning career to hide a narco-trafficking operation that extended from the ports of southern Spain to the frozen tundra of Lapland.

Delilah Shaw, now free from her gossamer dress and laid out with only a bikini bottom to protect her modesty, was a more difficult proposition to uncover. Black widow? Minor Royal? In the end I decided she was a frustrated housewife who had abandoned her family and set off in search of the sun.

Mr Romanelli was equally tricky. People kept coming up to talk to him throughout the morning. Not just Ian Dennison, but the smiley chap I'd shared the patio with took a photo and even Sagrario and Celestino, when they appeared, red-faced, after their tennis match, felt compelled to say hello. He was clearly well known and looked more like a politician than a film star, but I didn't recognise him.

One thing I could confirm, with all the investigative nous I'd built up over my three murder investigations, was that the Italian was a stone-cold silver fox. He may have been twenty years older than me, but I'd never seen such a ripped body – he made Danny look like a puny schoolboy. He could swim across the bay in no time and I couldn't stop watching his wide, muscular back which was covered by a tiger-head tattoo. It seemed to be roaring at me as he frolicked with his kids.

The German girls had been glancing at him the whole time and, when they finally got up the courage to approach, posed for a selfie with their three smiley faces sandwiched together. Delilah was the only one there who didn't take an interest in him. In fact, the only time she moved was to turn over to continue her roasting.

Halfway through the morning, the woman who I assumed was Mrs Romanelli appeared at the top of the cliff to shout down to her husband. She didn't sound any more cheerful than she had at breakfast and her family quickly collected up their possessions and scampered back to the hotel.

Perhaps that's just how she speaks? Scottish people always sound like they're about to start an argument, maybe Italians are the same.

I wasn't in the mood to point out to myself that two nations of people could not constantly be angry. Talk about a twisted mind.

When the morning was done, the beach was vacated and everybody retreated from the midday sun to have lunch back at the hotel. I, on the other hand, had come prepared. I had sandwich-making provisions left over from our road trip and I could hide beneath a blue and white parasol that was slightly too small for me but did the job. If it hadn't been for the occasional cry of a child, floating over from the dining room, and the sight of a small fishing craft, far out to sea, I might have imagined I was completely alone in the world.

For a few seconds it was bliss.

I felt the warm breeze on my skin and the sun just about catching the tips of my toes. The wind whispered, the sea audibly sighed but, the moment that rare feeling of tranquillity rose up within me, I remembered what was happening back home. My stomach knotted up like a ball of string and I couldn't stop the tears coming to my eyes.

David's plea for me not to attend the trial did nothing to assuage my guilt that I was sitting on a beach of my own while the prosecution painted him as a savage murderer. If nine-hundred miles and a luxury hotel couldn't distract me, there was only one thing that could. I reached into my drawstring beach bag and removed my battered copy of "Death on the Nile". I'd read it at least five times before, but immediately drifted off with Poirot to that equally beautiful setting far, far away.

Chapter Five

I spent the afternoon in my book trance, only snapping out of it to pull my ridiculously long limbs back from the scorching sunlight. Inevitably, despite my near military efforts to the contrary – sun cream, sun hat, parasol (which, in Spanish, literally means *stop sun*) – I still left the beach that afternoon three shades closer to a tomato than I had been that morning.

Back in my room, I had a quick shower of after-sun before changing for dinner. Walking down those elegant staircases, in what was, for me, a surprisingly appropriate evening dress, I felt like the hundred thousand pounds in my bank account (that I still wasn't quite sure what to do with). Sadly, there was a huge, golden mirror in the foyer which served to disillusion me of the idea. Under the light of the grand chandelier, my skin turned neon and my teeth glowed yellow for some reason. I looked like I'd made myself up to go to a Halloween rave.

Ramesh was working in the bar, pouring gin and tonics for the two German girls. Smiley breakfast man was there too, knocking back a whisky on his own. The place was far busier than at breakfast. There must have been forty new guests in the dining room and two waiters running about delivering food as Kabir oversaw the work.

"It's a coach party from France," he told me. "They're just here for the night. There's a conference in Santander tomorrow and there was a problem with their hotel." He didn't sound happy about it and pleaded for my understanding. "I couldn't turn down such a big booking, Izzy. I really couldn't."

He immediately bustled off to see to a frowning guest and I went to visit Ramesh at the bar. I got the message that he was pretending not to know me.

"Lemonade with a dash of lime, please, barman." I figured that sounded more grown-up than my usual drink of lemonade with a dash of lemonade. "And go easy on the ice."

He nodded respectfully and got to work.

"Are you here for Next Phase?" one of the girls asked as she played with the stirrer in her drink.

We're on holiday, Izzy. We can be whoever we like.

33

"Oh, yes. Yes, I definitely am."

The second girl beamed at me. "It's going to be amazing. We've come all the way from Austria."

Austria, Germany; we weren't far off.

Up close, the two ~~German~~ Austrian girls looked quite different from one another. The first had big brown eyes and dark features and the other was pale with golden hair. They wore the exact same expression though and I wondered if they were related.

"Where have you come from?" The blonde asked and I decided that my adopted persona for the evening would be someone who answers questions in a weird way.

"West Wickham."

They looked at one another uncertainly before taking a guess where that was.

"Great Britain?" the brunette replied. "Ah, yes. You have a fine political tradition."

Her friend agreed with this wholeheartedly. "Yes, our countries have very strong links. And they will only get stronger as the movement progresses."

I had no idea what they were talking about but I was having fun, so joined in with their nonsense. "Yes, I see a bright shining future for all of us."

This seemed to be what they wanted to hear and they smiled approvingly.

"Heike and I got a photograph with Marco Romanelli on the beach today." The blonde pulled her phone out and the selfie they'd taken was already set as her screensaver.

"You're so lucky." I was sure they would catch the tone in my voice, before remembering that sarcasm isn't the done thing on the continent. "I wish I had the guts to go and talk to him, he's dreamy."

They looked puzzled again and Heike, the brunette, felt the need to correct me. "Oh, no. It's his ideas that Lio and I connect with." Perhaps afraid that her message wasn't getting through, she continued in the loveably serious manner that Central Europeans often maintain. "We love him for his mind."

"Oh, exactly. That's what I meant. His mind is just... dreamy." The tennis match of their approval had swung in my favour and they looked relieved that we'd found common ground once more.

Ramesh sniggered quietly and I decided to boost my standing with my companions. "Were you listening to our conversation, barman?" I narrowed my eyes to glare at him before turning back to Heike and Lio. "You have to put these people in their place, don't you think?"

They both nodded appreciatively.

"That's right." Lio glanced at her watch and I could see she wasn't the type of Austrian to buck stereotypes. "We have a booking for dinner at eight o'clock."

"Why don't you join us for drinks after?"

I did a weird sideways head nod, like a monk in a silent order, and they waved from three feet away and went in search of their table.

"What's going on?" I asked Ramesh once they'd gone.

"Uncle put me behind the bar. He says I'm not to talk to the guests like they're friends but to talk to my friends like they're guests."

"Not that. I mean, why are all the people staying at this hotel so strange?"

He stopped polishing the glass he was holding and raised it to the light. "Don't ask me. I just work here."

I felt a tap on my shoulder just then and turned to see the bloke from breakfast leaning against the bar. "Excuse me, are you Izzy Palmer?"

"Last time I checked." I always know just the wrong thing to say.

He looked me over for a moment without speaking. I kind of liked the idea that he was a very conscientious courier, who preferred to take his time and get to know the receiver before delivering his package.

"My name's Álvaro Linares." Another pause, another quick flick of the eyes. "I read all about you in the papers."

"Oh, thank you very much." I didn't know what else to say.

"What is it? Two murders you've solved single-handedly already?"

Three, but who's counting?

"Three, but who's counting?" Oops, that was supposed to stay in my head.

"Could be dangerous here with you around!" He flicked his floppy fringe from his eyes and knocked back the last drop of his drink. Putting his glass down on the bar, he winked and walked off to a table in the corner of the room.

"See," I said, "another weirdo."

"Izzy, you're famous." Ramesh sounded less impressed than I would have expected. Clearly the job was already getting to him.

I knew that the Porter case in particular had been widely reported. A friend from uni had sent me a clipping from Le Poste in France. So I was already aware that word of my Miss-Marpling had reached mainland Europe, but it was no big deal.

Gosh. You're so humble, Izzy, not to mention modest! Has anyone ever told you how humble-

Shhh! There are more important issues to think about.

"Have you heard of this Next Phase thing?" I picked up my sophisticated drink and enjoyed the feel of the cool, wet glass in my hand.

Ramesh was busy checking that the paper cocktail umbrellas were all neatly folded away. "It's some kind of conference. The guy who runs it is staying here. I think he's a lifestyle guru or something." He stopped what he was doing and looked up at me cheerfully. "Uncle says I can have an hour off for dinner once everyone's eating. Will you wait for me?"

"I suppose so. But I'll struggle to resist ordering any jamón croquetas before you join me. They're practically my number one reason for coming to Spain."

His eyes flicked to the middle distance and I could practically hear his tummy rumble. "And chorizo and little Padrón peppers and potato omelette!"

"Ramesh," his uncle interrupted. "I'm not paying you to stand around talking."

"You're not paying me at all," my friend countered.

"Which is lucky for you or else I'd have to cut your wages." Kabir pulled himself up to his full height. For a short man, he had an impressive bearing. "Oh fine. Just take your break now, but I expect to see you back here after dinner."

He didn't stick around for his nephew's thanks but rushed off to put out fires in the kitchen, hopefully only metaphorically.

Ramesh and I had dinner together in a private dining room that was even plusher than the main space. The two waiters that Kabir had hired were from the nearby village and I got to amaze them with my slightly above average Spanish.

Eyes wide in wonder, Ramesh was equally impressed. "It's like there's a whole other person lurking inside you… and she's Spanish." He spoke through a mouthful of calamari. "Iz, what do they call that tomato bread they eat here?"

"It's called pan con tomate." I admit I was enjoying showing off to him.

"And what do they call Padrón peppers?"

I snatched one from the plate and popped it in my mouth. It was spicier than I was expecting and I had to have a slug of red wine. "They're pimientos de Padrón."

"What about chorizo?" Ramesh has a degree in computers (or something) and one of the finest mathematical minds of anyone I know. For a clever person, he can be a complete idiot sometimes.

"It's called chorizo, Ra. It comes from Spain."

"That's brilliant!" I think I'd blown his mind. "They have the same word as us."

After dinner, we returned to the bar and went back to pretending that we didn't know one another. This wasn't a problem as the resident cougar Delilah Shaw kept Ramesh busy all evening. The lobster-human hybrid, Ian Dennison was there too and told me in excruciating detail about his classic car importation business. His faint, barely present wife stood beside him, not saying a word while their kids ran around the dining room trying to stab one another with forks.

In desperation, I got Ramesh to add some vodka to my next drink. I struggled through the intricate particulars of the Dennison business empire and, just as I was about to make my excuses and disappear for the night, Marco Romanelli returned. Dressed in a pure black tuxedo, he looked like an Italian James Bond.

The forty or so French guests, who were taking their time over dinner, erupted in applause when they saw him. He put one hand in the air in the *really, it's too much!* gesture so common to celebrities. I saw no sign of his children, but, dripping with diamonds, his wife hovered beside him like an ultra-glam bodyguard. Petite but strong, with her daughters' olive skin and long black hair, she was at least ten years younger than her husband. She had the kind of looks that would make her famous on Instagram and yet her beauty was diminished by the permanent scowl that lived on her face.

Go on, Izzy! Tell her she'd be a lot prettier if she smiled more. You misogynist!

They made their way over to the bar through a sea of admirers. Marco stopped every three metres to shake hands with anyone brave enough to come close. I kind of wished I hadn't put on an act with the Austrian girls and had asked them who the highly worshipped figure in our midst actually was.

"Mineral water and a white wine, please." The woman ordered for them both without consulting her husband and Ramesh had to extract himself from the grip of handsy Mrs Shaw, who had been feeling his biceps over the counter since the commotion began.

Passing the mineral water to her husband, Mrs Romanelli said something about the importance of making an appearance and then going to bed.

Hey, our Italian comprehension is really improving!

Marco glanced at the heavily made-up British woman disapprovingly and turned to the person next to him to initiate a conversation.

"Are you here for the conference tomorrow?" he asked me.

I thought about telling the truth, but didn't know if the Austrian girls were lurking somewhere. "Oh yes, I wouldn't miss it for the world."

"That makes my heart sing just to hear it." He had piercing grey eyes and I could understand why everyone loved him. He was magnetic. Even if he'd changed the topic to talk about Ian Dennison's business, I'd have listened intently. "None of it would be possible without good persons like you coming out to support our project."

Perhaps it was his accent that got to me most though. It was like he'd taken my language and mangled it into something precious and new. I was afraid I would copy the irregular intonation and misplaced stress of his words.

"You're welcome." He was old enough to be my very young father but I'm pretty sure my tongue was hanging from my mouth right then, like a cat in a cartoon.

His wife gave him a serious look and he got the message. "I must be going on, but I look forward to seeing you at the exhibition centre tomorrow."

He seized my hand in both of his and squeezed a bit too hard. There was something frightening about it, some undercurrent of violence packaged within a kindly gesture. I was about to thank him for… I don't know what, but he turned and left before I could get a sound out.

"Miaow!" Ramesh exclaimed. It was good to see his true self shining through the servitude. "He is hot stuff."

I watched that ripple of admiration once more pass through the crowd as Marco Romanelli moved across the room. He was unique, charismatic and a little bit scary.

Chapter Six

I'd promised myself I'd make the most of my time on holiday – despite the constant dark thoughts at the back of my mind – but didn't manage to wake up until eleven o'clock the next morning. By the time I got downstairs, the only people about were Ramesh and Kabir, who were arguing in the foyer.

"I'm supposed to be on holiday, Uncle."

"Don't you give me that, boy. I'm letting you stay here for free." Kabir attempted to win his nephew round by changing his tone from stern to gentle. "Is it too much for you to give me a little help? I'm practically running this place on my own."

"That's only because you let the other staff go as soon as I arrived."

"Morning," I called from the stairs to warn them of my presence. "Any chance of some breakfast?"

"Izzy!" I loved the way that Kabir was always happy to see me. "The kitchen is closed but, if Ramesh is feeling generous, perhaps he could rustle something up."

"That would be very kind," I replied in my most diplomatic voice. I was feeling a bit guilty for not standing up for Ramesh the day before. "And after that I can help with the rooms if you like. There must be a lot of work to do after last night."

Kabir's look of exaltation grew. "Oh, Izzy, you're a wonderful girl. Why can't Ramesh find someone like you, instead of this terrible Patricia person who I've never even met?"

I decided to speak up on my friend's behalf. "Patricia's lovely. I've met her at least twice. She's just very busy. I'm sure she'll come to visit when she hears about this place though."

Kabir let out a weary breath. "Ramu, my boy, come over here."

Standing at the entrance to the dining room, Ramesh inched towards his uncle in reception.

"I'm very sorry." The hotelier's eyes glistened in the morning light which was flooding in from the front of the hotel. "This week has been incredibly stressful and I shouldn't have expected so much from you." He put his arms out and his nephew moved in for a hug.

"That's okay, Uncle." Ramesh displayed a forgiving smile. It was sweet to see that he was not the only one in the family who was in touch with their feelings.

"Go on, Ramu. Take half an hour off, but I expect you to have made up the rooms of the remaining guests by six o'clock." Kabir's hard-nosed instincts had returned. He thumped down the hatch on reception and disappeared into his office.

I looked at my friend sympathetically. "How about that breakfast?"

To the horror of the elderly Spanish woman who fulfilled the roles of cook, kitchen manager, sous-chef and skivvy, we raided the kitchen. Seeing her there, it was too good an opportunity to miss.

"Perdona, Señora. Sabes hacer lemon meringue pie?" I asked, and she looked frightened and began sweeping the floor more furiously in my direction.

We took our ham sandwiches and orange juice outside. Despite Ramesh's prediction that a storm was on its way, the good weather had not let up. We were alone on the patio and the grounds were silent. I couldn't hear anyone enjoying themselves on the beach and the tennis court and swimming pool were just as empty.

"They've gone off to this Next Phase thing," he revealed. "I got talking to that Álvaro bloke last night and he made it sound like they're all nutters."

"You know what it is then?" I asked through a mouthful of crusty Spanish bread.

"Not a clue. We should ask Dean. He seems to know most things about most things."

He'd come up with an inspired idea. I took my phone out and propped it up on the table to video call our favourite cyber-genius.

He wasn't super happy that we'd rung. "Izzy, you don't need to call me every time you have a question. There's a thing called the internet now which will help you find whatever you need."

Something wasn't quite right with him. He'd only answered with audio for a start. "Dean, where are you?"

"So, Next Phase was it? Yeah I've heard of them."

He couldn't fob me off that easily. "Dean, why aren't you answering my question?"

"Their leader Marco Romanelli was born in total poverty on the streets of Genova."

I heard a voice in the background and realised what was happening. "Dean, are you with my parents?"

"Urmmm, I'm not going to lie to you, Iz. I may be at your house right now." There was one of his typical breathy silences down the line. "But only because Greg got a new badminton net and they needed an extra person for doubles."

"Seriously?"

Typical Mum. She's always stealing my friends.

"Ahhh, say hello to Rosie for me," Ramesh put in, as if to reinforce my point.

I growled in frustration. "Fine, Dean, just tell me what I need to know."

"Okay. This Romanelli guy, born into poverty, inherited a fortune as the distant but sole remaining relative of the Carlucci fashion empire. Sold his stock in the company and bought out an Italian car firm which he turned into the hottest make going for mega-wealthy sheiks, shahs and internet millionaires. I thought about buying a Romanelli myself before I got the Aston Martin."

"Meh…" Ramesh stuck his tongue out in disgust. "If I'd known you were going to talk about cars, I would have helped Cook clean the kitchen."

"Yeah, come on, Dean. Get to the point."

"Romanelli wasn't satisfied with being a billionaire and decided to use his wealth to build a following. He started off on Italian chat shows, talking about his worldview and how things needed to change. It was benign enough at first – a mix between Karl Marx, Donald Trump and Marie Kondo. People ate it up and before long he was all over Facebook and on every TV programme." There was another pause and I could hear two of my dads having a knockabout in the background. "Izzy, how do you not know this? I thought you liked to read. Not the news, apparently."

"Ha ha ha. Hilarious." I used my fakest of fake laughs. "Move it along now."

"So Romanelli and his wife Gianna started a movement called Natural Order. They have this philosophy that everything has its place in the world and we've lost sight of what that should be. The poorest in society should have a job and somewhere to live, rare animals should be at home in the jungle or the savannah, and everything we

43

buy should be made in our own countries like they used to be.

"The problem is that the logical extension of this is that all the immigrants across the world should go back to where their ancestors came from. Natural Order attracted the wrong sort of crowd, their rallies grew violent and the Romanellis did nothing to discourage the extreme, fascist following they'd built up. Gangs of hooligans started trashing immigrant neighbourhoods in Natural Order's name; people were murdered. So Marco Romanelli was forced to stand back from the organisation he'd created and, though his wife continued to be involved, it eventually faded away."

I can't say that this is what I was expecting. "So where does Next Phase come in?"

"Next Phase is the obvious continuation of Natural Order, only presented in a more palatable way. It started out as a TV series. A kind of self-help concept to get your life in shape and, before long, Marco Romanelli had his face on every magazine again and he was organising conferences and seminars to promote his ideas all over the world."

"So is Next Phase any different from Natural Order?" Ramesh asked. I was impressed that the conversation had held his attention.

"On the surface it is. They've managed to distance themselves from the looting and violence at least. But I've read articles which claim that all the pseudo-Nazi rhetoric is still there, hidden under a pretty façade. I'd be careful with Romanelli if I were you."

"Dean, look at this!" Ramesh gleefully pulled out his mobile to point into the camera. "I got a selfie with him!"

"When was that?" I asked. The photo showed Marco with his arms around Ramesh, who a drunken Delilah Shaw was hanging off.

"Last night, after you went up. He practically saved me from that woman as well. He told her that she'd had enough to drink and should go to bed. Did it in this really smooth way so she didn't get upset. The guy is pure class."

I looked at him like he was missing his brain. "Ramesh did you not hear the part about him being a Nazi?"

No one is perfect, Izzy. Don't forget that chocolate bar you stole from Woolworths when you were eleven.

"No one's perfect, Izzy," Ramesh echoed my thoughts exactly. I should really stop telling him my secrets. "You once stole a chocolate bar from Woolworths."

"He's a Nazi!" As I struggled to get my point across, Dean interjected.

"Anyway, guys. It was nice talking, but Rosie's here now and we're going to start the match." He hung up before we had a chance to say goodbye.

Ramesh turned to me with a solemn look on his face. "Izzy, I'm worried that Dean might be a psychopath." He gripped his glass a little tighter. "What normal person takes less than five attempts to say goodbye to friends on the phone?"

Chapter Seven

That day was the most fun I had all holiday. Even though we had to clean out the rooms and make up the beds for the remaining guests, there was endless joy to be had.

We sped down the corridors on top of Ramesh's housekeeping cart and did time trials to see who could push the fastest. He was a surprisingly dedicated competitor and it was all frolics and laughs until he upturned the cart and sent me flying into a wall. After that, I limped off to the lobby to slide down the banister time and time again until Ramesh got a splinter in his leg.

Kabir came and told us off for wasting time so we headed back to the top of the hotel where the Romanellis had the suite next to mine.

I gawped once more on entering. "If I'm in the presidential suite, what's this one called?"

"Uncle told me these are The Royal Rooms."

It was hard to speak with my jaw hanging open. "Did a monarch stay here then?"

"Yep. Jóse Rovera, the used car king of Madrid. He's a legend in the industry apparently."

"Impressive."

The suite was set out like a large apartment with several bedrooms, bathrooms and a spotless kitchen area that I very much doubted the Romanellis would be making use of. In fact the whole place looked like it had been cleaned before we got there; there was not a pillow out of place or a curtain half-drawn.

"You do the kids' bedrooms and I'll get to work on the master suite," I suggested but Ramesh did not look happy.

"How is that fair? I'm the senior member of staff here."

"You're right." I figured he'd earned this small luxury. "I'll do the kids' rooms."

We went our separate ways and I took my vacuum cleaner and feather duster over to a world of stunning pink. The room I entered looked like it had been painted by a three year old girl who was colour blind. There wasn't an inch of space that did not contain some rosy hue. Even the furniture was pink. Somehow, even the mirror was pink.

I got to work stripping the beds, struggling to remember why I had offered to help and trying not to think about David for the thousandth time that day. I could only imagine what he was going through at the Old Bailey. Perhaps his solicitor had put him on the stand by now. Perhaps he would be ripped apart by the horrible prosecution barrister. Even if that Barton guy was only doing his job, he clearly took great pleasure in the cruelty he dealt out.

I was busy not thinking about this, and pulling the pillowcases off my forty-seventh pillow, when Ramesh came in holding a gun.

"Izzy, look at this!" Do you remember what I told you about Ramesh not always using the full capacity of his intellect? He was pointing the silver handled revolver straight at me.

"Have you lost your mind?" I instinctively dropped the pillowcase and put my hands in the air. "Did your parents never tell you not to pick up random guns and point them at people?"

He was all smiles. "Come off it, Izzy. I doubt it's real. It is heavy though."

"Ramesh, where did you find it?"

"In a cute little box in the Romanellis' bedroom."

I sidled out of his line of fire. "Yes, Ramesh. That will be a gun case. You're holding a gun."

His smile disappeared and he suddenly looked terrified. The weapon dropped from his hand and he let out a high shriek like a pig arriving at an abattoir.

As it fell through the air, time slowed down and I jumped for cover behind a pink armchair. I landed on the carpet and immediately put my hands to my ears, waiting for the inevitable bang. When seconds had passed and there was no sound, I looked out from behind my shelter. Ramesh was similarly braced for disaster but the gun was lying innocently on the floor between us and had not gone off.

"See, Izzy there was nothing to worry about." Ramesh spoke in a breezy, relaxed manner but he was shaking like a stick insect.

With my hand in a pillowcase, I picked up the revolver. I studied it carefully, making sure not to get any fingerprints on the weapon. It had a long barrel with a round tube added to the end to muffle the sound and an inscription on the handle which read 'To M.R. from FHD Jungend."

I turned my attention back to Ramesh. "Are you actually insane? Outside of characters in bad movies, what kind of person sees a gun and thinks, *I know I'll pick that up and show it to my friend*?"

"I didn't think it was real."

"It certainly looks real and it certainly feels real." I hesitantly put the barrel to my nose. "Oh, guess what? It smells real too."

"Sorry, Iz." He looked like a schoolboy who had been caught cheating on a test.

I took pity on him. "Come on, before we get in any trouble. Let's put it back."

We hurried through the main living area to the Romanellis' bedroom/aircraft hangar.

"Where did you find it, Ramesh?"

"It was in their wardrobe."

In the five minutes he'd been in there, he'd managed to make the room less tidy than before. There were dusters all over the bed and the cleaning cart was on its side again.

"What were you doing in their wardrobe?" With my arm outstretched like I was holding something smelly, I walked the gun across the room.

The way he was glaring at me suggested the answer was obvious. "I was looking at their clothes, Izzy. What else would I be doing?"

One of the mirrored sliding doors was open and a drawer had been pulled out. Inside it, a varnished wooden box displayed a silky interior. How Ramesh could have thought such a grand case would hold a toy gun was hard to comprehend. The box of bullets beside it was also a pretty big clue that it should be left alone. I was about to wipe the handle down when we heard a noise at the door.

"Quick, Izzy. Shove it in the case," he said and bolted from the wardrobe.

I put the gun into its neat slot as quickly as possible whilst still holding it through the pillowcase. I kicked the drawer closed and ran out to the main bedroom area where Ramesh was pretending to dust the curtains. As poor as his acting was, he looked less out of place than I did. Standing in the middle of somebody else's bedroom dressed in a sarong and an "I Heart New York" t-shirt, I can't say I blended in.

"What are you doing here?" Gianna Romanelli came to a sudden halt when she saw me.

"Urmmm, just cleaning really."

To my surprise, it was Ramesh who came up with an excuse. "I'm cleaning, she's supervising."

Mrs Romanelli did not look convinced. Eyeing me with her typically hard expression, she stepped past me to go to the bed stand. "My husband forgot some papers, I'm here to pick them up." She grabbed a folder and moved to leave.

Just when I thought we were in the clear, she spun round in the doorway and addressed me once more. "I have to say that, in general, you're doing a very good job. The hotel is immaculate."

"Yes, that's because of our strict one cleaner, one supervisor policy." I don't think I sounded very convincing. "We like to ensure that there's no slacking off. It's one of the many wonderful ideas that Mr Khatri has implemented." My hands together in front of me, I offered her my most innocent look.

She smiled for the first time since I'd seen her. She actually looked like a half-normal person for a moment. "Keep up the good work then."

"Thank you, Mrs Romanelli. We will."

I waited for her to leave before breathing again.

"Ramesh, there are two things you've got to do right now," I instructed. "Number one, wipe off that gun to make sure that your prints aren't all over it. Number two never *ever* touch a weapon again for as long as you live. If it was used in a crime and got traced back to you, you could end up in prison."

"Yes, Izzy. Sorry, Izzy." He looked suitably chastised.

Once I'd finished the kids' rooms, I went back downstairs for more janitorial fun. The only other interruption that afternoon was the old Spanish lady, Sagrario, barging in on me in the Dennisons' room.

"Oh," she said, looking confused.

"Can I help you?" I asked but, just then, her husband appeared.

"No, darling," he said, gently pulling her back out again. "Our room is on the next floor." He poked his head in to see me and apologised in broken English. "We sorry. Room wrong."

An hour later, when I thought I was finished for the day, I went to check on Ramesh's progress in the Romanelli suite. It didn't look like there'd been any.

"You really are terrible at cleaning." The duvet was only half inside the cover, he'd left footprints all over the bathroom and the floor was covered in croissant crumbs, which definitely hadn't been there before we entered. Add all that to the fact he was asleep in the island-sized bed and he had not done a perfect job.

He yawned, placing a hand over his eyes to shield them from the sun. "It's not my fault. All that dusting and polishing made me tired and I had to lie down."

"That's all right, mate. I think you're more suited to bar work."

He sat up in bed and I notice something shiny around his neck.

"Ra, what is that?"

He peered down at himself uncertainly. "Oops, I thought I'd already put that back."

It was the diamond necklace that Gianna Romanelli had worn the previous night. I had to admit, it was stunningly pretty. I've never been very materialistic or one of those girly girls who only thinks of sparkly things, but I would have sold a lung to wear that necklace for the night. Not that I let Ramesh know that.

"What is it with you and things you shouldn't be touching? Put it back and finish tidying!"

My generosity had its limits and, with my work done, I left him to it and headed off to the beach. Though it was a little overcast, the air was the perfect temperature and the sand beneath my feet was as hot as a barbecue grill. I put my towel down, lathered on the sun cream and the heavens opened to wash it straight back off again. The day had turned in the space of five minutes and, by the time I got back to the hotel, I was soaking wet.

That evening was a much quieter affair than the night before. There was no coach party to crowd the dining room and the other guests didn't get back until after dinner. Despite that, there was still plenty of drama.

I spent most of the evening at the bar with Ramesh. Uncle Kabir joined us for dinner in the near-deserted restaurant. He told me embarrassing stories about Ramesh's teenage crushes back home in Watford and my friend sulked throughout. There was no lemon meringue pie to be had but the crema Catalana did a respectable job in its place.

Yum, crema Catalana – like custard but more… Spanish.

The only other diner was Delilah Shaw, who, it turned out, had no interest in that day's conference and had spent her time in the spa. Thanks to the sauna and sunbeds she'd been using, she looked like a shrivelled grape that had been left behind after harvest.

"I feel invigorated," she told us several times, shouting across the room to our table. "I was overdue some *me* time today and that's just what I got."

"I think she could do with a little less *me* time if you ask *me*," Ramesh muttered under his breath.

When the Next Phase party reappeared at around eleven, Marco Romanelli was stern and distracted. He entered the hotel flanked by the Austrian girls, with his wife, daughters and other disciples following a little way behind.

"Inspirational, that's what it was," Lio told him.

Heike seemed to agree. "It's not just what you say but the way that you say it that inspires me."

The group walked up to the bar and, with a click of the fingers from Marco, Ramesh set to work preparing him *the usual*. This turned out to be a Negroni with a slice of orange in a short glass. Ramesh really did make an exceptional barman.

The elderly Spanish couple headed upstairs to bed but the whole noisy Dennison family took a table for some snacks. I was amazed that Cook didn't mind serving them so late.

"This isn't late," she told me in typically blunt Spanish when I relayed the order. She grimaced and pointed at the clock above the sink. "Who eats dinner before ten o'clock?"

I watched the new arrivals to work out what had upset Romanelli but whatever it was soon passed. With the help of Ramesh's refreshments, the man of the hour appeared to calm down. His wife was dangling off his arm, positively beaming at him, as he got busy entertaining his fans.

With the Dennisons, the Austrians and even Delilah Shaw hanging on his every word, he told the story of his days on the streets and the time he'd had to fight his way through three young punks who wanted to steal his last hundred lira.

Just as he was really getting into the story, a switch flicked inside him. "Of course, I left that life behind me a long time ago." He'd gone from being a barroom raconteur to an evangelist in the space of a sentence. I had no doubt that these were two personas he regularly made use of in his public speaking. "I was twenty-four when a young priest discovered me passed out in the street and told me about a better life. He taught me what it meant to be a good Christian and I became more involved in the church in Genova. But it wasn't until a trip he organised for young people to this very region of Spain that I think I really found myself. And six-months later, I discovered I'd inherited a fortune…" with a twinkle in his eye, he delivered the punchline. "…so that helped too."

His audience broke out in giggles just as Álvaro appeared in the entrance. In a single moment, Marco's face dropped and his glass flew from his hand to smash into the wall, a few feet from its intended target.

"Get out of here," he screamed. "And, if you come anywhere near me or my family again, the thing that flies at your head will be faster, sharper and deadlier."

Álvaro hadn't moved from his spot by the door but a smile slowly formed on his face. In reply to the threat he said nothing. Instead, he waved one hand to me at the far end of the bar and turned to walk up the grand staircase in the lobby.

Marco Romanelli retained that furious, bloodthirsty look for a few moments before ironing his face flat once more. He peered around at his companions and began to laugh, in the friendly, nothing-is-the-matter-here manner he usually employed. "Sorry everybody, but I really can't stand that guy. Now, what was I saying?"

I'd made another promise to myself to go to bed early, so I could get to the beach before everybody else. But there was no way I was going to let the evening pass without talking to Ramesh to dissect what had gone on. Sadly, that meant waiting another half hour until everyone had gone to bed.

"I told you, these people are all crazy." I was helping him load dirty glasses into the dishwasher. Even Cook had left by this point.

Ramesh seemed less excited. "Who do we know that isn't crazy?"

"Yeah, but this is serious. The guy is rich and powerful. He's the leader of an ideological organisation and he just threatened to shoot somebody in front of ten witnesses. Add that to what we found in his wardrobe earlier and he's clearly not the kind of bloke you'd want to cross."

Ramesh let out a world-weary sigh and shut the dishwasher door. "Izzy, you really have to get beyond this fantasy that, wherever we go, some dark crime is about to take place." He sounded like a man who'd been up since six that morning working in a hotel.

Feeling a bit stupid for getting so worked up, I accompanied him out of the kitchen. We said goodnight in the foyer, where he left me to do a shift in reception and I went upstairs to my luxury penthouse suite.

Chapter Eight

I kept one half of my promise and woke up at eight thirty the next morning. I decided to skip breakfast before the returning sun got too strong. The walk from the hotel to the beach was a pretty one. On leaving the hotel gardens, soft, platinum sand cushioned my path and that special pointy grass, which only seems to grow near the coast, poked up out of the ground all the way to the cove.

Gulls screamed from on high and the sound of the gently breaking tide called me forward. I had a brief feeling of exaltation as I stepped onto a beach that was all mine. For a little while, as I sat on my towel watching the sea, the whole, wide universe seemed infinitely wonderful.

So it was a shame when that perfect morning was disturbed by my least favourite part of my new career. I have to admit that, to achieve my goal of Poirot-like excellence in the field of detective work, I will require plenty of corpses, but that doesn't mean I like it when people die.

The girl in the sand was only a few years younger than me. Her eyes sparkled even after death and she was pretty in a way that seemed effortless. She had a beauty spot on one cheek and strong, dark features. The open wound on her forehead had been washed clean by the tide, but the bruise around it was a nasty shade of black. Around her neck, a small cross on a chain, with a purple stone in the centre, danced about in the water.

There were tears in my eyes as I searched on my phone for the Spanish emergency number and eventually dialled one one two.

"Hay una chica muerte en la playa," I said when the operator answered my call, then had to ask them to slow down as I've always been terrible on the phone in Spanish.

I was tempted to search her pockets for ID but decided I'd pushed my luck enough with the police recently and didn't think I could get away with it in a different country. I called Ramesh to stay with the body and make sure it didn't get pulled out to sea so that I could be there when the Policía Nacional arrived. Fifteen minutes later, three blue and white cars pulled up at the hotel.

I wasn't sure how good Kabir's Spanish was (it turned out to be perfect) or whether the officers would be able to speak English (most of them could) but at least I could explain what I'd found and lead them to the beach when they arrived. I'd been reading up on crime scene preservation recently and had already told Kabir to make sure that no one left the hotel before the police had spoken to them.

"I know her," one of the officers said as soon as we got there. He was young and eye-meltingly handsome. I was trying to be sombre and serious but, in his tight, summer uniform, which appeared to have been painted onto a body that was rippling with muscles from the tip of his finger to-

Izzy, a girl has been tragically murdered. Your boyfriend is back in London going through hell. Stop perving and get on with your job.

Sorry, I got a bit carried away there.

There were four officers present, in addition to the two who'd stayed back at the hotel. The most senior was a tall, thin woman with an angular face and body who looked permanently unimpressed by the world around her. The other two instantly returned to the hotel in search of supplies and the young, deeply tanned *agente* had knelt down to look at the dead girl, showing the impressive muscular definition in the back of his throbbing-

Izzy, snap out of it! You're making this sound like a Mills and Boon novel.

Sorry, won't happen again.

"She's from my village," Officer Sexy declared. "Her name's Maribel Ruiz."

"Put some gloves on and look for ID," his superior barked. "It's no good making assumptions."

"Shouldn't we wait for forensics?" He was clearly pretty choked up at the discovery.

"No time for that, the sea could wash away any evidence that's left. We have to seize the moment."

Is that really what she said? Do you really know the Spanish for "seize"?

Well, it was something like that.

As if she'd just remembered I was there, the senior officer turned and addressed me in English. "You said there was no one near the body when you first saw it, yes?"

"That's right," I replied, clearing my throat a little as the emotion was getting to me again. "It was just me here."

She turned away and muttered in Spanish. "A strong swimmer could have made it round the headland. The sea was calm last night." It sounded as if she was trying to convince herself of this theory more than anyone.

"It's no good, Inspector. She's buried in deep." The junior officer was excavating the girl as much as he could with the tide still washing around us. Every time he moved a handful of sand out of the way, water would well up and fill the space he'd made. "She would have washed out to sea otherwise."

As he moved the sand, I caught glimpses of the red summer dress that the dead girl was wearing, and, unless the killer had left a handbag with the body, it seemed unlikely there would be any ID to find.

At that moment, Kabir appeared with one of the officers carrying a spade and a large metal board that looked like it could have been used as a wheelchair ramp.

"I thought these might help," he shouted to us in a melancholy tone. "Terrible thing. Just terrible."

The two young officers made use of the supplies. The first attempted to dig a trench, though the sand kept shifting, while the second pushed as hard as he could on the metal screen to protect the crime scene from the tug of the water. They eventually succeeded in their task, but, by the time they'd finished, the tide was almost out and the forensics team had appeared to take over the immediate investigation.

"Miss Palmer," Officer Lovely said. "Perhaps you should go back to the hotel and we'll come to talk to you once we're done here."

I wanted to reply, perhaps even tell him how sorry I was for the loss of his friend, but then I caught sight of his pretty brown eyes and the gold chain that picked out the nape of his neck, just above that strong masculine chest with its well-defined-

Izzy!

I got *distracted* and the only words that came to mind were, "Perdona, dónde está la catedral?" It was the first sentence I remember learning in high-school Spanish class and didn't quite express my sympathy as I'd been hoping. It could have been worse, I could have just mumbled a list of Spanish ingredients at him.

He looked at me like I was one egg short of a tortilla. "Sorry?" He replied in English.

I closed my eyes to try to focus on the task at hand, but when I opened them again he was still just as beautiful. "Mi gato es blanco."

I turned around and started towards the hotel, "Sorry for your loss." I shouted back over my shoulder, as I cursed myself for coming across as a complete, raging moron.

When I got to the dining room, everyone had already heard the terrible news. The Romanellis were sitting in silence near the buffet, the Dennisons were dressed for the beach and making a fuss that they weren't allowed to go out and the two Austrian girls were discussing the situation with the police. I was actually a little relieved to see Lio. When I'd first found the body, I'd mistaken it for the pretty Next Phase groupie.

It's so sad that we lose our humanity as soon as we die. A body is "it", not he or she but it; like any other lifeless object.

The wretchedness of the situation was making my brain surprisingly poetic.

Kabir, Ramesh and Cook were the only employees present that day and were doing their best to maintain the high level of service people had come to expect from The Cova Negra.

"It's just not on," Ian Dennison was telling whoever would listen, as his typically mute wife remained silent. "We're supposed to be here to relax. This is just the kind of thing that ruins a holiday." He was clearly not concerned about the body on the beach.

As I arrived, Álvaro Linares came over with some questions for me. "Did you recognise the girl, Izzy?"

"No, of course not," I replied absentmindedly. I was trying to watch the reactions of the assembled guests.

"Was Inspector Bielza in charge?" He wasn't giving up.

I turned to look at him and suddenly questioned what his interest was. "What do you want, Álvaro? You keep interrogating me but I haven't a clue who you are."

"I'm sorry, I should have introduced myself properly. I'm a journalist. I'm based in Santander but I've been following Next Phase for the last couple of months as they've campaigned around Europe."

Marco Romanelli's anger from the previous evening suddenly made sense. If there are two kinds of people that nobody likes, it's politicians and journalists. Well, and dentists and used car salesman.

And estate agents. Don't forget estate agents!

"So, I'm guessing you haven't been giving Mr Romanelli the best write-ups."

He smiled, clearly proud of the effect he'd had on the man. "Then your famous talent for deduction has triumphed again."

"What made him so angry at the conference yesterday?"

His smile became a smirk. "I took the opportunity to ask him some pertinent questions. I'd kept a low profile until then, but I guess you could say that I ambushed him."

At that moment, the senior detective returned to the hotel.

"Your attention please." She raised her hands in an authoritative gesture.

"That's Inspector Nerea Bielza del Toro," Álvaro explained. "She's hard as a nail and twice as sharp."

"Ladies and gentlemen, I'm afraid that I have to inform you we have found a body on the hotel beach."

"Do you suspect foul play?" The journalist immediately asked.

Bielza's bird-like gaze twitched to land on Álvaro and she replied in her native language. "I'm not ready to discuss that at this moment, Linares. And you would be wise not to interfere in the investigation." Apparently unflustered by his question, she addressed the crowd once more. "I expect you all to stay inside the hotel so that my officers can gather information and talk to you when the time is right."

"Hey, you listen here." Ian Dennison inevitably stood up to complain. "My family and I have paid for a week at the beach, not a week shut up in some crumbly old hotel."

"What is your name?" The Inspector's words were like a ninja star, thrown straight at Dennison's head.

"My name is not the issue right now, what I want to know is-"

"You will sit down and listen." A spark fired and Bielza was enraged. "A young woman is dead, and it's my job to find out what happened. You will be able to return to the beach when interviews have been carried out and the body has been removed. Now, what is your name?"

The Brit abroad had lost all his fire. "Ian Dennison, ma'am. I didn't mean nothing by it. It's the kiddies, you see. If they can't go to the beach, they'll make our lives a nightmare."

As if in confirmation, the Dennison brood glared at the Inspector and Mrs Dennison flinched.

I watched the reactions of the other guests. The old Spanish couple were taking fifteen minutes to choose which type of ham they wanted for breakfast and didn't seem too concerned. The Austrian girls had lost all their usual bubbly positivity and were sitting at their table with their heads solemnly bowed. But it was Marco Romanelli I was most interested in. It looked like the world had been pulled out from under his feet and he was left falling through space. His face was scarred with fear, horror, dread.

"Based on the preliminary evidence, we believe it is necessary to keep you here until further notice."

Gianna Romanelli spoke up to say her piece. "We were supposed to be leaving today." She looked around the other faces as if searching for supporters. "We have another conference to prepare for in Madrid."

Bielza had her response cued up ready. "We'll be as quick as we can but, if necessary, you'll have to stay another night. I've spoken to the hotel management and there are plenty of rooms."

There was some murmuring around the dining room as she said this, it was clearly not a popular decision. It occurred to me that she wasn't telling the whole story. She'd never have thought of locking the hotel down if she wasn't sure it was murder.

Ramesh shimmied over to me, pretending to offer a drink from his tray. "Okay, Iz. I take it all back. Wherever you go, there is a dark crime just about to unfold." He went back to work, clearing plates and glasses.

As Inspector Bielza recommenced her announcement, the young officer who made me feel oddly warm and queasy inside walked into the dining room and mumbled something into his superior officer's ear. Her previously blank expression changed as he spoke. Her eyes cast down and her pointy chin jutted out a little more. He stepped aside and her gaze flitted around the room vaguely.

"I have to attend to the scene of the crime now," she said, her voice wavering slightly. "I'll leave you in the hands of Agent Torres and his colleagues."

Despite being sparsely populated, the room suddenly ignited with the sound of angry voices.

The brawny young officer came to talk to me. He let out a deep sigh before saying anything. "How am I going to tell her family? They are good people. I know them since I was a child." He looked at me as if he hoped I could make it better.

I thought about putting my hand on his arm but knew that, if I did that, I wouldn't be able to form a sentence again. The journalist had gone over to the breakfast area so I could speak freely. "She was murdered, wasn't she?"

"We're not sharing this information," he replied, in a way which communicated, *yes, that's exactly what happened*. This was only reinforced when he said. "It's good you're here. You know, I read about you in the paper. They called you *Señorita Marple*." He started to smile at this and then, presumably remembering the terrible situation we found ourselves in, frowned in distaste.

"Obviously, I'll try my best to help." It was a rare moment to hear someone compliment my detective skills without dismissing me as a lucky amateur. Even the newspaper write-ups and local TV reports had treated me as little more than a curiosity.

It had nothing to do with luck. I was good at being a detective. I knew that now and was tired of pretending otherwise. A murder had been committed and I would do whatever it took to find the killer.

Chapter Nine

As the police tended to their enquiries, I had my own investigation to begin. Kabir had his ears open to whatever was going on so I followed him to his office to find out what he knew.

"This isn't something for young ladies to get involved in," he told me from behind his desk.

I did not appreciate his rather old-fashioned response to my enquiry. "Did Ramesh not tell you? I've already assisted the police with three murder investigations."

He looked unsure how to reply. "Yes, but, Izzy…"

I thought you were done pretending? Tell the truth. We did more than just assist.

"I'm being modest. I should have said I solved three murders."

"Three murders!" he looked impressed. "My apologies, Izzy, this is definitely something that young ladies should get involved in. What do you need to know?"

That's more like it.

"Last night, was the gate locked? Could anyone have got into the hotel from the front of the property?"

"No, absolutely not. We are upgrading the security system at the moment, but the exterior is well monitored and the fence is alarmed. I would know if anyone came in."

"So then how did the girl get on the beach?"

He raised one finger, to make a correction. "Oh, yes. She came in but no one else. It was around two o'clock in the morning, Ramesh was on shift on the desk and buzzed her in."

"And what did she say? Where did she go after that?"

"That's what the police asked me. They came to get the surveillance footage from the hotel cameras and I showed them what happened when she arrived. All she said on the intercom was that she wanted to visit a guest. Ramu was half asleep and didn't think to ask which one. The video cameras at the front of the hotel show that she walked up the drive and round the side of the building towards the beach."

"What about other guests? Did they show up on any cameras around that time?"

Kabir glanced down at his desk dejectedly. "The only cameras installed inside the hotel are the one here in reception and one in the main lobby. Somebody could have gone down in the lift and accessed the beach through the garden and we wouldn't have caught them on any camera."

"So, we can't rule anyone out then? If no one else came into the hotel last night, the killer must still be here."

"Well… I suppose that's true." His normally direct manner had disappeared. "Such a terrible event as this one could tarnish the reputation of The Cova Negra. Or, even worse, we could be swamped with murder tourists who come here to relive the crime."

"Is that a thing?" I asked, forgetting for a moment my own morbid obsession.

"Yes, Izzy. It is very much a thing." He nodded seriously. "There are all sorts of strange people in the world."

It suddenly occurred to me that, despite the fact he was my best friend's uncle, he was a suspect like everyone else. "Kabir, you have to trust me this week. I can't say that I'll be the one to work out what happened, but I'll try my hardest to find the killer." I waited for my words to sink in before continuing. "You must tell me what you know as soon as you know it."

"Okay Izzy. I will, I really will." His usual warm smile had returned. "But the police have taken the footage away and the Inspector told me their experts are already examining it."

"What about this morning? Did you see who was first up?"

"I didn't get the chance," he said with a roll of his fingers on the desk. "You were the first person I saw down here, the others appeared for breakfast after nine o'clock."

I was probably getting ahead of myself. It was hard to investigate a murder without knowing anything about the victim. The fact is though, that Marco Romanelli was travelling with a gun and had looked like death itself when the news had come in about the girl on the beach.

A million possibilities flooded my mind.

Was she another Next Phase groupie? Or perhaps a young lover Marco didn't want his wife finding out about? The girl was local, which could mean Álvaro needed investigating as much as the man he was following. Or maybe the two old Spaniards knew the girl and invited her to the hotel.

I thanked Kabir and went to see Ramesh to find out whether he'd heard anything. I'd learnt at Vomeris Hall that it's often the staff who know the most about what goes on around the place and, for that week at least, Ramesh was chief dogsbody. I found him propped up in the kitchen, practically asleep on his feet.

"I feel terrible, Izzy. If I hadn't let her in… If I'd at least asked who she'd come to see… she might never have died."

We got to work drinking thick, Spanish hot chocolate that Cook had kindly whipped up for us. It was completely inappropriate for the hot weather, but sweet, delicious and endlessly comforting.

"Don't beat yourself up about it, Ramesh. It's not your fault. You were barely awake. You're still barely awake." The miserable expression on his face was slightly undermined by the chocolatey moustache that formed above his lip.

"Most of the guests don't seem that bothered." He wiped off the back of his hand. "The way some of them were talking, you'd think they were the ones who'd been murdered and dumped on a beach. That Ian bloke is a total waste of space."

"His family aren't much better." I took a teaspoon to scrape out the last traces from my mug. "His kids are little hell raisers and his wife doesn't say a thing about it."

This at least brought a smile to his face but it was soon gone again. "I just can't believe how cold they're all being. Marco Romanelli was the only one who was moved by the situation."

"Yeah, I noticed that. Did you overhear anything he said?"

"Well, yeah, Izzy. I heard them speaking a bunch of Italian and I'm pretty sure they weren't talking about the Mario Brothers."

"What about Delilah Shaw? She's been acting weird the last two nights. Perhaps she knows something about it."

"It's possible, I suppose," Ramesh looked deep into his mug, as if the pattern of chocolatey residue could spell out the truth. "She was chatting away with that old Spanish couple just now. It's funny how everyone here speaks English."

"Never mind that, what were they talking about?"

"She was banging on as usual. You know what she's like; she doesn't approve of anybody in the world who isn't exactly like her. I think she was complaining about young people and hoping that the Spaniards would be sympathetic to her nasty rhetoric." Ramesh clicked his fingers. "That was it. She was saying how the girl probably brought it on herself."

"And what did the Spaniards say?"

"It was funny, I thought they'd just go along with her to be polite, but the old woman really told her off. She said it was wicked to be so heartless when a young girl had died. And the old man joined in to say that it's not just the young who end up in sticky situations and that she should have more compassion."

"I bet Delilah really loved that."

Just then, Cook began to grumble more loudly. She'd been fussing around the kitchen the whole time, unimpressed by our lingering. It was clear she didn't want us on her territory so Ramesh put the mugs in the dishwasher and we left the kitchen together.

"I don't suppose she could have done it?" Ramesh asked, his face stony serious.

"Nah, it's never the cook." I was about to remind him that she'd gone home before the murder occurred when we emerged in the dining room and Álvaro came up to us.

"Listen, Izzy, I'm sorry about before. I really think we should talk."

"Don't worry about me," Ramesh said. "I'm sure there's some work to be getting on with." He wandered off to see his uncle who had emerged from his office and was in mid-conversation with the Romanellis.

Álvaro pulled me over to the side of the room, away from prying ears. "I know something about Marco Romanelli he wouldn't want getting out. Tell me what the girl looked like on the beach."

I was getting tired of the journalist's pushy manner. I guess it came with the job, but he wasn't doing himself any favours. "Why would I tell you that? You're just as likely to be involved in this as he is."

"I promise you, Izzy, the Romanellis are dangerous. It wouldn't surprise me for a moment if Marco was the murderer. He's ruthless. I've seen it time and time again. The further I look into his organisation, the darker it gets." He paused to fix me with his determined glare. "Tell me what you saw on the beach, what harm can it do?"

I studied him for a moment, trying to get a feel for what sort of person he really was. He was older than I first realised, late thirties maybe. Up close, his skin was strangely lined and papery and there was no warmth in his eyes. I could see some of the ambition there that I'd noticed in Marco himself. But it was true, even if Álvaro had killed poor Maribel and left her on the beach, describing what I'd seen would give him no great advantage.

"The girl's a brunette, which hardly makes her distinctive around here. I'd say she was in her mid-twenties, with a round, pretty face and green eyes."

"And a mark on her cheek. How do you call it in English? A little brown thing in the shape of a heart below her right eye?"

"A mole?" I pictured the girl more clearly in my mind. "That's right. How did you know?"

I could see that my response had shocked him. He looked over at Marco who had returned to his daughters at their table. "This is bad, Izzy. I've been a fool."

"Álvaro, I've struggled to understand a single sentence you've said to me since we met. What do you think happened and how are you involved?"

Still glancing around the room nervously, he pulled me further from the other guests. We were right in the corner, whispering away to one another like overly conspicuous spies. "I've been able to discover a lot of nasty stuff about the Romanelli Empire. Sources have told me that the violence linked to their organisations is directed from the top down, but no one will go on record against him. They're scared."

I had no reason to believe everything the journalist had to say, but would have obviously listened to his story if Inspector Bielza hadn't interrupted us again.

"Ladies and gentleman," she said in a dramatic tone which instantly caught the attention of everyone there. "I'm afraid that we are now dealing with a murder investigation. Which means you are required to stay in your rooms until we come to get you for your interviews. If anyone does not obey this command you will be arrested."

Unsurprisingly, Ian Dennison was not happy about this. "Hey now, this is not on. If you lock my kids up in the bedroom, you'll have more than one murder on your hands. They need to go to the beach!"

The young officer stepped forward to talk to calm him down but the inspector didn't need any help. "I'm afraid that's not possible,

Mr Dennison. Nobody will be leaving this hotel until we find the murderer of Maribel Ruiz."

Chapter Ten

I was the first to be called for my interview. I don't suppose it's standard procedure to conduct formal enquiries in a hotel conference room, but, with so many people to talk to, it was the obvious choice. I had no doubt that any suspicious characters would be dragged down to the station for further questioning.

It reminded me of my first police interview, six months earlier. I'd been terrified as I sat through my grilling from Irons and Brabazon, certain that I would say the wrong thing and incriminate myself. And here I was again, up in front of a steely detective having just discovered a dead body. The difference this time was that I was an old hand at police interviews and there was no way I was going to get all nervous and say something stupid.

Inspector Bielza watched me through those raptor's eyes of hers. "Why are you here, Miss Palmer?"

I took my time before replying. "Urmmm… You asked me to come?"

"Not here in this room!" She shook her head and I realised I'd already said something stupid. "Why are you in Spain? Why are you at this hotel?"

"Ohhhhh. Well, it's a bit of a long story actually. You see a while back now, I discovered my boss's dead body in his office. The police suspected that I was involved but I had nothing to do with it. In fact it turned out that it was my boyfriend who'd killed him." I came to a halt with a smile on my face, hoping I'd said the right thing.

Izzy, stop talking so much.

"Yes, Miss Palmer we all know about your incredible *detectiving abilities*." She ended the sentence with bendy-finger air quotes. I've never trusted people who make that stupid gesture.

She shouldn't be so smug. Detectiving isn't even a word.

"Oh, you read about it too, did you?" I was surprised how far my fame preceded me. It seemed I was better known in Spain than I was back home. "Well, anyway, after all that – and then my other boss getting killed, and the time I went to a caravan park and my neighbour there was murdered…" I stopped myself and cleared my throat. "After all that, I needed a proper holiday so my friend Ramesh, whose uncle owns this hotel, suggested we come here."

She slowly crossed her legs at the knee. She may have heard of my previous success with murder enquiries, but she did not seem impressed by it. "Well, thank you for that very complete reply. Had you ever seen the dead girl before today?"

"No, I hadn't."

She looked at me like she didn't trust me to give such a short answer. "And do you know how she was connected to the other guests in this hotel?"

"I'm afraid not." I thought about adding to my answer, but decided it was a bad idea. Then I changed my mind again and did so anyway. "I already have a few theories though."

"Oh really." She crossed her arms this time. "Please, tell us what we're missing."

"I'm not suggesting you're missing anything, I'm just saying that there are certain conclusions we can already draw."

"Go on." She glanced at Agent Torres who was sitting next to her. Their table was positioned in front of the curtainless window so that the light came in behind them and they looked like two silhouettes on a wedding invitation. It was beginning to hurt my eyes. "I have an eagerness to hear your idea."

Ha, thinks she's so clever. Her English is only about 98% perfect.

It was time to show them what I was made of. "Okay, first up, the girl is in her mid-twenties."

"She's twenty-seven," the junior officer explained.

"Right, so she came to the hotel alone in the middle of the night to meet one of the guests, but who could that have been? She is Spanish and the only two Spaniards staying at the hotel are old enough to be her grandparents and, from their accents, come from a region in the far south of the country."

I was getting into a groove now. "It might seem too much of a jump, but given the hour, I'd say it's most likely that she was here to meet a man. If we exclude the live-in staff, one of whom is my best friend and the other his uncle, there were only three men staying at the hotel last night. One is an oafish, overweight Brit who, having spent more than three minutes in his company, I find it very difficult to imagine a pretty, young Spanish girl being interested in."

I paused to make sure they were still following. "That leaves us with two possible suspects. The first is a well-known journalist, who you recognised him immediately. I suppose it's possible that Álvaro Linares could have asked a source to meet him late at night. Or even that he was romantically involved with this girl, but, in either case, it would have been more discreet and more logical to arrange a meeting away from the man he is investigating and a place he could be tied to."

She smiled, but there was little joy in it. "I see. So you're suggesting that Marco Romanelli is behind the murder."

"It stands to reason." I admit that I'd started to get cocky.

"Does it really?"

"Absolutely." For a moment, I thought she was genuinely impressed. "He's not only a world-renowned public figure, he's a millionaire and the most handsome man here. A young woman might easily agree to meet Marco Romanelli in an unfamiliar place after dark if she thought she could get something out of him. Who knows what that was in this case? Fame, money or something else that adults get up to late at night."

Izzy, you prude. You're not seven anymore. You can say the word sex without getting into trouble.

Inspector Bielza was full-on grinning by now. "What a remarkable mind you have, Miss Palmer." The moment she opened her mouth I knew I'd made a mistake. "The only issue with your hypothesis is that the video cameras show that Marco Romanelli left the hotel at one o'clock last night and did not return until four this morning. The preliminary findings of our forensic pathologist suggest that Maribel Ruiz was murdered shortly after she walked through the gate at two o'clock."

"Oh," I managed to get out. "Okay. It wasn't Romanelli after all."

So, in the end, Bielza was not bowled over by my uncanny skills of detection, nor did she take me on board the investigation to assist in the hunt for the killer. Once she'd run through the standard questions I expected from her, she let me go again with little comment.

"Do I have to stay in my room?" I asked, determined to get something out of the experience. The whole thing had been conducted in English, so I hadn't even been able to impress her with my foreign-language skills. "Or, can I help Ramesh and Mr Khatri look after the hotel?"

She paused to think before answering, once more inspecting me with her attacking gaze. "You can help them, if you must."

I nodded subserviently and left the room. As I was crossing the foyer to look for Ramesh, Officer Handsome caught up with me.

"It is not important to me what she has said in there," he told me in his endearingly sincere tone. "I want you to help us. I want to make sure that we find Maribel's killer. And I'm not convinced that Marco Romanelli is so innocent like the Inspector insists." What is it about men with faltering English that I find so insanely attractive?

It suddenly occurred to me that ten seconds had gone by without me saying anything. I won't lie; I was looking at his muscles again. If I saw a man staring at a woman's chest, instead of paying attention to what she was saying, I'd call him out as a misogynistic dinosaur. I'd start an online petition to make him apologise. I would most likely raise the issue with my member of parliament. But, sadly, I am a bad, bad hypocritical person and I hope you can forgive me, as this will not be the last time it happens.

Phwoar! I'd peel him like a banana!

Stop it this second. I'm bad enough already without you getting involved.

I'd shell him like a nut!

I forced myself to say something, anything! "I'll do whatever you command."

"Pardon?"

To save myself, I found the one safe part of his body that didn't turn me into a drooling idiot when I looked at it. I stayed squarely focussed on his chin. "I mean, I'll help however I can."

He glanced over his shoulder to look back at the conference room and, as there was no one on duty in reception, led me over there to make sure we weren't overheard. "I don't trust Bielza," he said, his eyes flicking about the foyer. "She will not be enough hard on Romanelli. She went to his conference yesterday. I think she is a fan."

"Perhaps if you tell me more about the victim, I can help you." I waited for his reply and received a serious nod for my trouble. "What do you know about Maribel? Could she be connected to Romanelli?"

He glanced around to check that his colleagues weren't listening. "I was never close with her, but we are from the same small village and our mothers are friends. I'm sure she was just a normal girl. She finished university last year, some kind of science, I don't remember what. She's sweet, popular and has had the same boyfriend for years."

His voice grew hoarse and he had to pause to collect himself. "She could not be involved with these fascistas if it is what you are thinking. Maribel was the opposite of them. I know because she used to go on protests in Madrid. She loved any social cause. She was against domestic violence, pollution, tax cuts for hospitals. Whatever you can think of, she did get excited about it."

Raw emotion coursed through his voice once more. "I have to talk to her mother now. She will want to hear it from me. This is the hardest thing I have to do as a police."

I searched for something to say to comfort him but there was nothing in either language I speak that would do the job. During one of my trips to Spain when I was at uni, I spent the summer in a village on the Costa de Almería. It was probably not so different from his. Everyone knew everyone until the whole place felt like one great big family. He was mourning the loss of a cousin and about to tell his aunt that her daughter was dead.

"Good luck, Torres," was all I managed to come up with and even that sounded cold and impersonal.

"Jaime," he told me, smiling because there wasn't much else he could do. "You can call me Jaime."

I watched him leave the foyer then pause on the steps outside to send in one of the officers who was standing there. If I hadn't felt bad enough already, I certainly did now. One of the few criticisms I think it is fair to make about my beloved Dame Christie, is that she often doesn't have enough compassion for her murder victims. Poirot is so caught up in solving a case and Miss Marple so sure of those around her that they sometimes forget the harsh reality of death.

Says the woman who has spent the morning dribbling over el Agente del amor.

Shhhh! I'm making a serious point.

A young woman was gone from our world and, if I was feeling this bad about it, I could only imagine what her friends and family would soon be going through. For a little while after Jaime left, I desperately longed to be as tough as Poirot or the old maid of St Mary Mead.

Chapter Eleven

In an ideal world, I would have gone to my bedroom, cuddled up to Elton John and had a good old cry. But then, in a perfect world, Maribel Ruiz would not have been killed. I went looking for Ramesh in the dining room but the only person in there was Delilah Shaw.

She was still sitting at her table, surrounded by a vast selection of food when she saw me and called over.

"I told the police… I said, you can arrest me if you want, but I'm not going anywhere. I'm not doing anybody any harm here and I don't want to be locked up in my bedroom. It's a question of civil rights."

"I'm sure they're just doing their job." I found her very difficult to talk to.

"No doubt they are, Miss Palmer. And I'm just eating my breakfast." She gave me a wink then and started to laugh. "It's not my fault if it takes me a little longer than normal this morning."

The woman really rubbed me up the wrong way. She's one of the few people I've ever met who is worse sober than drunk – and she was pretty bad when she was drunk. I thought of what Jaime had gone off to do and the anger darted up inside me.

"What are you even doing here, Delilah?" I could no longer hide my revulsion. "If you didn't come for the conference, what brought you to this place?"

She raised one of the many glasses of juice in front of her but did not drink. "I'm on holiday, Izzy."

"Yes, but who are you?" As I watched, I felt like the mythical Greek king who was doomed to spend eternity just millimetres away from the promise of refreshment. I had no idea how thirsty I was until I saw her not drinking.

"Oh, what a disappointment." She put the glass back down and it almost broke my heart. "I know who you are. Oh, yes, I've read all about the great Izzy Palmer. I hoped that you would at least recognise my name."

Delilah Shaw? It does ring a bell, sort of. Wasn't there a Delilah on Britain's Got Talent once?

Thanks for your help brain. And actually, no, there wasn't.

It finally clicked. "The columnist? You write for that rag back home don't you?"

She sneered, before taking a malicious bite of her croissant. "Got there in the end! And I wouldn't call our bestselling newspaper *a rag*. Just because your perspective might not agree with mine, that doesn't mean you can diminish it." A tone of officious self-righteousness had entered her voice and I remembered where I'd heard it before.

Delilah Shaw was the token ideologue on the phone-in show that my mother used to listen to when she drove to work in the morning. She was famous for saying whatever it would take to shock and offend people. She didn't believe in free hospitals, interracial marriage, or helping the poor and once claimed that cancer had been sent down by God as a punishment for human obesity. She was not my kind of person.

"I've been coming here for years, you know. I can't help it if somebody's been murdered. I've been haunting these halls longer than anyone."

"So you've got nothing to do with Marco Romanelli, whose political views just happen to tie in neatly with your own?"

That awful smile hadn't left her face. "Nothing whatsoever. I'd barely heard of this Next Phase thingy before I got here." She leaned forward and continued in a whisper. "All a bit too European for my liking!"

Already tired of the conversation, and aware that it wouldn't help me find out what happened to Maribel, I decided I'd had enough. "Have you seen Ramesh around?"

"Oh yes, I've seen him." She emitted another lustful cackle.

I turned my back to her as huffily as I could manage and went off to the kitchen.

"No chocolate. No lemon merengue!" Cook screamed at me in Spanglish as soon as I was inside.

"Hi there, Cook. Have you seen Ramesh?"

"No cake. No cake!" She was not happy to see me.

I figured it was safer to look elsewhere so cut back through the dining room, without a glance towards the notorious Miss Shaw, and up the foyer stairs.

"Oh, this is embarrassing," the old Spanish woman, Sagrario, said, peering about her as she wandered around the first floor landing.

She looked lost and I was about to escort her back upstairs to her room, when her husband arrived to do just that.

"I'm very sorry. My wife she confuses some time," he said and I switched to Spanish to calm them both down.

"Don't worry about it. But make sure the police don't see you. You could get in trouble being out of your room."

Celestino nodded appreciatively and his wife glanced around at the gilt-framed paintings of Cantabrian hills and beaches which were hung on every wall. "I got the wrong floor again, didn't I? They all look the same." She giggled then and there was something very girlish in it that I couldn't fail to admire.

"Come on, Sagrario," I took her free arm and directed her to the stairs. "Let's get you back to your room."

"What a very nice girl," she smiled widely, her eyes full of optimism. "You're not from Spain though are you?"

"That's right," I replied. "I'm from London. In England."

"She knows London," Celestino told me. "Our daughter lives there."

"She's about your age. Do you know Rosa Martinez?" That cheeky glint shone in her eye and I could tell she was teasing me.

I smiled back at her. "Not personally. London is a big place."

She continued to charm me like this until we got upstairs and I said goodbye to them both. As far as I could tell, everyone else was safely shut away in their own rooms. I finally found Ramesh in my suite, stuffing himself with food from the maxi-minibar.

"I had to hide here, Izzy. Uncle Kabir would have made me help prepare lunch otherwise and you know what I'm like in the kitchen."

He was sitting on the floor in front of the gigantic television. Elton was at his side, helping himself to the plates of cold meats, crisps and cake that Ramesh had laid out.

"I don't blame you." I grabbed a lemonade from the fridge and sat down on the floor with him. "It's too hot to do anything anyway."

We sat there saying nothing. "World's Grumpiest Animals" was playing a highlight reel of its best moments on the TV before us and we cracked up at every sarcastic moo and sleepy bark we heard. Even Elton seemed to be enjoying it. It had been a long morning and I hadn't eaten anything, so the sandwiches I made using two slices of cake and a piece of ham were very much appreciated.

Urmmmm.... Izzy?

Yes, brain?

Why are we sitting in front of the telly when there's a murder to solve?

Because... we're on holiday?

My brain gave me the silent treatment and I knew it was an argument I couldn't win.

At that exact moment, Ramesh grabbed the remote control and muted a koala who was having an argument with a pig. "Izzy, I think we should talk about the case?"

"Oh, not you too."

He ignored me. "You've got a responsibility to work out who killed that girl. Not just for your reputation, but for the future of the IP PI agency."

"That's not what I'm going to call it and, the thing is, there's all this pressure on me now. Jaime – the gorgeous police officer – and Álvaro and even that horrible Delilah Shaw read about me in the paper and they all expect me to solve the case. But we don't know anything about the girl who died, we have no evidence to work with and all the suspects are shut away in their rooms, so what can I do?"

He crossed his arms, unimpressed. It was unnerving because that's just the kind of thing I do when he says stupid things. "Actually, Iz, you're wrong. There's tons of evidence to consider. We might not know anything about the victim, but we've got plenty on the suspects."

He'd made a good point, so I tried a different line of attack. "But it's sunny out, it's too hot to think, and I bet that, if Miss Marple had lived in a warmer climate, she would have been much more reluctant to go poking around in murder inquiries."

"Oh yeah? So how did she manage so well in 'A Caribbean Mystery'?" I knew I should never have encouraged him to watch the Christie shows on TV. "Stop being lazy, and get on with it."

I let out a sigh like the disgruntled llama we'd just seen. "Okay... so if we dismiss the possibility for the moment that any of the kids are involved, that narrows it down to... ten people. Ten people! We're never going to solve this. Five or six suspects should be the absolute maximum."

"Izzy!"

"Fine. What do we know? We've got an extreme right-wing pundit who just happens to be here at the same time as a dubious lifestyle guru with a racist following. There's Ian Dennison, the current holder of "World's Most Boring Man", not to forget his wife who lacks the capacity of speech. Then there's the Spanish journalist who won't spit out everything he knows. Two suntanned Austrian stunners who love Marco Romanelli for his mind not his ridiculously well-toned physique. There's Romanelli's super serious wife and two sweet little old Spanish holidaymakers who I might have to adopt as my grandparents. Is any of this helping?"

Ramesh raised one finger triumphantly. "Yes, because you forgot about my uncle and me. You never ever take me seriously as a suspect in your murder inquiries, Iz, and I'm really not happy about it."

I barely registered what he said because I was in shock. "Twelve suspects! Twelve! That's impossible. There's more chance of me winning an Olympic medal for synchronised swimming than solving this."

Having filled his tummy, Elton came to lie down on my feet. He was all warm and fuzzy and I buried my toes right into him. It made me wonder where his buddy Kiki had disappeared off to.

Ramesh looked as grumpy as the giraffe that was glaring at me from the TV. "Oh, come on, Iz. I never get to be involved in anything, this is my chance to be a proper sidekick. You know I've always dreamed of playing second fiddle to a more capable investigator. Let me be the blank surface you reflect off and I'm sure we'll crack this case-"

"All right, all right," I interrupted him. "But what we need is to be methodical." I stood up to pace up and down the pastel living room. "Poirot is always complaining that Hastings has no method. We need structure and order. We need a plan if we're going to work out who killed this girl."

Ramesh failed to conjure up the words of encouragement I required. "Don't look at me. My only hunch at this point is that my uncle did it because he's a heartless, opportunistic slave-driver."

"Then let's try to knock some of those suspects off the list. Whatever you say, I know you didn't kill some random girl on the beach. Unless you're suggesting you murdered her because she woke you up in the middle of your nightshift?"

He looked a little depressed again, then huffed and gave in. "Fine, the pressure's too much for me. I admit it! I didn't kill her. I kind of wish I had now, just to prove you wrong."

"Okay, eleven!" I allowed a little smile to take over my face. "Things are looking up. What about your uncle? Could he have been having an affair with the young lovely on the beach?"

Ramesh narrowed his eyes and tilted his head somewhat dubiously. "My uncle is gayer than Elton John's hairdresser so I very much doubt it."

"The real Elton John's hairdresser or your cat's hairdresser?"

Ramesh thought about it for a second, then shrugged. "Either."

"Right, that's not the only reason Kabir might have wanted someone out of the picture, but let's forget about him for the moment. And Mrs Dennison can go too, she's far too busy with those monstrous kids and I doubt she'd have the energy to get up in the middle of the night and make it all the way to the beach just to kill someone. What about Gianna Romanelli, do you think she could be involved?"

"She does wear trouser suits," Ramesh said as if the significance was obvious.

"And?"

"Really, Izzy? Do you never pay attention when I'm reading Vogue? How many times have I told you? Never trust a woman in a trouser suit. Hillary Clinton, Theresa May, Victoria Beckham." He counted them off on his fingers. "They are all dangerous individuals."

I looked at him, still dumbfounded by his opinions after five years of friendship. "Uhhh, okay... We'll leave her in. So what are we down to? Nine suspects now?"

"Yeah... But, I was thinking, can we really dismiss the possibility that one of Ian Dennison's barbarian children didn't sneak out of their rooms last night to kill the poor girl? At breakfast yesterday morning, the boy spilt scalding hot tea on me and I swear he did it on purpose. Plus Romanelli's oldest daughter must be at least fourteen; she's practically an adult."

"Okay." I took a deep breath and totted up the final number. "That's twelve. We're back up to twelve suspects!"

Ramesh's face split open in a very smug grin. "Yes, Izzy but we've refined that list substantially. It may be the same number we started out with, but I have great faith that the names upon it are of a higher quality than before."

I considered killing him for a moment but, just then, there was a scream from the suite across the hall. Ramesh jumped to his feet with enormous excitement and raced to the door. I tried to be a little more discreet about it by casually strolling after him.

We were both standing in the doorway as Marco Romanelli burst from his room. He came to a sudden halt on seeing us there and nervously tried to explain. "My wife's jewellery has been stolen and some other things too. She said there were two strange people inside the room yesterday. I'm going to tell the police."

He hurried off down the stairs and Ramesh grabbed my shoulders, overjoyed. "You know what this means, Izzy?" I did not know what this meant. "I'm a suspect again. Somebody is going to treat me like the criminal I know I have it in me to be!"

Chapter Twelve

I decided it would be a good idea for us to explain to the police that, despite Ramesh's grand ambitions, we were not master jewel thieves.

Marco Romanelli didn't speak any Spanish and the officers who were not otherwise occupied had no English, so I was in the strange position of having to translate from Spanish into English for an Italian.

"And was there anything else?" The skinny, middle-aged agent enquired when Romanelli had gone through the list of jewellery, tablets and a portable speaker that had been taken.

Marco looked hesitant for the first time since I'd met him. "Well… In fact… Yes. We had a gun."

The officer raised one eyebrow suspiciously as you would expect from an experienced investigator. "A gun? You travel with a gun?" I didn't need to translate that part, Marco understood immediately.

"Not for protection. It was a present," he sounded apologetic about this fact for some reason. "The leader of a German youth movement gave it to me. It was in a wooden case."

"Yep," Ramesh confirmed. "It was there yesterday, we saw it when we were cleaning the room."

I stamped on his foot to get him to shut up. It didn't work but it made me feel a bit better.

The officer wrote down all the details and, as Kabir was in with Inspector Bielza, it was down to Ramesh and me to accompany the search of the occupied bedrooms.

"Here, listen," Ian Dennison said when we knocked on his door. "It's one thing you locking us up when we could be out on the beach, but that doesn't mean you've got the right to come barging in here going through all our stuff." His grunting voice was as melodic as a snoring walrus.

"There's been a burglary," I explained. "They just want to check none of the stolen items are in here."

He opened his mouth to complain but just then his wife came to the door. She looked distressed and in a barely audible whisper, said "I've just realised my watch is missing too."

"Not the Rolex?" Dennison's jaw dropped. "Where did you have it last?"

Her reply started quiet and faded into silence.

"This is all we need," her husband replied, before opening the door to us all the way. "I guess you'd better come in then."

By the time we left, they'd discovered that a phone, their camera, and two handheld computer games were also missing. "We had 'em yesterday. I put everything up in the room before dinner. Was probably those Frogs. I've never trusted the French." He spat the last word out like he'd swallowed a fly.

"It couldn't have been them," his wife timidly pointed out. "They left yesterday morning."

"Bloody marvellous," he said, ignoring her entirely. "Bloody marvellous."

We went to Heike and Lio's room next. It was easy to imagine that they'd been robbed as they appeared to have very few possessions with them. In fact it was hard to understand, going by their budget phones and limited possessions, how they could afford to stay in a place like The Cova Negra. Nobody had stolen their Primark t-shirts or unbranded trainers though and their passports had been locked in their safe.

Makes you wonder why the Romanellis didn't think of doing the same with the diamonds they were carting around.

I suppose diamonds are pretty common possessions for rich people. Perhaps it didn't occur to them to lock them up safely in a posh place like this.

Celestino and Sagrario had also been victims of the unidentified thief. After we knocked on their door, they discovered that Sagrario's rings were missing and Celestino couldn't find his wallet. They couldn't be sure when the items had been taken though, as their valuables had been left in the room when they'd attended the conference.

We showed the officer to Álvaro's room next.

"There's nothing missing," he assured us. "You can come and look through my things if you like but I wouldn't be a very good thief if I hid them in my own room." There was a disgruntled tone to his voice and he curled his lip a little as the officer entered.

He stayed behind in the doorway. "I still want to talk to you Izzy, but not with him here."

"Don't mind me," Ramesh said, completely missing Álvaro's point. "I won't tell anyone."

"I think he's talking about the police officer, Ra," I explained to my unimaginative friend.

"It comes with my job that I never trust the police." It was hard to know how to react to Álvaro's increasingly combative persona. He was shifty and paranoid like a spy in a cheesy movie.

"Well, let's get a drink later," I said lightly and the journalist kept up his mysterious shtick.

"I need to talk to my editor but I'll find you when I'm ready." He glanced down the corridor then went off to check that no evidence was being planted.

Ramesh was ecstatic. "This is so much fun. It's like one of those murder mystery weekends where you take on a character." He thought for a second as we walked towards the lift. "I'll be Mandrake Carmichael, the international oil baron financier and you can be-"

"I think I'll stick with Izzy Palmer, thanks."

The remaining rooms on that floor had been empty since the French coach party had left. Most of their doors were open and I could see there were pillowcases and sheets strewn about the place.

"I thought you told your uncle you'd finished all the rooms?"

"I have!" He looked a bit guilty. "I've finished starting cleaning and later I'll start finishing cleaning."

We returned to the ground floor to see if Jaime Torres was back. He was already in the foyer when we got there and I could see from his expression that his visit to Maribel's family had not been an easy experience.

Inspector Bielza emerged from the conference room before I could speak to him.

"You," she pointed at Ramesh. "You might as well be next."

Without waiting for a reply, she turned around and disappeared once more through the large double doors. Ramesh glanced at me nervously and followed her into the room.

"How did it go?" I asked Officer Brawny.

Stay focused on his chin, Izzy. Whatever you do, don't look him in the eyes. He's like medusa, one glance and you're dead.

85

"It was terrible," he explained. "Her mother's devastated. I've never seen someone cry so much. I didn't know what to say to her."

I didn't want to appear insensitive, but he'd asked me to help him and perhaps the information he'd gained could lead us to the killer. "Can we go somewhere to talk?"

He called across to his colleagues in slangy Spanish that I didn't understand and motioned for me to follow him to the patio. Stepping outside into the heat, my ingrained British instincts desperately sought out shade, while he was happy to stand in full sunlight overlooking the gardens. I put my hand to my eyes to shield my poor, sensitive face from the sun. This had the added benefit of muting his vibrantly good looks.

"I told you before, Maribel was just a normal girl. She wouldn't have had anything to do with these Next Phase people. I asked the mother and she said that Maribel didn't go to the conference yesterday. She was in the village all day and went out in Santander with her friends in the evening. A bunch of them were starting back at university this week."

"You must know something." I was using his impressive frame to hide from the sun and must have looked insane, ducking down like that. "Is there anything that could explain what happened to her?"

"At the moment, all I can tell you is what the pathologist has been able to work out. She was hit with a hard object."

"You mean blunt?" Who was I to complain, I'd barely spoken a word of Spanish to him.

Annoyed not to have remembered the word himself, he tipped his head back. "That's it; a blunt object. But that wasn't what killed her." He paused to find the courage to get the words out. "She drowned when the tide came in."

I put this together in my head, still squinting into the sun the whole time. "So whoever killed her, knocked her out first then buried her in the sand and waited for her to die."

"Yes, there were rocks under her dress to keep her in place, that's what told us for sure it was murder."

"But it's still an odd way to kill someone." I moved us on to the next topic. "What about her family, what do you know about them?"

He shook his head like the whole thing was too much to dwell on. "I'm telling you, Izzy. They is all good people. She has cousins and aunts and uncles and they'll be crying just like her mother."

"Is her dad still around?"

"He died in an accident when she was a kid. I remember him a bit but no one really talks about him. My grandparents still call her 'the widow Ruiz' though."

I let out a sigh, feeling frustrated at the lack of progress. I should probably confess that I'd been staring at his chin for so long by this point that I was beginning to find it incredibly sexy. I had to keep reminding myself to focus.

Izzy, focus!

"Have you got any idea what might have happened?" he asked and it almost felt cruel to tell him how far from the truth I still was.

"I'm trying my best, Jaime but it's not easy to investigate like this. Your boss doesn't want my help and, for the moment, I can't talk to the other guests. If you have any idea what I should be doing, you have to tell me."

He looked even sadder than when I'd first seen him that morning. The weight of events was pulling him down. His shoulders were rounded, his head bowed and it looked as if he wanted to give up and lie on the floor where we stood. He was about to reply when a fellow officer knocked on the patio doors and signalled for him to come inside.

Jaime started walking back towards the hotel. "All I can tell you is that the killer is still here. I know that will be enough for you. Bielza will do whatever she can, but you'll get there first." Pausing in the doorway he smiled shyly. "I'm sure of it."

He marched off and I wanted to stand on that pretty terrace peering out to sea. A bit of quiet reflection on the mystery I was facing would have done me the world of good. But I could feel my skin flaking off even as I stood there, so I bolted back into the hotel.

Chapter Thirteen

It was another couple of hours before all of the interviews were concluded and the guests were allowed out of their rooms. The two Dennison kids ran downstairs screaming their guts out and shot from the hotel towards the beach with unrestrained joy. Their mother ponderously followed after them, but Ian didn't appear. I was sitting in the dining room when they thundered through.

"Whisper whisper whisper nap whisper whisper," she explained apologetically before chasing her kids through the floor-to-ceiling doors which had been opened to let the warm breeze in.

Perhaps that's why her husband stayed upstairs – he's never trusted French windows!

Nah. That's not one of your best jokes, I'm afraid.

Ramesh had been cornered by his uncle and made to help get ready for lunch and I had some research to do on my phone. Once I'd checked just how long it would take to swim from the next bay to The Cova Negra, I got busy reading up on Next Phase on my phone. My search only served to back up what Dean had told us about the Romanellis' organisation. I dug a little deeper into the reports of violence that the movement had inspired, but there was no solid evidence to lay the blame at Marco's feet.

On the Next Phase website, a list of past conferences revealed they had already been through the major capitals of Europe, barring Madrid where they were due to finish three days later. Santander struck me as a rather small destination for their roadshow, but perhaps they wanted some time on the beach before heading home.

The thing that surprised me most was the gallery on their Facebook page. There were shots of Marco with important politicians from various countries and the fans who came to his rallies. There were hundreds of photos in all, and Heike and Lio appeared in several of them. There were at least five pictures of the girls with their hero. A few were in crowds with other people, but there was one shot of the three of them together. Their hesitance on approaching him for a photo two days earlier suddenly didn't ring true.

"Izzy?" someone called to pull me out of my rabbit hole. "Why don't you come to the beach with us?"

Timing it to perfection, Lio and Heike had appeared in the dining room.

"Yes. It is a good idea that you come with us," Heike said in her slightly robotic voice. "The police have given us permission. So long as we do not leave the hotel grounds."

I had no reason to say no and every desire to find out more about them, plus I was still in my beach gear from that morning.

"Yes," I replied, accidentally mimicking their unnatural tone. "It is a good idea and I will come with you."

As we walked along the path to the beach, they spoke of that morning's events.

"It's terrible what happened," Lio lamented.

"We heard she was about our age."

"Yes, terrible." I didn't sound very sincere as I was busy trying to work out what was up with the two of them. They kept looking at one another in that suspicious way they had and I could tell I was being tested.

"We searched for West Wickham on the internet maps." Lio made this sound as if it was a very serious issue.

"That's right," her friend added. "We did not understand why you mentioned it because West Wickham is a truly small and unimportant town."

"It's not that small." I suddenly felt protective of the place I'd been desperate to get away from my whole life. "It's got a Dominos and a Pizza Hut."

They looked deadly worried about me, but then a smile broke out on Lio's face. "We finally put it down to the famous British sense of humour."

"We do not find the same things funny at all." Heike still looked concerned. "In fact, British comedies are not popular in Austria."

"That's right." Lio shook her head sadly. "They are not popular at all."

Suddenly feeling rather protective of British comedy, I stepped onto the beach and my worries disappeared. A zing of joy passed through me as I remembered that the world is not all murder and darkness and it's hard to be glum when confronted with such beauty. It didn't last long as I soon spotted the sole remaining officer who was standing next to one of those "An incident occurred here…" signs. At least the body had been removed and the forensic team had returned to the station.

Heike and Lio wanted to place their towels right by the waterline with no shade or protection from the sun. While they coated every inch of their deep brown skin in cooking oil, I got to work on my own routine.

Applying sun lotion for me is practically a workout. I get two big handfuls of the stuff and then go crazy slapping it on all over myself. Even with my ridiculously long limbs, I can't reach my whole back though. So, like a window washer who's running out of soap, I squirt some on my shoulders and shimmy and jump up and down in the hope it will cover that bit in the middle that's impossible to get to. I'm a seasoned pro now and it only takes me a quarter of an hour to do my whole body. Of course, twenty minutes later I'm back at it again.

Glistening prettily, Heike and Lio watched my performance in stunned silence.

Those maniacs! Haven't they heard of skin cancer?

"You know, it's Mr Romanelli I feel sorry for," the blonde beauty explained as I collected two parasols and stuck them in the sand to claim my territory.

"Yes, that poor man." I think I'd moved past sarcasm by this point and perfected just the right tone of voice to sound as earnest as they constantly were.

"When this is reported in the news, those awful journalists will start saying horrible things about him again." The two of them clearly shared some kind of hive-mind as they were capable of continuing one another's discussion with barely a pause.

"They always do." Heike sounded particularly unnerved by the issue. "They treat Mr Romanelli so cruelly."

"So you don't think there's anything in the rumours then?" I was tired of going along with them and decided to stir things up. "I mean, there were some pretty bad things connected to his old organisation."

The pair looked up at me like I'd just insulted their grandmother. Lio was the first to snap back. "That had nothing to do with Marco."

"He was just a…" The brunette turned on her side to ask her friend a question. "How do you say-"

"Scapegoat," Lio interrupted. "Mr Romanelli was a scapegoat. It's not his fault if people do crazy things."

Heike blinked in agreement. "If anything, his ideas would put an end to conflict like that."

The two girls nodded back and forth to one another, showing that a consensus had been formed and any other opinion was now irrelevant. I could see that challenging them would not help my cause.

I picked my words more carefully this time. "No... You're absolutely right. I meant to say that it was terrible that people abused his name in that way. The last thing a beautiful movement like Next Phase needs is extremists messing everything up."

They let the air out of their lungs like they'd been holding their breath for the last thirty seconds.

"I'm so glad we see eye to eye." Heike looked at Lio to make sure she was saying the right thing. "I would hate for us to argue."

"I'm really sorry." My words hung between us as I thought up an explanation. "I probably only said those thoughtless things because I'm jealous that you got a photo with Marco."

Lio started laughing and I wondered if this was an example of Austrian humour. It was way over the top and, when Heike joined in, she sounded even less natural than her friend. They stopped at the exact same moment and silence returned.

I think it bears repeating that these two are world-class weirdos.

I'd finally got to the question I was most eager to ask them. "Had you ever met him before this week?"

Heike looked uncertain so she deferred once more to her more confident companion. "Oh, no. This is our first Next Phase conference."

"Weren't they in Vienna a couple of weeks ago? Didn't you think of going there?"

"Yes, but..." Heike faltered once more and received a stern look from her friend. "...but we thought we'd make a holiday out of it. We love Spain."

"Yes we love Spain," Lio added with all the passion you might use to talk about your favourite brand of toothbrush or floor cleaner. She relaxed a little then and smiled brightly. "Let's go into the water. We have a beach ball to play with. Izzy, will you join us?"

"You go ahead. I think I'll stay here and read my book for a while."

The two girls stood up and, with one of their trademark nods, daintily pranced off across the sand and into the sea.

They're lying.

Of course they're lying. Nothing about them is real.

I'd been so taken in by their stereotypically Teutonic weirdness that I'd failed to realise it was all an act. They'd lied about meeting Marco and they'd lied about their connection to Next Phase. Good actors plan out a backstory for their characters. I had no doubt that Ramesh could tell you any number of details about his alter ego, Mandrake Carmichael, but Heike and Lio hadn't told me a single thing about their real lives. The only topic they could talk about was Next Phase.

Maybe they're the thieves and they're just pretending to be interested in the movement as a cover story?

I grabbed my book from my bag and spent the next twenty minutes attempting to read a single page as various explanations swirled around my mind.

Chapter Fourteen

By the time I left the beach for lunch, I was thoroughly frustrated. My hour there had only dragged up more questions and I felt further than ever from mastering Poirot's methodical approach to detective work.

My brain certainly wasn't helping by singing the whole time.
Oh we do like to be beside the seaside!
Oh we do like to be beside the sea!
Oh we do like to stroll along the prom prom prom,
Something something something something diddly om pom pom!

I tried repeating business-minded buzzwords like "Method. Order. Technique," to help me focus, but I was so busy chanting them in my head, I forgot to apply them.

You have to admit, twelve suspects (fifteen if I was being truthful with myself) is a lot for anyone to get through. Okay, there are ten in "And Then There Were None" and there are thirteen key passengers in "Murder on the Orient Express" but Christie had been writing for decades when she came up with them and this was only my fourth case.

Besides in "And Then There Were None" that number drops pretty quickly. Why can't some of our suspects be killed off?

I stopped halfway along the path back to the hotel, angry at myself for having such a thought.

It's not that I want anyone to die, I'm just saying it would make our job easier.

I ignored my dark instincts and continued back to the hotel. By the time I'd showered, changed and made it to the dining room, it was time for lunch. Sagrario was sunning herself on the terrace while her husband spoke to Ramesh who was busy serving. Heike was already at a table, but Lio hadn't appeared and the only other people to have made it down were Mrs Dennison and her kids. There was still no sign of Ian or the Romanellis and Delilah Shaw can't have been hungry after the breakfast she'd devoured.

Kabir was zipping in and out of the kitchen, distributing starters to the occupied tables. Gianna Romanelli appeared and was looking about for her family and things were almost back to usual. If it hadn't been for the occasional crackle of a police radio and the presence of

Inspector Bielza in the corner making notes, I might have been able to imagine it was a normal holiday.

I followed Ramesh to my usual table, and was just about to order, when the illusion was shattered.

I'd never heard a gunshot before. There was a weird silence just before it happened, like all sound had been extinguished to add resonance to the moment. Three succinct bangs in quick succession shocked everybody into stillness. They froze us in place like a superhero's ice-ray and, for five seconds, all we heard was the running of guests on the upper floors and seagulls screeching outside.

I told myself I was being dramatic and it was probably just a car backfiring or balloons popping, but then the Inspector burst into life. She jumped to her feet, shouted to her subordinates to follow her and was halfway up the stairs before I could even move. For once, there was no inappropriate grin on Ramesh's face as I caught his eye. His uncle was so distressed that he had to sit down in the nearest chair to cope with the drama and Gianna Romanelli still hadn't found her kids and looked terrified.

"Stay down here, Izzy," Jaime shouted to me from the upstairs landing as I reached reception. "It could be dangerous. Everybody stay down here."

"What happened?" Heike's voice sounded less mechanical than normal. "What was that sound?"

I didn't answer. There was nothing to say and no way to say it. All the guests who had been present in the dining room came to stand next to one another at the bottom of the stairs and we remained there in stasis. We were unable to go forward or back, stuck in that moment until some outside force could jolt us free.

Celestino had collected his wife from the terrace and, with one arm around her shoulders, now whispered some soothing explanation. A fairy tale, to keep her calm.

"It's Álvaro Linares," one of the officers announced as she ran back downstairs to block off the front door. "He's dead."

Lio followed the officer down from her room and I watched Heike to see if this revelation could trigger any reaction but she remained calm. It was Celestino whose response surprised me. Still huddled close to his wife, he had tears in his eyes. The detective in me wanted to know why he would cry for someone he didn't know but another much more human part of me understood that such sympathy was only natural. He was crying because a man had been murdered and there was no excuse for such a thing.

Everything happened at once after that. More police officers shot down from the first floor like starlings flying about the hotel. Jaime came to talk to Kabir in the dining room and the two of them worked their way around the perimeter to ensure nobody could escape.

"Where is your husband?" the female officer barked at Gianna in Spanish but the Italian still looked stunned.

"She wants to know where Marco is."

Gianna peered between the two of us, unable or reluctant to form the words required of her. "I thought he was down here…"

"Dad's up in our room," her eldest daughter replied, coming in off the patio just as Kabir was about to lock the door. Her little sisters were behind her and all three carried tennis rackets and sports bags. "What's happened?"

No one answered but the skinny, older officer who had reappeared at the top of the stairs left to locate the missing Romanelli.

There were important questions to be asked and I didn't wait for the officer but turned to Mrs Dennison myself. "Where's Ian?"

"His room…" she replied and made a confused whimper as Jaime translated for his colleague.

"I thought he was desperate to go to the beach?" the dashing lawman snapped and I got the impression he'd received an earful on the topic that morning.

I figured I'd help pile the pressure on. "You said he was having a nap two hours ago. What's he been doing since?"

The poor woman began to tremble but, just then, Inspector Bielza reappeared with Ian beside her. "Found him in his room," she shouted to the junior officers in Spanish. "Has anyone seen that dreadful woman?" They looked back uncertainly. "You know, she looks like Belén Esteban. Big lips, too much makeup."

I didn't know what she was talking about, but the other officers laughed gravely at her comment.

Must be Spanish humour.

Jaime and the sole female agent ran to the lift just as Delilah Shaw appeared from the direction of the leisure centre with a towel wrapped round her. A few minutes later, the forensics team turned up again. I bet they hadn't expected to deal with a double murder when they woke up that morning.

Once Marco had been located and all of the missing players were in place, Bielza chose a spot halfway up the grand staircase. Just behind her, one of the golden-framed mirrors reflected a beam of sunlight onto her like she was the protagonist in an old movie. She was ready for her close-up.

"We are in the presence of a murderer." She waited for the resultant buzz to die down before continuing. "I might have been willing to believe that the first death could have occurred without your involvement, but that is no longer possible. No one has left the hotel since Señor Linares was murdered and, unless there's someone hiding upstairs that my officers failed to find, I can now count the potential suspects on one hand."

Her presence and intensity were impressive. Standing high on the stairs above us, she was a colossus; a great unbending force who might pick any one of us from the crowd to devour or turn to dust. She cast her gaze around the assembled hotel guests and it drilled into each of us, guilty or otherwise. I knew I hadn't done it, but that didn't make it any less painful to stand before her.

"I have a good feeling for which of you is the killer, so I wouldn't get too comfortable just yet."

She held the attention of every last person there. From the pool boy to the waiter, the cleaner to the barman… No, wait a second, that's all the same person. I'll start again… From Delilah Shaw and Marco Romanelli right through to the police officers who were arranged in an oppressive semi-circle around us, no one uttered a word for fear Inspector Bielza might have more to say.

When just the right amount of time had passed, she broke her own masterfully engineered silence. "No one is to leave the hotel. My officers will be stationed here from now until I arrest the killer." Her searchlight vision panned across us once more. "I hope you enjoy your stay."

Chapter Fifteen

Okay, so; Marco, Delilah, Lio and Ian. That's a more workable number.

Four? If anything it's too easy. We might as well go down to the spa and have a nice afternoon to ourselves. We could pick the killer from four possible suspects in about twenty minutes.

Stop being so cocky.

As the others went off to have lunch, I approached the inspector. In many ways, Nerea Bielza del Toro was everything I aspired to be. She was confident, brave and powerful; a woman who inspired fear and admiration in equal measure.

She remained on the stairs, watching the crowd disperse and I had trouble getting my words out. "Álvaro was investigating Next Phase and knew Maribel. We all saw Marco threaten to shoot him last night. Are you still so sure that Romanelli isn't involved?"

She looked at me with her typical dubious glare. Her mouth was so straight and rigid you could have used it as a ruler. "I appreciate your colourful theories, Miss Palmer. But Marco Romanelli was not in the hotel when the first victim was murdered. There is no possible way he could have been in two places at once."

The way she spoke then surprised me and I could tell that she was holding something back. "So where was he?"

"How do you mean?"

"Where was Marco Romanelli when he wasn't at the hotel?"

I'd provoked my strongest reaction yet from the cast-iron lady. She narrowed her eyes one tiny fraction.

"Listen, I'm not trying to be difficult." I was hoping a more reasonable approach might win her around. "The longer this takes, the more damage it does to my friend and his hotel. Kabir is a lovely man. I don't want him suffering because of all the terrible things that are going on here. We've had two murders and a string of robberies. He's only been in charge a couple of months, it won't do his TripAdvisor rating any good."

She pursed her lips and took her time. "Okay, Miss Palmer. What exactly do you want from me?"

She was standing three steps above my own. It was an odd sensation to have to crane my neck to look up at someone and I felt a pang of sympathy for some of my shorter ex-boyfriends.

"Let me into Álvaro's bedroom. Let me get a feel for what happened in there. Maybe I can help." I was less than confident that she'd grant my request. "Come on, what harm can it do?"

"I don't know how the police do it in Britain, but we do not let amateurs or aficionados poke around crime scenes." I was about to argue with her again when she continued. "But, if you wait until the forensics team and the pathologist have finished their initial investigation... maybe I'll let you in."

I did that embarrassing thing where I punched the air like the hero in a 1980s action movie. "You won't regret this, boss!"

She looked at me like I'd lost my mind. But, in actual fact, I was beginning to see the case clearly for the first time. Theories ran through my head. Connections formed between the four suspects and the two victims. I could see a way through to the truth now. All it had taken was another dead body.

You're welcome.

Of course, knowing what to do and carrying out a plan are two very different things. I made my way into the dining room to look for Marco. I was sure, if I had him on his own, I could work out how he was involved. I hadn't reconciled the paradox of his absence from the hotel when Maribel was murdered, but he was still the obvious killer and my investigation was only just starting.

"Izzy, can I have a word with you?"

Ian Dennison was the first roadblock on that journey to the truth. Marco was right there, on his own, waiting for his family to return from the bathroom and Ian bloody Dennison stood between the two of us.

"I'm a bit busy now."

"It's just... I didn't realise who you were at first. It was my wife who pointed it out. You see, we live in London, so we saw the news reports about you and I think I've got something important that you might want to hear."

In the time it had taken him to say this, my window of opportunity had closed. Marco Romanelli's family had returned and accompanied him over to a table for lunch.

"Go on then, Ian," I replied with a sigh. "What is it you've got to tell me?"

"You see, the thing is. Our room is just opposite this dead bloke's and I heard him shouting down the phone. Just before he was killed, I heard him shouting something over and over again."

I admit, boring Ian Dennison had surprised me. I assumed that whatever he was going to tell me would be of absolutely no use whatsoever. I lowered my voice to a whisper. "Great, what did he say?"

"Oh, I don't actually know what he said. It was all in Spanish. I don't speak any foreign myself."

"So why did you think this would be helpful?"

"Well… It shows he was angry with someone. It shows that someone would have wanted him dead."

Before I could shout at him, slap him or bite him, I took a breath and calmed myself down. "We know somebody wanted him dead, Ian! They shot him three times with a gun."

"Yes, but maybe if you checked his phone records, you can work out who it was." He spoke in a manner which suggested I should have been the one to think of this and, while he had a point, it seems unlikely the killer rang Álvaro to tell him they were coming by for a visit. It was more likely that he'd been talking to his editor as that is exactly what he told me he was going to do.

I decided to find out what other dramatic facts he was party to. "What did you do when you heard the gunshots?"

He narrowed his eyes conspiratorially, like he was about to deliver the key piece of evidence to solve the case. "That's the thing, I'd fallen back asleep and wasn't really with it. I'd only wanted to lie down for twenty minutes, but the nap had knocked me right out." He bit his lip and looked up at the ceiling to show that he was having a good old think. "It's probably the jetlag."

I didn't have the energy to explain that you don't get jetlag several days after a two-hour flight. "So you didn't go out of your room to see who shot him?"

He started laughing then and his fiery cheeks jiggled. "Go out there when I was all sleepy and there was someone with a gun? I'm not a total moron."

Oh? Just a partial one?

"Thanks, Ian. I'm sure this information will come in very useful. You should tell the police every last detail."

He looked pretty pleased with himself and went off to bore Inspector Bielza with the same story.

There was no way I could talk to the Romanellis with their children there so I settled for Delilah Shaw. Actually, I was pretty hungry and decided to make it a working lunch.

"Mind if I join you, Delilah?" I pulled up a chair before she could say no. "We had such a nice chat this morning, I thought we should pick up where we left off."

She tilted her head like she thought I was a simpleton. "What would you like to talk about, dear? Britain's healthcare problem or the scourge of free breakfasts for the poor? Now, don't get me wrong, I'm not against children eating per se. I just don't think it should be funded by the taxpayer."

I grabbed a menú del día from the neighbouring table and was scanning the options. What a dilemma. Not only did I have to choose a witty comeback to her diatribe, I had to make my mind up between minestrone soup, goat's cheese salad and melon with ham as a starter.

"How about you tell me where you were when Álvaro Linares was murdered?"

"How about you mind your own business?"

"Just answer the question, Delilah. Or do you have something to hide?"

As she allowed a tense silence to whirl around us, I set about choosing my main course.

Izzy, if you don't go for the paella I won't speak to you again for a week.

Oh, fantastic!

I waved the menu in the air to get Ramesh's attention. "Ra, I'll have the melon followed by the monkfish please." I turned back to Delilah Shaw. "Now, I think you were about to tell me what you were doing at the time of the murder."

"Fine," she took a sip of sangria. "I'd gone for a swim, I don't like swimming in the sea because the sand and scum gets all over me, so it was wonderful to have the pool all to myself. I snuck off there when the police weren't looking and it was pure heaven."

"Did anyone see you?"

"I just told you," she spoke as if I was nothing more than an inconvenience to her. "The wonderful thing about it was that I was alone the whole time."

"Did you hear the shots from the pool?"

"Yes."

"So why did you take so long to arrive in the foyer?"

Just then Ramesh delivered her first course. She took a piece of melon in one hand and sucked on it so that the juice ran down her fingers. It was gross, noisy and strangely aggressive. "Oh," she replied breathlessly, like she'd come up from a very long kiss. "I thought it was just kids playing."

"So you've got no alibi, could easily have run down from upstairs and you expect me to believe you weren't involved?"

She pouted her puffy lips coquettishly. "I would hope that my previously sterling character would be enough for people to believe that I am not a murderer." She licked her thumb clean and then moved on to the fingers. "Did you know that white people are far less likely to be murderers?"

"How strange," I had to bite my lip to stop myself saying what I really thought. "In Agatha Christie novels, all the murderers are white."

This time, she was the one without a comeback as my own first course arrived.

Everyone was sitting down by now and it felt odd to be eating all together but far apart. It wasn't like the previous nights, we were united by recent events and, as much as I disliked many of the people there, my mother's love of community must have rubbed off on me. I was half tempted to stand up and say, *Come on, everybody, why don't we shove the tables together and make it one big party*?

Instead, the only communal element to the experience was the fact that we all had to put up with Ian Dennison's ten-year-old son moaning that there were no sausages on the menu and all the food was weird. When he was done, the sound of cutlery on our dinner plates was almost too depressing to bear.

I decided to keep on at Delilah, to at least break the silence. "I don't suppose you'd met Álvaro before?"

She put the shrivelled skin of her melon down and pouted once more. "How would I have come across some random Spanish bloke?"

"You're both journalists, aren't you?"

"Opposite ends of the scale, Izzy." She let out a tittering laugh. "By all accounts, he was some liberal lefty and I'm... Well, I'm a little different from that."

"I thought you said he was some random Spanish bloke? Sounds like you know him a little after all."

The amusement fled from her face. "One hears things, in my line of work. It's my job to know who people are and what's happening."

"So that you can criticise them and disapprove of everything?" I answered her. "Yes, you do that so well."

Delilah glared at me and, despite the fact I was white, middle-class and British, I had clearly made it into the not very select group of people she despised. She fell into a spiteful silence and, with every chunk of food she bit off, eyed me as if I was the next course. It was like eating dinner with Hannibal Lecter, only the conversation was less engaging.

I was glad when Jaime peeked into the dining room to get me and I could finally escape her company.

She delivered her parting words of discouragement with a grimace. "You know what you are, Izzy Palmer?"

"A detective? A woman of above average height? Go on, I'm sure you want to tell me."

"Like every last *millennial* on the planet, you're a flash in the pan. You're having your fifteen seconds of fame right now, but it won't last. The problem with you kids is that you don't expect to work for anything. It took me twenty-five years to get where I am. All you had to do was date a murderer to get a few column inches. My advice: start your own Instagram or sell some racy photos to the tabloids while you can. Because in a couple of months, no one will remember who you are."

It was hard to know how to respond to such bile.

Izzy, stab her with your fork. The police will understand why you did it. No one will blame you.

Trolls like her live for that sort of a reaction. So, instead, I went for, "Well, it's been a genuine pleasure, Delilah. What are your plans for dinner?"

Chapter Sixteen

The only good thing about my lunch date was that, as we were in Spain, the food was delicious and nutritious. Sadly, I'd only got through the starter when Jaime called me so I was still starving.

"I don't know what to make of this, Izzy," he explained in Spanish as he accompanied me upstairs. "I mean, I can understand someone wanting to get rid of a journalist; they're always causing trouble. But what could connect Álvaro to Maribel?"

I stopped in the first-floor corridor to talk to him. "Actually, when I told him what the body on the beach looked like, he recognised Maribel. I can't be sure, but I assumed he was using her for his investigation into Next Phase. Everything that's going on here, it has to come back to Romanelli."

"I think you must be right," he replied and continued down the hallway towards Álvaro's room. "Bielza said you can have two minutes before they take the body away."

There must have been sixty rooms in total but, with hardly any guests, the hotel appeared hollow and fake. Walking past all those empty rooms was unsettling because it felt as if anything could be behind those quiet doors. The stolen goods, a lurking killer or yet more fresh corpses to discover. That fear of the unknown was far greater than my apprehension on approaching my second murder scene of the day.

Jaime opened the door to me and the officers inside greeted us before stepping out to wait in the hall. They gave us our shoe covers and gloves and we entered the room.

"Like I said, two minutes."

Álvaro's body was slumped over the end of his bed. The back of his head looked like someone had taken a sledgehammer to it and his blood had splashed all the way across the sheets. I don't know that much about splatter or blood patterns, but I got the impression he'd been shot standing up then fell forward onto the mattress. He looked like a child at bedtime prayers. His knees were bent and his hands close together but he would not speak another word.

From the look of it, the bullet had exited through the top of his head as there was blood on the ceiling and…

Yuck, do you have to go into such disgusting details?

I ignored my brain and tried to sound professional. "He must have unlocked the door, let the killer follow him into the room and been shot from behind as soon as they got inside," I said and Jaime nodded quietly in agreement. "I wonder if he thought he was welcoming a friend when he let them in."

"It's impossible to say, but one of my colleagues is talking to the telephone company to find out who he'd spoken to before he died. His phone is missing."

Álvaro's remaining possessions had been scattered across the room. Whoever had killed him was clearly looking for something. There were papers and photographs lying in piles on the floor on the other side of the bed and a laptop cable plugged in, but no computer in sight.

"Have they taken any evidence away?" I asked.

Jaime looked distraught once more and I wondered if these two bodies were his first on the job.

Amateur!

"Not yet. I think you must have won inspector Bielza around. They've taken photos of the scene but she told the team not to remove anything until you arrived."

While I couldn't help but take this as a compliment, it also made me wonder what was going on with the senior detective on the case.

I walked around the edge of the room without disturbing the scene. The photos by the bed were a selection of the shots I'd seen on the Next Phase Facebook page, mixed in with old pictures of Marco. There was one of him in a gang of boys in an Italian marketplace, the ten of them posing with great confidence and Marco at the front of the pack showing off a tattoo on his arm. But there were more prints which I could not connect him to, photos of the local parties in a Spanish town. Under the banner "Fiestas de Santa Maria del Mar 1992" another group of young people were huddled. There were a series of photos from that time but Marco wasn't in any of them.

"Is that your village?" I asked Jaime. "Santa Maria del Mar?"

He nodded and joined me to look over the photos.

"Do you recognise anyone in that group?"

He was silent for a moment, then, with something approaching a smile, said, "That's my aunt Carolina. She hasn't changed. But some of the younger ones are harder to recognise."

"What about Maribel's parents? Do you see them there?"

He pointed down to a photo of two guys in their twenties who were waving at the camera. "I think that's the father, he was a character. He died in a car accident a few years after that was taken. Maribel was only little when it happened."

The father was wearing the cross that Maribel had been found with. It was small, gold and unremarkable except for a purple stone in the middle of it which glinted even in the photograph.

"What about the mum, can you see her anywhere?"

He shook his head. "No, I'd recognise Susana. She's not there. But what I don't understand is what Álvaro is doing with these photos." He leaned closer to look at the group picture where his aunt was holding a sign saying *Free Hugs.* Everyone around her looked carefree and exhilarated. My own limited experience told me that, if there's one thing that Spanish people love, it's their local fiestas.

I went back to the doorway and crouched down to look the victim in the eye before I left.

"I'm sorry, Álvaro." I found myself saying out loud. "I should have believed you from the start."

Part of the problem with being a detective (or even just reading a ton of mystery novels) is that you begin to suspect everyone of having bad intentions. Instead of considering Álvaro to be a potential ally, I'd been overly suspicious of his motives. Rather than pursuing him to find out what he knew, I'd let my opportunity pass and now it was too late.

The morticians had arrived with a stretcher and body bag to cart the journalist away. The forensics team would be in next to cart off anything worth taking and Bielza was already out in the corridor to move me along.

"So, any new theories?" She stood with her arms folded over her neat blue uniform.

I wasn't in the mood to spar with her. "Not yet. Just a lot of questions and the feeling that Álvaro's death could have been avoided."

She looked as though she wanted to answer back, then changed her mind. I wasn't trying to criticise her and I could see that she knew that.

I said goodbye to Jaime and left them to their work, with a feeling of futility once more permeating my thoughts.

Wow, it's a rollercoaster being in your head today.

I thought you weren't talking to me?

On the positive side, that's the fifth body we've seen and you barely flinched at the blood and brains and skull bone sticking out all over the place.

Actually, thinking about it now makes me a bit queasy.

I am not Hercule Poirot or Jane Marple. Every dead body I see gets to me in some way. Even horrid old Bob, who deserved exactly what he got, was no great joy to find. But I liked to think that this weakness in me – this sensitivity – was a gift. I could feel the sadness of each event and I was sure that it helped me to understand how such things could happen in the first place.

With the sorrow of Álvaro and Maribel's deaths at the front of my mind, I decided I needed time to myself somewhere. Walking and thinking has to be the greatest tool in a detective's arsenal and there were so many questions floating about in my head that I figured such a break was overdue.

A whole list of mysteries had written itself out for me. I desperately needed to know why Maribel had come to the hotel. This was the obvious one that had been rattling around inside me all day, but, in the periphery, plenty of other questions lingered. I had to find out why the Austrians were putting on an act, what Álvaro had known about Marco Romanelli, who was stealing from the other guests and what Delilah Shaw was really doing at the hotel.

What about, who the murderer is? That would be a good one to work out.

I had theories to each but no definite answers and so, before going out to clear my head in the garden, I decided to focus on a question that was in my power to resolve.

In addition to the lift beside reception, there were two sets of stairs in The Cova Negra hotel. The main staircase in the foyer was the obvious one to use, but there was a second smaller one at the back of the hotel. I knew that nobody could have used the lift at the time of Álvaro's death because we would have seen them from the dining room. But, until I tried for myself, I couldn't be sure whether Delilah

Shaw could have got all the way from Álvaro's room, through the hotel leisure suite and out to the foyer without being seen.

I followed the staircase down to the ground floor and discovered that it came out right by the indoor swimming pool, which was just as luxurious and over-the-top as the entrance to the hotel. There were Doric columns rising up from the water and the ceiling above it was dotted with tiny lights like a starry night's sky. In one corner, a water nymph was holding an overflowing pot which splashed down melodiously into the main pool.

The whole place was spotless. Not a lounger was out of place and the towels in the cupboard by the door were in perfect order. Either Ramesh had suddenly become good at his job or no one had been in there that morning. And even if she had been there, Delilah could have run upstairs to Álvaro's room in less than a minute.

That's not quite true. You can do it in about a minute. A person with normal-length legs might take a little longer.

It's irrelevant anyway. Delilah's hair was dry when she came downstairs, I can't imagine her messing up her perfectly styled locks with a swimming cap either so it's pretty clear she was lying.

It helped to have an idea of the layout of the whole hotel so I explored a little further. Between the leisure centre and the dining room there were several meeting spaces but they were locked when not in use. I looked into the spa and it was still steamed up from whoever had been in there last. I wasn't sure that any of this would be important, but I was trying to be methodical again. I needed to establish the facts as clearly as possible, instead of relying on haphazard chance.

As I came out from the corridor to the swimming pool, I spotted Marco and Gianna talking by the lift. I hung back to watch them but their conversation barely lasted ten seconds when Gianna kissed her husband and pushed the button to open the doors.

I was a little over-excited to see him alone and bounded over enthusiastically.

"Mr Romanelli, I was going for a walk in the gardens, would you like to come with me?" I sounded like a stalker, auditioning my next celebrity target.

I had him trapped in against the lift and there was no getting away.

"Well… I was supposed to be leaving this morning so I can't say I have any other plans." He paused, perhaps trying to think up another criterion that could rule the possibility out. "Okay, Miss Palmer. After you."

He pointed outside with his usual gentlemanly charm and I nodded and walked ahead. I went about twenty steps before realising how weird it was to be racing away like that so I waited for him to catch up.

"You know who I am, don't you?" I asked once we were outside.

He made another gallant gesture of acknowledgement. "They called you Signorina Marple in the Italian papers. I read all about the way you solved the murder of Aldrich Porter, it was very impressive."

I was getting more used to this sort of compliment but still found my cheeks warming up a little when it came from Romanelli.

Don't fall for his charms, Izzy. Remember, he could be a Nazi!

Nobody is perfect, brain. You once convinced me to steal a chocolate bar from Woolworths.

"It's very kind of you." We descended the steps from the terrace to the formal gardens behind the hotel. "But I'm afraid that, this time, you're my main suspect."

He did not seem concerned and laughed at this. "Well, I can understand you thinking that. I am no murderer, but I can see why it would suit you to believe this thing."

We were walking along a gravel path between two large flower beds covered with precision-cut bushes and the odd, hardy rose still sticking out. I'm pretty sure it was an Italian style garden, which seemed appropriate considering who I was talking to.

"You won't mind telling me where you went last night then?"

He recoiled a little at this question then quickly gathered himself. "I was here in the hotel. You were with me."

"No, after that. After everyone had gone to their rooms. You got in your car and drove somewhere. Where did you go?"

His pace suddenly increased as we walked around a large pond in the centre of the garden where the fleur-de-lys fountain was noisily squirting water down into the lower basin. "Oh… After that?" He laughed his tuneful laugh once more. "The thing is, Izzy, I could tell you anything and you have no way of knowing it's true. So, why even ask?"

It was a question I'd thought about a lot. I wasn't the police and the suspects I spoke to weren't compelled to talk to me. "Sometimes a lie can tell me much more than the truth would. Whatever you say will be worth hearing."

"Okay then, how about… I went to the circus. How do you like that for an answer?"

We had reached the wall at the end of the garden. In front of us was a patch of grass which covered the fifty metres between the low, stone barrier and cliff edge. I had my enormous floppy summer hat on, and wasn't worried about the sun for once, so stopped there to talk to him.

"That wasn't an answer. It was a performance." I stepped a little closer to study his face as we spoke. "There's a difference between acting and answering. I'll rephrase the question. Where did you tell the police you went last night?"

He raised his eyebrows a little to tell me that it was an obvious ploy but not entirely without merit.

Very good body language interpretation there, Izzy. Not everybody can read eyebrow semaphore with such alacrity.

Shut up, you! You're just annoyed because I chose the monkfish over the paella, which, may I remind you, we didn't even get to eat!

"I told them I had driven in to Santander to experience the nightlife. I went for some tapas and a few drinks in a club. You can probably find the photos on Twitter somewhere. I'm quite well known these days and people often want to take selfies with me."

"So you had a few drinks here at the hotel, then drove into the city and had a few more drinks there and then drove home again. Weren't the police concerned about your driving when you told them this?"

He leaned forward to whisper in my ear. It reminded me of the first time I'd met him, it was a gesture filled with both malice and charm. "Between you and me, I told them I stuck to lemonade."

Lemonade! The drink of champions!

He smelt of expensive cologne and the red wine he'd consumed at lunchtime. His attractively lined cheek was so close to mine that, if I'd turned my head, I would have kissed him. Such was the power this man had that, for a moment, I genuinely considered it. I was relieved when he straightened back up and I could get a hold of myself once more.

I moved on to my next question. "When the news came in this morning of the girl's death, you looked horrified. Did you know her?"

He had the answer ready prepared on his tongue. "How could

I know her? I haven't even heard her name. I don't think there's anything wrong with showing emotion. A girl has been murdered. If I'd sat there casually eating my breakfast like nothing had happened, I could understand you wondering why. If anything, my reaction shows I had nothing to do with the murder."

"But how would such unbridled emotion fit with the message of Next Phase?" I let him think on this before continuing. "I have to admit, I wasn't familiar with your movement until this week, but everything I've read about it since suggests that your old-fashioned, macho followers would not approve of you crying into your morning coffee."

This was enough to trigger his contempt. He clicked his tongue behind his teeth and began to stroll back towards the house. It was not a sign that the conversation was over, but that he was the one controlling it.

"Oh really? I thought you told me that you were here for the conference. Have you been lying, Miss Palmer?"

Bleeding heck, this guy is good.

You reckon? Well I'm better.

I increased my pace to pull level with him. "Heike and Lio? I was going to ask you about them. Are you paying them to be your cheerleaders? Or they do it out of the goodness of their hearts?"

"My organisation includes all sorts of wonderful people."

"Álvaro Linares was very interested in the type of people you attract, wasn't he?" I asked and he stopped once more beside the fountain. "Why did you threaten to kill him last night?"

His lips curled back against his teeth and I could see I'd really got to him this time. "That man was a liar. He wrote terrible things about me in the press and thought he could get away with it."

"So you killed him?"

He barely gave me time to finish the question before roaring his answer back. "No, I lost my temper and threw a glass at him. That was all."

Just then, his daughters appeared from the hotel in their beach clothes. He smoothed his face out and waved to them.

"Where were you when Álvaro was murdered?" I knew he wouldn't answer, but gave it my best shot.

"If you'll excuse me, Miss Palmer. I'm going to enjoy some time with my family before we move on to our next destination." He was already walking away from me, but I couldn't let him have the last word.

"I wouldn't be too cocky just yet, Mr Romanelli," I shouted after him. "Your next destination might be a cell in Santander police station."

Marco's thick black eyebrows drew together in critique and I felt a little guilty for saying it with his kids there. His eldest daughter was the first to arrive and had clearly heard what I'd yelled.

As her father ushered her sisters away, she stopped for a moment and looked at me.

"Valentina," he called and she shook her head anxiously and scurried away.

Chapter Seventeen

I had a problem. There was one obvious suspect who wasn't at the hotel at the time of the first murder. Three people who could have been involved in both killings but had no obvious motive and ten or so others who, for the moment, I would have to discard.

"I still say Ian Dennison's son was involved." I found Ramesh by the back door of the kitchen, on his break with Cook. "That little hell-seed told Delilah Shaw I fancy her. She was bad enough already, squeezing my bum all the time. I feel like a tenderised steak."

Cook was smoking a fat Cuban cigar and, between puffs, would sympathise with Ramesh with a weary, Spanish sigh.

"Ramesh why are you smoking?"

"It's the job, Izzy. It's the relentless grind of life in the hospitality sector. You can't imagine what it's like. I've only been at it three days and I've already turned to nicotine."

"Belén Esteban!" Cook suggested. "The killer is Belén Esteban!"

I still didn't know who that was so I ignored her.

"It can't be Ian Dennison's son. For one thing, the chance of a ten-year-old boy indiscriminately murdering hotel guests is pretty infinitesimal, but more importantly he was with us at lunch when Álvaro was shot dead."

Ramesh thought for a second. "What about that old Spanish couple? They're kind of creepy."

"Ramesh, I thought you wanted to help me with this investigation. Not just suggest people who can't possibly have been involved in the murder."

He bowed his head despondently. "I'm sorry, Iz. This working life is eating me from the inside out. I can't even come up with convincing theories for who the killer could be."

I didn't like to point out that his previous track record was not much better. Instead, I put my most sympathetic face on and, avoiding a cloud of filthy smoke, gave him a friendly punch on the arm. "I appreciate you trying, buddy."

"The one like Belén Esteban!" Cook tried again. "Much makeup, big lips. Dresses like prostituta from the twenties. You know!"

"Delilah Shaw?"

The middle-aged Spanish woman, in her standard-issue, blue kitchen uniform, exploded with joy. "That's her! She's the killer, I know this. She's got face of killer."

I could see that she and Ramesh were born to work together. They had a surprisingly similar attitude to life.

"Thanks for the suggestion, Cook."

It's funny how, every time you report a Spanish person's speech in English, it's full of mistakes and yet, when you speak Spanish, it's like you're a native.

I ignored my brain and my two companions' theories. "Listen, Ramesh. I haven't got much time. Who knows how long the police will keep everybody at the hotel. I can't see Bielza forcing the Romanellis to stay here after tomorrow."

"I'll come with you," he responded and stubbed his cigarette out on the brick wall. "My next shift is about to start."

He said goodbye to his colleague, using the international language of grunting and she raised her cigar to us in salutation before puffing out an enormous, black smoke ring.

"You can do it, Iz. I know you can," Ramesh said as we skirted the building. "And I'll try to think up some really good ideas while I'm cleaning. Maybe I'll land on the killer myself this time."

I wanted to believe him, but things were not looking good. There were still suspects and witnesses to talk to. Still ideas to explore but I felt like I was missing something obvious.

It's not as if anyone's paying us. Why don't we go down to the beach again and relax for a while? Or what about the swimming pool? There's nobody in there, we can splash about and make all the noise we want.

How about I choose paella for dinner? Will that shut you up for the rest of the day?

Silence! I promise you. Pure, uninterrupted silence from now until bedtime.

There was only one police car left at the front of the hotel so I imagined that the other officers were off investigating potential leads. As we mounted the front steps, I noticed a taxi pulling away, but I didn't think anything of it until I got inside.

When we walked past the police guard and into the foyer, I was surprised to see two new guests checking in. A woman dressed in a spotless cream dress and matching hat, which I could totally picture my mother wearing, was standing at the front desk making a fuss.

"I'm Bu-Bu La Mer!" she boomed in a powerful American voice. "What do you mean you haven't got my booking?"

The man standing behind her said nothing. Dressed in a tight black suit, which showed off his broad frame, he moved his weight from one foot to the other intimidatingly. I couldn't see his face but, from his pose – hands behind back, legs apart – it was safe to assume he was her bodyguard.

"OMG!" Ramesh only uses abbreviations when he's really excited about something – so maximum thirty times a day. "I love Bu-Bu La Mer!"

"Who's Bu-Bu La Mer?"

He looked at me like I'd recently had a lobotomy. "You don't know Barbara La Mer? How is that possible?" He looked at me like the lobotomy had been a massive failure. "She was a gigantic star in the eighties. She was in that movie 'Woofable.' You know, the one about the talking dogs and that series, what was it called?" He thought for a moment. "'Every Silver Lining Has A Cloud'!"

"I'm pretty sure you just made that up. I've never heard of either of them."

Ramesh ignored me as he was busy geeking out on his celebrity crush. "I had her posters all over my walls when I was a kid. I thought she was so sophisticated. I have to talk to her."

Without waiting for me, or my opinion on what he was about to do, he stormed across the foyer. "Miss La Mer," he screamed. "I'm such a big fan. It's an honour to have you in our hotel."

Behind reception, Kabir was looking worried. "I don't have any record of the booking."

"Forget the booking, uncle. This is Barbara La Mer! Put her in the best suite we have. And if there's not one available, kick Izzy out of hers." All starstruck, Ramesh looked over at his heroine. "Don't worry, Miss La Mer. We'll sort out this misunderstanding in no time." It was odd to see him so efficient and businesslike.

"It's about time someone with brains turned up," La Mer said to her bodyguard. I thought perhaps I recognised the voice but her features were hidden by her hat and glasses.

"Of course," Kabir added. "We're not open to the public at the moment, but we'll make an exception for you, Miss La Mer."

"Izzy," Ramesh shouted to me. "Take the luggage to the third floor and no dawdling."

I was a bit put out that I'd ended up at the bottom rung of The Cova Negra staff ladder. Strangely overpowered by Ramesh's orders I walked across to the flamboyant actress and carried her first two cases to the lift. I was about to return for the others when her bodyguard appeared, his face covered by a pair of large aviator sunglasses and his head down to guide the cases inside. I held the door open for him and Ramesh arrived with our celebrity guest.

"It's such an honour," he repeated and ushered her into the lift.

Bu-Bu La Mer's hat was almost too big to fit inside. Two great peacock feathers arched across it and it instantly cleared a space around her like she wanted to ensure people kept their distance.

The door closed and Ramesh pressed the button for the third floor then instantly burst out laughing. Grabbing me by the shoulders, he screamed, "And that, Izzy Palmer, is the power of amateur dramatics!"

Bu-Bu La Mer pulled the hat from her head. "Hello, Izzy darling!"

"Mum? What are you doing here?"

She joined in with Ramesh's noisy joy. "I came as soon as I heard. Ramesh called me this morning and we were on a plane in Gatwick by ten o'clock."

"That does not explain what you're doing here." A thought suddenly occurred to me and I turned to her fake bodyguard. "Danny? Why would you go along with one of Mother's ridiculous plans?"

Mum removed her equally oversized sunglasses. "Well Greg's on a retreat this weekend. And somebody had to drive me to the airport."

There wasn't much I could say to that. The lift dinged and the door opened.

"You will be in the Celebrity Suite." Ramesh had their key at the ready. "I don't know why it's called that. According to uncle no celebrities have ever stayed here."

"Until now, darling," my mother replied, waving her hat through the air with a flourish. "Until now!"

As Ramesh opened the door to the last remaining suite, Danny came to look at me. He put his hands on my shoulders then pulled me in for a hug. "It's so good to see you, Iz. I really mean that."

My tummy quaked, my muscles contracted and my brain felt all funny as he held me tighter. I was fourteen years old again. That's the effect he could still have on me.

"It's only been about three days, Danny." I ducked out of the hug and hurried into the room in search of answers "Alright, Mum, you've got some explaining to do. I only told Ramesh about the first murder at eight thirty this morning, how did you have time to buy new luggage and clothes, get plane tickets and get to the airport so quickly?" An even more important question came to mind. "And how did you have time to coordinate a backstory for your characters with Ramesh?"

Mum wasn't listening because she was too busy staring around in wonder at her hotel room. "Don't worry about any of that, darling." She spun her floppy hat through the air into her bedroom. "The important thing is that we are here now and we can help you solve this murder."

"Murders, plural, Rosie," Ramesh corrected her. "Another one bit the dust this afternoon."

Danny's eyes grew three sizes bigger. "It wasn't that Marco Romanelli bloke was it?"

"No, it was the journalist." Ramesh slunk over to Danny conspiratorially. "You know, the one I told you about. Nice beard, poor dress sense."

"Everybody, slow down." I was still trying to figure out what they were doing there. "Mum, why are you pretending to be famous?"

"That was my idea, Izzy." Ramesh was extremely proud of himself. "You're always saying we need to be more methodical, well *I* am a *method* actor." He put his arms out to the side like his audience had just demanded an encore.

"Yes, but why did you bother?"

He slumped down onto the sofa and, in two clicks of the remote, "World's Grumpiest Animals" was back on. "Oh… dunno really. Just thought it would be fun."

Mum stepped forward to elucidate. "And I went along with his plan because now I can go undercover at the hotel and find out everybody's dirty little secrets." She had returned to her deep southern accent. It was far superior to the New York one she had tried in the past.

Danny was still rushing around the place with his tail wagging. "I don't want to freak anybody out, but I just peeked into the bathroom and we've got our own jacuzzi!"

"That's nothing. Wait until you see the wardrobe!" Ramesh jumped up from the sofa to pull Danny into the bedroom.

It was always going to happen one day.

You said you were going to be silent!

Oh, come on. That was too good to resist!

While the boys checked out the ample storage space, I yanked my mother over to the balcony and shut the door behind us.

"Mum, what are you doing here? There have been two murders already, it might not be safe for you."

She was too busy admiring the view to give me her full attention. "They wouldn't dare kill me, darling. I'm British!"

I knew I would only lose such an argument so moved on to my next complaint. "I can't believe you brought Danny here. You know I have a boyfriend."

"Yes, my love, and I'm sorry to tell you that the trial isn't going well."

"That's not the point." My voice was already breaking. "I love David."

"And I love David too, you know I do," she said with all the sympathy she could muster before completely changing her tone. "However, I think it's in everyone's best interests if you break up with him as soon as you can and get together with Danny."

I stared at her, unable to believe she was serious, even after decades of being unable to believe she was serious. There were no words to sum up how I was feeling so I went with a low groan, like a cow passing a kidney stone.

"I'm sorry to say it so bluntly, Izzy, but I'm Team Danny all the way. It would be so fantastic if you got together." She looked up at the sky dreamily. "My two wonderful children finally united in love."

"I'm pretty sure you don't need me to point out how weird that sounds."

"You know what I mean. Danny's like a son to me and you-"

Just then, something entirely unexpected occurred. I started to cry.

"Oh, Izzy, my poor creature."

I don't know if it was the news from the trial, the double-murder investigation I was making no progress with or Danny's arrival, but everything had got too much for me.

"I know I don't talk about these things, Mum. But I do feel them." I paused to find the right words. "I wanted to be with Danny for so long but, when David came along, I thought that part of my life was over." I fell quiet again and stared out across the horizon. "The truth is that everything is messed up and I've no idea what to do about it."

She looked at me for a moment and took my hands in hers. To be honest, I'm surprised she could understand me through the tears. "Izzy, you are one of the strongest people I know. I'm sorry if I've made things worse by bringing Danny here but you will get through this the way you always do."

Her sympathy made me cry even louder. I was grateful that The Cova Negra had soundproof windows because I really didn't want Danny hearing me. "I'm not sure I will, Mum. If David ends up in prison, I haven't a clue how I'll handle it."

Her pretty face crumpled into a frown. "You really do love him, don't you?"

"Of course I do." I attempted to dry my eyes with the back of my hand, but, as I was still crying, it didn't do much good. "Have you only just realised?"

She looked a bit guilty. "I'm sorry, darling, I really am." I wasn't used to hearing her speak like this. She was calm and serious. "I knew you liked David, but you only went on a few dates together. I never imagined you'd take it so much to heart."

She put her arms around me and it felt so good to be held for a moment.

"I take everything to heart, Mother. I'm not the kind of person who can turn my feelings on and off so easily. No matter how I feel about Danny, I can't just switch my affection over, especially if David is found guilty."

She pulled away to look me in the eyes. "You know your problem is that you bottle everything up." Her voice was firm, like she was telling off a wayward child. "It's time you came to terms with whatever is going on inside you. And if primal screaming and chakra channelling don't work for you, how about telling me how you feel once in a while?"

I didn't have any answer to that so I pulled her back in for another hug.

After a minute of blissful silence, she looked at me once more.

"Izzy Palmer, future head of The Clever Dick Detective agency-"

"I'm not calling it that."

She continued, unperturbed. "Izzy Palmer, there's a murder to solve and I'm going to help you. So why don't we go back inside and you can fill me in on the case?"

I still wasn't sure that I was ready but nodded and let her lead me back inside.

Chapter Eighteen

"So, let me get this straight." Mum was holding court in the lounge of her suite. She'd taken a whiteboard marker and had scribbled up the titles of three important categories on the blank TV screen. Suspects, Clues and Hypotheses; everything we needed to get to the truth. "All the evidence points to Marco Romanelli and yet it couldn't possibly be him. What about his wife, could she be in on it?"

"I don't see how," Ramesh replied. "She was with us in the dining room when Álvaro was shot. And also, Rosie, you say the evidence points towards Marco but we still don't know why Maribel was murdered."

"Then what if there are two killers?" Mum asked.

"Bit unlikely isn't it? Two maniacs at the same beach resort?" Ramesh spoke as if Mum was talking nonsense, which, coming from the man who once started an online petition to erect a statue to Diana Ross in Trafalgar Square, was a bit rich.

"No, darling. Two killers working together. Maybe Marco dealt with Álvaro and his accomplice did away with Maribel?"

There was silence for a moment as we considered this possibility, before Ramesh once more broke it. "But why would they have bothered?"

"Don't you see?" Mum was alive with ideas, bouncing from toe to toe in front of the screen. "By killing two people, they throw suspicion off their real motives. Perhaps Maribel was collateral damage and the whole plan was hatched to silence Álvaro."

There was another pause, another whirl of thoughts spinning through our heads.

"I think you need to look deeper into the other suspects." Danny was clearly enjoying the first moments of his holiday. He'd pulled out a bottle of champagne from their minibar and was quaffing it from a cocktail glass. "What about those Austrian girls? You don't know the first thing about them. It looks like they're tied up in this Next Phase business. Could they be Romanelli's fixers or something?"

"Well the blonde was missing during the second killing," Ramesh replied. "Perhaps they took it in turns to do the deed."

I was leaving my squad to do a bit of the work and enjoying their process of deduction. Sometimes, the only way to solve a problem is not to focus on it. Hearing my assembled loved ones throwing their theories around, had sparked up some ideas of my own.

"From the way Álvaro spoke to me, I think he knew what Maribel was doing here last night. But with him out of the picture, how are we going to find out what that was?" I thought for a moment but the answers I came up with only stirred up more questions. "Danny's right, we need to know more about the Dennisons, the old Spanish couple and the Austrian girls. Even if they weren't involved in the murders, their presence here could still reveal something about the case."

"Well, I know exactly what I'm going to do this evening," my mother replied, pointing her red marker at us dramatically. "I... or rather, Bu-Bu La Mer is going to get a table with Marco Romanelli. Us celebrities have to stick together." She flicked her eyebrows to the ceiling, also highly dramatically.

"And I'm going to sit near you looking steely and aggressive." Danny tossed his suit jacket aside to show a bulging holster strapped under his arm.

Ramesh instantly lurched towards him. "Is that a real gun? Can I touch it?"

"Ra! How have you not learnt anything after what happened yesterday?"

He pulled back, looking disappointed, and Mum called us all to attention. "Okay everybody, you know what you have to do. I'm going to spend some time making myself look fabulous before dinner. Danny, guard the door. Izzy, keep investigating and, Ramesh, we need you to make up an extra bed on the sofa."

Ramesh groaned, no doubt aware that he still had his afternoon shift to get through. Feeling more energised than I had all day, I stood up to leave. Who would have thought that all I needed was my mum?

"Izzy, can I have a word?" Danny caught up with me as I got to the suite's own entrance parlour. "I wanted to ask you something."

My heart started up a marimba beat and my palms got all clammy. I'd spent the last month avoiding any confrontation with Danny and here we were, halfway across the continent, alone together.

"Yes, Danny?" My eyes locked onto his and I remembered every lonely night of my teenage years that I'd spent dreaming of the boy next door.

"Do you really think it's safe? I mean, there's already been two murders. The killer could strike again."

To be honest, I never really considered the possibility that I could be in danger. It was yet another thing to worry about. "I can handle myself," I lied. "I'll be fine,"

"Okay… But let me know if you need a bodyguard." He smiled his generous smile and, this time, my whole body quaked.

I could really have used my brain giving me a silent, verbal slap right about then, but it was busy keeping shtum. I stood there, staring goofily at my lifelong crush until he headed back into the suite.

As I walked downstairs, I decided to reach out to another member of my dedicated support staff.

"Listen, Dean, I need your help."

He didn't sound very happy to hear from me. "Well that is a turn up for the books." In fact, he was full-on cranky. "What is it this time?"

"You know you love doing stuff for me?" I replied in a no doubt adorable tone. "And you're so much better at interneting than I am."

"Go on, Izzy. Spit it out."

"I need you to find any link you can between Marco Romanelli and Delilah Shaw."

He was silent for a moment. "Who's Delilah Shaw?"

"She's a nobody. Just some aggressive journalist on a morning phone-in who's always telling people how terrible they are."

He puffed out a breath. "Oh, yeah. Rings a bell actually. And how would she know Romanelli? He's surely too big a deal to hang out with someone like her."

"That's what I want you to find out for me. You know I'm on a case, right?"

Another awkward pause. "Yeah, I've been texting your mum. I heard that the bodies are piling up already?"

"How do you even know that?" My mother's communication network has always been a thing of wonder to me. "I only told her about five minutes ago and I've been with her ever since."

He ignored my question. "Listen, Iz, I've got to go. Your dad is taking me out for some drinks tonight. Says he's going to be my wingman."

"I really don't know which part of that sentence I find more disturbing. Yes I do… your wingman?"

I came out at the top of the stairs in the foyer. The police had returned and drawn a crowd too for some reason. The Dennison double demons were trying to get a look at what was going on and I spotted their parents, the Spanish pensioners and Gianna there too.

With a final huff, Dean gave in. "I'll get you the information when I have a minute. If the two of them have done anything together, the internet will reveal their secrets – it always does. Oh, and tell your mum that her website and Wikipedia entry are almost done."

"Wait, what website?" I asked, but he'd already hung up.

As I got to reception, Lio was being escorted through the front door by two uniformed officers. Inspector Bielza shouted out orders to various underlings before leaving the building herself.

"What's going on?" I asked Jaime, whose turn it was to stand by the door checking who was leaving and entering the hotel.

"I can't share that information with members of the public."

I realise now why I had been so attracted to him since we first met. He was the perfect Latin reproduction of Dr Danny Fields – right down to the puppy dog eyes and tight-fitting clothes. This revelation made me feel a bit better about myself. I'd essentially only been thinking about one other man whilst my boyfriend was standing trial for murder, not two.

I got the impression he was putting on a show for his colleagues, so lowered my voice and tried again in English this time. "Are they arresting Lio?"

"Her name isn't Lio," he replied in a whisper. "It's Sabrina Muller. She's not even Austrian, she's German and she's been lying to us this whole time."

I knew she was German! Oops… sorry, sorry. I'll be quiet, I promise.

"Have you found something that links her to the murder though?"

He glanced about at the crowd as if he was expecting trouble. "I told you, Izzy. I'm not allowed to share any other information with you."

One of his colleagues had passed on his way to speak to Kabir and, once he was gone, Jaime added, "This Sabrina person has a criminal record. Violence going back years. Bielza put a request for information out and the German police sent us her record." The short female officer I'd seen that morning came through the rotating door and gave Jaime a suspicious look when she saw him talking to me.

I didn't want them thinking badly of him so, in intentionally poor Spanish replied, "Thank you, Officer Jaime. You are very kind and hard-working."

He nodded and I walked back across the foyer, hoping to find Heike. She wasn't in the dining room or on the terrace and I was about to head to the beach to look for her when she appeared on the path. By this stage of the holiday, her skin had turned a shade of brown that was somewhere between caramel and cinnamon.

"Heike, I was looking for you. They've arrested Lio."

"I can't say I'm surprised," she replied without emotion, her eyes peering up at the hotel.

"Your friend could be in serious trouble."

"She's not my friend and, I'm sorry, but I'm on my way to the spa." She walked off ahead of me into the hotel and I tried to understand the sudden shift in her personality.

"I have some questions to ask you." I trailed after her across the dining room.

"Well, then I hope you like saunas." Her whole attitude, and even her voice, had changed since I'd spoken to her that morning.

There wasn't much else I could do so I accompanied her to the hotel's leisure centre. When we got there, she removed the towel she'd been wearing and, dropping it to the floor with significant sass, went through the door into the sauna and began to steam the place up.

I ditched my sarong and T-shirt and braved the sauna. The place was hotter than a bonfire and it made me dizzy to step inside.

She was sitting on a wooden-slat bench and, just to make me feel more comfortable, she'd removed her bikini. "Most people like saunas in the wintertime, but I think there's nothing better after a day on the beach. Do you mind if I add a little more steam?" All the sweetness I'd expected from her was gone. She was cold, rigid and precise.

"Please, go ahead," I said because I'm a polite idiot.

"It gets rid of all the toxins from your body, you know? It's the perfect thing after a swim in the sea." She sounded like she was no longer working for Next Phase and had moved on to sauna promotion.

I wanted to ask her my first question but was busy trying not to faint. My head was all spacey, my body appeared to have fallen asleep and my throat felt like it was closing in on itself. "I just heard that your… your companion's name is not really Lio."

"That doesn't surprise me." She was being less forthcoming than I would have liked. To be honest, I'd have preferred her to spit out everything I needed to hear in one easy chunk so that I could run back out of hell as soon as possible.

"How did the two of you know each other?"

"We didn't." She really wasn't making this easy.

"Despite the number of times you like to mention Marco in any given sentence, I know you're not Next Phase devotees. So what were you doing here together?"

The steam was so thick that I couldn't see her face though she was sitting right in front of me.

"It sounds like you've already worked that out." Her voice cut through the dripping wet air. "The Romanellis paid us to be their fans; you know, promote the organisation, look good in photos, that sort of thing."

She was right, I'd come to this conclusion but it was still surprising to hear it confirmed. "Are you actresses?"

Her laugh came out frosty, despite our surroundings. "Not exactly, but let's just say I'd done a lot of acting in all my previous jobs."

I ignored the innuendo and continued with my questions. "How did you come to work for them?"

"I was on the streets in Hamburg when Lio found me. That's the only name I ever knew her by, so don't expect me to tell you much about her. She said she'd got a cushy job and that, if I spoke English, they needed another girl. She'd been sent out to find someone, I hadn't seen her around before then."

"What did they want you to do?"

She leaned forward and her beautiful brown eyes loomed out at me through the steam. "They told me that our primary duty was to spread the word about Next Phase wherever we went. Normally that meant going out on the night before a conference to drop it into conversation with gullible men. It was easy to get people fired up about those kinds of issues."

I took my time, turning each word over before replying. "That's what they told you, and what did the job turn out to be?"

She smiled like she appreciated my inference. "During the

conferences, we had to keep any unwelcome guests from getting too close to the Romanellis. You'd be surprised how effective two pretty girls can be at persuading people to move along. Marco said we were better than any bodyguard."

"So that was it? Nothing more sinister?"

She hesitated and a tiny bit of the vulnerability she'd shown around Lio re-emerged. "Of course there was, we had to sleep with politicians, journalists; whichever men he told us to. But I'd been expecting that from the beginning."

Even through the steam, I could tell there was something she hadn't said. "That wasn't all, was it?"

There were five seconds of silence and, when she did reply, a hairline crack had cut through her voice. "Álvaro." She breathed in deep and slowly back out again to cope with the heat. "He wasn't like any of the other journalists we met. Flattery and flirting didn't work with him. He was obsessed with bringing Marco down, but he was kind to us too. He knew we were working for Next Phase and he offered to help us get away from them."

A thought fired in my head. "Did you give him any dirt on the Romanellis?"

"No, never. But then nothing I know about Marco is really that bad. The worst I can say about him is that he likes to party and has a wandering eye. That kind of thing might have been interesting to Gianna but I doubt it would have made it into the papers."

"So what did Marco make you do to Álvaro?"

"We didn't kill him if that's what you're suggesting. Lio had just gone upstairs when he was shot. I doubt she'd have had the time to find a gun, kill Álvaro, get showered and changed and come back down."

"But Marco made you do something, didn't he?"

She let out a troubled sigh. "At the conference yesterday, Álvaro got up in the middle of the auditorium and screamed accusations at Marco. He said he knew all about Marco's past and that he was going to bring him down. Until then, he'd never made a scene like that and it took ages for us to pull him away. It was in the middle of the keynote speech and Marco was furious. When the conference was over, he told us to do whatever was necessary to destroy Álvaro's reputation before the end of the tour."

"And what did you think that meant?" I took a cup of water from the tap by the door and poured it down my back. Rather than cooling me off, it made me feel like I was the element in a kettle as yet more steam fizzed off me.

"I wasn't paid to think. Lio said she would deal with it and I kept quiet. But when Álvaro came back here last night and Marco lost his temper, I saw that demon side of him that he'd always kept hidden. With someone like Marco, you know it's there, lurking beneath the surface, but when it finally emerges it's raw and terrifying and you can't look away."

Until that moment, I hadn't paid attention to the fact that her English was now almost perfect. Even her accent had improved and I realised it was another part of the act she'd been putting on. It made me wonder if I was still falling for her tricks.

"So… why are you telling me this? Why answer my questions now?"

A single second of laughter puffed out of her. "I don't owe the Romanellis anything." She straightened in her seat and the steam swallowed her up once more. "I figure the job's coming to an end one way or another. Either Marco's going down for these killings or we finish up in Madrid and they'll have no further use for me."

"So you think he did it then?"

She answered with another question. "Who else would want Álvaro dead?"

"That's the big question." I paused to think about everything she had told me and there was still one part of the mystery that didn't fit in. "Did you ever meet a Spanish girl called Maribel Ruiz? She had long brown hair and a heart-shaped beauty mark on her right cheek."

"She doesn't sound familiar, but there were some Spanish girls working for Marco before I came on board. I think he likes to imagine he's doing us a favour by plucking us from the streets, just as his own benefactor did."

Her comment caught me off guard. "Marco inherited his money from his family's business. There was no benefactor."

Standing up at last, she re-materialised before me to pull her bikini back on with a knowing grin. "Sure. You can believe the highly unlikely story that he's the last, lost relative of the Carlucci family if you want to, but let's just say that my past and Marco's are far more similar than you might imagine and he would ever admit. He told me one night when he was drunk; he was a grifter and, when he met the old Carlucci woman, he found his ultimate trick."

She opened the door and the steam rushed from the sauna, apparently even more desperate than I was to get out of there. "Wait. Do you think that's what Álvaro discovered? Was that what he was threatening to reveal?"

I stood up to chase after her but as soon as I stepped into the dressing room, my body grew limp and I felt myself falling. The floor zoomed up to kiss me and the room went black.

Chapter Nineteen

It didn't take me long to come round but, when I did, I had a bruise on my head and I still felt like I was dissolving.

"Izzy, are you okay?" I could hear Heike's voice before I opened my eyes.

Ramesh was there too. "Please, don't let her die! I couldn't live without my Izzy."

I rolled over onto my back and looked about.

"Glad to see you're still with us." The pretty brunette smiled down at me sweetly. There was an unexpected burst of compassion in the look she gave me and her coldness appeared to have melted away.

"It's a miracle!" Ramesh fell to his knees in exaltation. "Thank you, Lord. I will never doubt you again." Coming from a half-Hindu, half-Christian family, I'm not sure even he knew which god he was praying to.

I sat up, still feeling weak. "I'm fine." There was a towel rolled up where my head had just been and a glass of water on hand. "Thanks for taking care of me."

"It was all Heike," Ramesh admitted. "I've been a mess since she came to get me."

"How's your head?" She was a hooker with heart.

"I'm fine. It's my own stupid fault for standing up so quickly. I should have eaten more for lunch."

"Perhaps we should call for an ambulance?" the presumably still Austrian girl replied.

I was feeling steadier so I pulled myself up onto a bench. "No, honestly, I'm fine. It was the heat that made me pass out, not the bruise."

She nodded, and wrapped a towel around herself. "Well if you're sure you're alright, I'll leave you with your friend." She looked at me to check this was okay then took her possessions and left.

"Are you certain you're not dying, Iz?"

I smiled at my faithful companion. "Of course not. And there's no time for lying about in a daze."

"That's a relief." His tone changed. "Uncle will shout at me again if I don't get all my work done this afternoon. I have to finish cleaning out the empty rooms from yesterday. You wouldn't believe the stuff people leave behind. I found a phone, some phone chargers, a bunch of books, a Bluetooth speaker, more phone chargers, an unopened packet of bacon sandwiches – which were delicious – and a load more phone chargers."

I rested my weight on his shoulder as we left the leisure centre and headed back to reception. "You know, you really should talk to Kabir about getting some more staff. It's not fair the way he's taken advantage of you."

A grin shaped Ramesh's face. "He's family. What else would you expect?"

"That doesn't mean he should use you as a slave."

"Don't worry about me, Iz. I'm actually starting to enjoy myself. The good thing about doing the bedrooms is that I get to eat all the little coffee biscuits I could ever dream of. I'm supposed to lay them out with the tea-making facilities, but who's going to know?" Still smiling like a manatee, he picked up a box from reception and headed over to the lift.

I thought about talking to Jaime again as he was alone now, but there were other people ahead of him on my list. I spotted Celestino and Sagrario playing cards in the dining room and decided I should cross them off first.

"Do you know how to play Escoba?" Celestino asked me as I sat down at their table and he dealt out their cards.

"I know solitaire? Is it anything like that?"

The corners of his mouth turned upwards the tiniest bit, but it didn't break his concentration as he picked up his hand to view the cards. "You better sit this one out, pay attention and I'll deal you in for the next round." He was a man who took his cards seriously.

"I was talking to Marco Romanelli earlier." As I spoke, I watched their faces for any hint of emotion. "He's a wonderful man, so full of grand ideas. I'm sure that if Next Phase is given a fair go, it could change the whole political system in Europe. Wouldn't that be wonderful?"

Sagrario picked up a card from the table but didn't look at me as she answered. "Yes, wonderful."

"Celestino, what was it that attracted you to the movement in the first place?"

His eyes flicked in my direction and I was sure that he knew what I was doing. "It's like Marco says, we need change." This was all he offered, but I could see the annoyance on his wife's face.

I kept pushing, determined to get the reaction I was after. "Of course, it will only work if we apply all of Next Phase's ideas. Doing things by half will get us nowhere."

"Yes, that's right." Sagrario nodded with her eyes still glued to her cards.

"It's one thing to get businesses nationalised again but we also need a balance in our society." I was making this nonsense up as I went along. "Now, I'm not a racist, but it's obvious that people should stick to their own."

I'd finally provoked a tut from the old lady. I could see that I would have no luck getting any information out of stone-faced Celestino, but his wife was a different bucket of salmon.

"Don't get me wrong, I have foreign friends, but it's like in the animal kingdom, certain species live in certain environments. It doesn't take make sense for us to be scattered across the planet. Holidays are one thing, but Englishmen should live in England and Spaniards in Spain. And, as much as I like them, it's only right that the Africans should go back down to Africa."

That did the trick. Sagrario was suddenly raging. "So then, who would work in our hospitals and pick our food? It's that kind of disgusting attitude which set Spain back fifty years under Franco. A whole generation died trying to protect us from bigotry and I never thought I'd live to see such ideas return to Spain." Her words faded out and she raised her hand to her mouth.

Her husband looked across at her but didn't panic. He tossed a card down and turned to address me. "I think it is wonderful that we live in a world where everyone is free to express their opinions."

I could see right through him. "I knew it! You two aren't fascists. Romanelli and his gang are the last people you'd want anything to do with. Tell me the truth, why are you really here?"

Sagrario kept her mouth shut this time and her husband scanned the room to make sure that no one could hear. "Know your enemy, Izzy. If we're going to stop these barbarians, then we have to understand them. That's why we booked this hotel; to see Romanelli up close.

And that's why we went to the conference yesterday."

"So, what are you? Political activists?"

Sagrario still looked terrified, so Celestino did all the talking. "I prefer the term guerrilla journalist. In 2008 after the financial crash, we lost everything. We had an ironmonger's shop in Seville and it went bust. We survived for a while but, when the bank took our house away, we ended up in a shelter. That's where we decided that we would never let a government rob us again. We set up a blog to expose corruption. We've made it our goal to stop this kind of thing before it can infect the country. We can get closer to people because they think we're just a sweet old couple."

I was doing some sums in my head adding bits of information together leaving others aside. "So you must have known Álvaro?"

Sagrario switched her focus to me. "We'd crossed paths, but we maintain our anonymity so that nobody knows who we really are."

"Okay then, just to summarise; the two of you are here because you are undercover septuagenarian guerrilla journalists, hell-bent on stopping Marco Romanelli's movement?"

Sagrario's sweet little old lady face brightened up at this. "That's exactly it, dear."

I copied her sunny expression. "And how often do people fall for that excuse?"

Celestino joined in. His deep, booming laughter thundered across the empty dining room. "It's the first time we've tried it. What do you think?"

Sagrario was looking worried so I tried to put her mind at ease. "I'm not trying to get you into trouble. I just need to know why you're here. I can't see how you would be involved in either of the murders, but, to work out who was, you have to tell me why you've been lying."

The old man's expression was suddenly hard and fierce. "That's for you to work out. Why should we give away all our secrets, just because you're a pretty girl who happens to speak a bit of Spanish?"

"Yeah, why should we trust you?" There was something nasty in Sagrario's tone that put me on edge.

"Because, before long, I might not be the only one who sees through your sweeter than sweet act. The truth has a habit of exposing itself."

Having relaxed into the conversation, there was a change in

Celestino. He rounded his shoulders, pulled his hands into his body and stared down hard at his cards. "Sagrario, it's your turn." I would get no more out of him.

I waited, as they played their game, in the hope that Sagrario would open up to me once more. It was useless. Celestino won the hand and I left them to it, still none the wiser of the rules of the game.

First Heike and Lio, now the Spanish couple. It was hard to believe that anyone was who they said they were. Delilah Shaw was the one person in the hotel who seemed most suited to the Next Phase ethos, and she claimed she had nothing to do with them. It's a detective's job to find the truth, but what if everyone around you is lying from the start?

I walked to the terrace to get my thoughts in order. Ian Dennison was already out there sitting under a parasol with his wife as their two kids ran around the garden pulling up flowers and occasionally punching one another. The weather was just right. The sun was high in the sky, a few wispy clouds floated about and the air was a perfect thirty degrees. Every time I ended up on the terrace, it made me want to sit down with a book, order an ice-cold lemonade and exchange real-life murders for fictional ones.

"Oi, Izzy Palmer?" Dennison called over and I knew that "Death on the Nile" would have to wait. "Have you worked out who the killer is yet?"

I pulled my sunglasses down my nose and looked over at him. "Yes, Ian. My working hypothesis is that you're the culprit."

"Hey, that's a good one, that is." He laughed but it didn't sound real. "Hey, Sharon, did you hear that? She thinks I'm the killer."

Mrs Dennison let out a nervous giggle of her own.

"I'm not joking," I replied, raising my voice. "You do realise that you're one of the very few people whose presence was unaccounted for at the time of both killings?"

He suddenly didn't look so cheerful. "What are you saying? "He turned to his wife once more. "Sharon, what's she saying? I was asleep both times. I told the police. I told them, I was asleep both times." The more nervous he got, the more he repeated himself.

"Exactly. Asleep in your bed with no witnesses." It was my turn to address his wife. "Mrs Dennison? Can you say for sure that Ian didn't get out of bed last night and come down to the beach?"

She peered at her husband before replying in an almost inaudible voice. "I... I sleep with earplugs in because of Ian's snoring so... Well... no, I can't say for sure."

Dennison was sweating even more than normal. "This is ridiculous, why would I have killed those two people? They didn't mean anything to me." His voice went a whole octave higher.

"I'm not so sure about that." If only everyone was as easy to manipulate as Ian Dennison. "You keep saying how much you admire Marco Romanelli, perhaps you thought you'd solve a few of his problems to get in his good books."

He was jerking and glancing about now, like an angry cockerel. "This is insane, I can't believe what I'm hearing. I'm not a murderer!"

"So tell me what you're really doing here this week. I know you didn't just come for the conference."

He gestured to his wife with one elbow. "Sharon and I thought the kids might like some time on the beach. The conference was a bonus."

"Tell me the truth, Ian." I turned my chair to face him and the legs made a terrible screech on the concrete. "I don't believe you for a second. You couldn't care less about Next Phase, could you?"

He rose to his feet and pointed one finger at me. "How dare you. I'm a racist me. I love all this *send 'em back to where they come from* stuff. It's about time someone stood up and did something about..." He struggled over the next word and there was no conviction in his tone. "... foreigners."

"Oh, sorry I take it all back. So it's just a coincidence that Marco Romanelli owns a luxury car firm and you have a company that imports and exports expensive cars."

For a moment, the only sound on the terrace were crashing waves and screaming kids. Big red Ian froze where he stood. I believe the term is *snookered*.

He looked to his wife but she didn't have much to say at the best of times. When his reply did come it was garbled and hesitant. "I... I don't know where you get these ideas. I'm... I... Well, I'm just here for the sunshine. The kids go crazy if they don't get a dose of sun from time to time. In fact, I'd better check on them. You can't let them off the leash too long or they start to bite people."

He went off across the patio and down the steps to the garden. I almost felt sorry for his kids, who bore the brunt of his humiliation. He instantly slapped them around the ears and told them off for whatever they'd done. His wife glanced back at me and it was clear that she knew more than her husband was letting on.

Chapter Twenty

Spiralling; that's another good word. Though it felt like I was going round in circles, I had to believe I was getting closer to the truth with each turn. I thought about calling mum's hairdresser Fernando to get his spin on the case, when Bu-Bu herself arrived on the patio with her entourage.

"It's the famous actress, Bu-Bu La Mer!" Ramesh ran over to the Dennisons to explain. I could see he was doing a similar hype job for my mother as Heike and Lio had done for the Romanellis. "Didn't you just love her in 'A Spy to Remember'?"

Gawping at Mum as they walked across the terrace towards the outdoor pool, Ian and Sharon mumbled to one another in impressed tones. Bu-Bu herself had ditched the flowing cream outfit and was now wearing a full-length, spangled dress that Shirley Bassey would have considered over the top.

"You have to play the part, darling!" She told me when she saw me looking on in disbelief, bordering on horror.

"And what part exactly are you playing? Unconvincing drag queen?"

With Danny following behind, holding her sparkly train, she approached the table and took the seat next to mine. Still in character, Danny stood with his back against the wall to scan the terrace, occasionally putting one hand to his face as if receiving a message through an earpiece.

"Come on, Izzy. It's been hours since I saw you, what have you discovered since then?"

On paper, my mother was the last person I needed butting in and yet I'd learnt from experience that my loved ones invariably helped me join the dots in complicated cases.

"That's a real puzzle," she reflected once I'd filled her in. Her complete lack of theories was almost more shocking than the combination of pink, orange and turquoise on her dress.

I may have let my disappointment show. "Is that all you've got for me?"

"Give me a minute, darling, give me a minute." She looked across the gardens and out to the jagged coastline. "I can't think like this…

Danny, my sweet, could you fetch Bu-Bu a glass of something tasty?"

Her fake bodyguard nodded, spoke into the imaginary microphone in his hand and headed off towards the bar.

"Let's say that Marco was behind it after all. You still think that's the logical explanation, but how could it be possible?"

She'd put into words everything I'd been thinking in just two sentences. This did not make answering the question any easier though.

"I've gone through all the different options. The only thing that makes sense to me is that he was working with somebody else. Let's imagine that Maribel started a relationship with him in order to dig up dirt for Álvaro. If Marco found out and decided he had to silence her, who would he trust to cover up the murder? I can't see his wife helping him if he'd cheated on her."

Mum removed her sunglasses and bit the end of one arm perplexedly. "What about his eldest daughter, you said she looked at you funny today. Could she be in on it?"

"Doesn't make any more sense than his wife helping him. In fact it makes less sense." My words emerged a little too aggressively and my mother put her glasses back on and leaned back in her chair. "I'm sorry, Mum but I've gone over it time and time again and nothing's fitting together."

Danny reappeared with two brightly coloured cocktails. He placed them on the table in front of us and winked at me behind his glasses.

Mum put her hand on mine and gave it a little shake. "You mustn't get worked up, my angel. There's no pressure on you to solve the case. No one is paying you, the police are here to do their job. So, if you don't manage to work it out, it's no big deal."

I let out a huff that my mother must have heard in every argument we'd had from the time I was thirteen until I left for university. "Well it's a big deal to me. There's no Poirot novel where the twist is that he can't find the killer. I wouldn't read that book, would you?"

She stretched her hands beyond the shade of the parasol and into the sunshine like she was dipping them into water. "You've always been the same, Izzy. Your problem is that you take life far too seriously. Things always go more smoothly if you relax once in a while. Look at me; yesterday I was a retired teacher, at home in suburban London, and today I'm a world-famous film star, living it up at an exclusive Spanish resort."

"Well, Mum… I appreciate you being here." Even if she had little more to offer than her company, I was still glad she'd come. The apparent impossibility of knowing anything for sure was starting to get to me.

"Shhhh! I don't want the press finding out I have an adult daughter, I've been telling everyone for the last fifteen years that I'm thirty-nine." She gave me a wink of her own and tried to comfort me once more. "Don't look so worried, Izzy. Ramesh and I have big plans for dinner this evening. Let's just take things one step at a time and you'll be on the right trail before you know it."

When I was a teenager, my mother's eccentric behaviour would send me into fits of shame. I thought that everything she did was designed specifically to embarrass me but, over the past year, I'd come to realise what a treasure she really was. She could be blunt and uncouth, loud and obvious, but she was still my mum and I loved her more than anything. Well, joint first with Dad, Greg, David, Danny, and Ramesh at the very least. And besides, since she worked out who killed Mr Porter before I did, I felt I owed it to her to listen to what she had to say.

A thought suddenly popped into place in my head. "Mum, you're a genius!"

"I know that, darling," she replied in a rather sad voice, "but I'm still waiting for the rest of the world to realise."

"I have to take it a step at a time. I've spent the whole day focusing on who the killer is, but I forgot about all the little questions I have to work out before I can get there."

Danny made a crackly radio sound and mum beamed with joy. "Fantastic! So where do we start?"

I went back to the list of questions in my head. "The gun? No, the thefts. Somebody went round the hotel yesterday stealing valuables from guests' rooms. Álvaro and I were the only ones who didn't have anything taken. As a journalist though, there's a good chance he would have kept all his important stuff with him. Also, when he came home, he went straight up to his room while the rest of us had dinner and drinks down here. I need to work out who the thief is and whether they knew the gun would be there before they took it? Perhaps that was what they were after in the first place."

"What about the two girls, the Austrians? You said they had a shady past, perhaps they were behind the thefts."

I thought for a minute before answering. "I suppose it's possible, and Lio did disappear for a while last night while most of us were down here."

Danny, who had been listening into the conversation the whole time, cleared his throat and put forward a suggestion. "Excuse me, ladies. Have you considered that the real motive for the robberies wasn't the valuables but that the thieves were looking for something in Álvaro's room? What if they couldn't find it but snatched the gun instead and returned the next day to silence him for good?"

For a second this made a lot of sense to me. "That's a nice theory, but it all sounds too risky. Imagine Marco wanted to kill the journalist. He'd need to be sure he could get away with it or else the murder would get him in more trouble than whatever Álvaro had discovered. And the fact is, Marco doesn't have an alibi."

"Yes, but-"

I would happily have ridden that train of thought with Mum and Danny for as long as it would go but, just at that moment, Gianna Romanelli appeared on the terrace. She was juggling mobile phones as she went down to the gardens to cut across to the beach. I jumped up to run after her and, still in bodyguard mode, Danny trailed after me, glancing around for snipers and paparazzi. I had to stop and shoo him away as I didn't want Gianna being scared off. By the time I caught up with her, she'd finished her call.

"Do you mind if I walk with you?" I asked and she looked at me in that coldly judgemental manner she had.

"Of course not," that magical smile of hers, which was all the prettier for emerging so rarely, appeared on her face. "I love walking on the beach in the evening. There's something unique about it."

"Oh, me too. Whenever we went on holiday when I was a kid, I'd spend hours with my mum combing the beach for shells."

We'd reached the sandy path and I motioned for her to go ahead of me through the narrow gate.

She let out a contented hum as she took in our surroundings. "Every time I step onto a beach, I feel like a child again. I love the mountains and the forest and, with Marco, I've travelled to jungles and deserts and everywhere in between, but the beach will always be so special to me." Some of the poetry that danced through her husband's speech was present in her own. "For me it's where the human world ends and pure nature begins. We will never control the sea entirely. Maybe one day we will bulldoze every last tree on earth, but the seas and oceans will remain."

Though I am a massive fan of poetry, I decided it was time to pull the conversation round to more urgent topics. "I think you know who I am…" I was trying to explain what I wanted without scaring her off. "…and so I'm pretty sure you can guess what I need to talk about."

Her smile diminished a little. "It's okay, Izzy. You can ask your questions."

"I need to know if you think your husband could have killed Álvaro or the girl on the beach this morning."

There was something very calm about her that I hadn't expected. More often than not, when I'd seen her over the last few days she'd been shouting at her family or into a phone. But there, with me, she seemed peaceful. "Marco is a figurehead. He's a role model and a symbol to so many people that it was inevitable we would attract the occasional psychopath. I don't think for a second he was involved in these murders. But that doesn't mean they weren't carried out in his name."

She stopped and buried her feet in the sand right there where we stood, like a child playing a game. "The police told me this afternoon that one of the girls who was working for us has a history of violence. I'd only ever known her as a kind and thoughtful girl. She was punctual, hard-working and dedicated to our cause. It goes to show how difficult it is to genuinely know somebody."

She looked back up at me, studying my face once more. "But I know Marco. We've been together for twenty years. He is my life and I am his. Whatever people might say about us, we're not violent, we are pacifists. We just want to make the world a better place and we know how to do that."

"Do you know who else thought that?" Her lilting voice had soothed my frayed nerves but I still had to answer her mixed-up rhetoric. "Stalin and Hitler and Chairman Mao all thought they knew what was best for their people and millions suffered as a result."

"Yes, but they weren't pacifists." Though she spoke with humility, I could sense the same undercurrent of aggression which was present in her husband. It both scared and fascinated me. Perhaps she could change the world, but I had no doubt there would be casualties along the way. "Next Phase is a philosophy. We just want everything the way it should be." Like a lot of poetry, she was edging ever closer towards abstraction.

"Where did your husband go last night after everyone else was in bed?"

She started walking again and we skirted around the perimeter of the beach. "One of the reasons Marco and I have a happy marriage is because we are different. He likes going out and partying and I prefer staying home with our daughters and a good book. And then, when he comes home, we both have things to talk about." I was coming to realise that everything she said sounded like it had been lifted from a self-help manual. "Marco went into the city for some drinks with old friends. He came back after the girl was killed, as I'm sure you already know."

I searched for my next question and, when my words failed me, she took control of the conversation once more.

"Can you imagine what it's like to be me, Izzy?" That stern, serious expression she normally wore dominated her face. "I had very little money growing up but married one of Italy's richest men. I run an international movement with only a few staff and look after our three children when Marco is off on television shows or being interviewed for magazines."

There was a tremble in her voice and I thought I was finally seeing the real woman beneath all the buff, shine and expensive makeup. "For the last two decades, I've been called every terrible name you can think of. I've been told that I use my looks to get what I want but also criticised for not being feminine enough. People have accused me of callousness when, if I was a man, they would have praised me for my bravery. The truth is that the only way for women like us to succeed is to be stronger than the men who seek to put us down."

I had completely forgotten by this point what question I'd asked her. I found myself floating away on her strange rhythmic speech patterns and I was no longer sure whether I'd recovered from my fall.

The right question finally landed on my tongue. "So, if your husband isn't a murderer, who do you think killed Álvaro?"

She smiled again and the contrast was as great as if she'd pulled a mask on. "That's not my job to say." We'd reached the waterline and she glanced dreamily along the serrated edge of the cliffs, like she was searching for something that would never be found. "But I can tell you this… if you do anything to endanger the unity of my family – if you try to pull Marco away from us because of your hunch – I will do whatever it takes to protect them. And, pacifist or not, if you cross me, I will find a way to destroy you."

Her eyes were locked on mine and, in a moment, every last possibility rushed through my head. Right then she was a victim and a devil, my prime suspect and my hero. Not wanting to cry, there was only one other option; I burst out laughing.

"Oh, my goodness," I said and each word was transformed by my weird cackle. "You're terrifying!"

She did not find it amusing and grew more serious. "It's not funny!" She'd started shouting. "I'm warning you not to mess with my family."

Instead of doing the sensible thing and shutting up, I laughed even louder. "No, I know it's not funny. Honestly." Bit louder again. "I really mean it, I think you're as tough as a brick wall." There were tears in my eyes by this point. "I've no idea why I'm laughing."

Like a popular kid who no one is paying attention to, she let out a melodramatic "Eek!" and marched away across the sand. I was howling by then, really letting rip. I sat down on the stand to avoid getting a stitch and, when I did, the laughter immediately changed into whole-body sobs.

Urmmm, Izzy? Are you alright?

No paella for you, buddy.

I don't care about the paella. I'm worried about you. What's going on?

Me!? I'm fine, I am. Don't worry about me.

We both knew I was lying. Of course I wasn't fine. Nothing was fine. I'd run away from England and tried to pretend that was okay. But I had no idea what was happening to David as he faced near certain imprisonment which had only come about because of the evidence I'd gathered. It didn't matter who I loved or why, what mattered was that I'd deserted him and I couldn't forgive myself.

Not knowing what else I could do, I pulled my phone from my bag and dialled his mum's number. There was no way I could solve a murder or pick a suspect until I found out what was happening back home.

As the tears poured off me, the phone started to ring and I braced myself for the answer.

Chapter Twenty-One

Back in my bedroom, I had a good long chat with the girl in the mirror. "Get it together, Izzy. It's not all about you, there are more important things at stake here."

Excuse me but, if you're going to talk to yourself, could you at least- NO!

The girl looked pretty that evening. Her brown hair had caught the sun a little and her skin actually looked tanned for once. Plus I'd dressed her up in a completely appropriate dinner dress with matching black heels so that she ended up feeling pretty good about herself.

Well, you deserve it after that phone call.

David's parents had not been able to offer the inspirational good news I'd been hoping for. His barrister simply wasn't able to fight back against the dark arts the prosecution employed and things were looking grim. Having already cut me off, David had become increasingly distant from his family but they said they would keep me updated all the same. It made me even sadder that they could still be so nice to me.

I finished getting ready, took one last peek in the mirror and headed out the door. I had just made it to the stairs when I felt my phone buzz and fished it out. There on my screen was a photo of Marco Romanelli with Delilah Shaw. It was a few years old, but there was no mistaking them. They were standing on a stage in front of large sign which read "New Voices for Free Spee-" I guessed there was a c and an h cut off the end and the accompanying message from Dean confirmed it.

This what you're looking for? Romanelli and Shaw were at a convention a while back. They were talking on a platform called "New Voices for Free Speech". From what I can tell, it's a fairly militant organisation calling for the end of all immigration to the UK. Marco was the key speaker. This is the only shot I could find of the

two of them together. I had a look at social media from last night and Marco popped up at a restaurant around one fifteen but there's no sign of him again until he took a selfie in a club at three in the morning. Hope it helps.

    I couldn't be sure what good the information would do. All it really proved was that Delilah had been lying when she said she didn't know who Romanelli was. I could understand Marco not acknowledging her, especially considering what a scene she'd made of herself, drunkenly hitting on Ramesh for the past few nights. But it didn't make sense that she would have denied her association with the rising star of the far right.

    Two more messages pinged back to me, both with photos of Marco on his night out. They were fairly innocent snaps with him and his waiters at the restaurant and another with his fans in the gloomy club. It would be down to the police to work out when the photos were actually taken and whether they would rule Marco out of the investigation, but the gap in time between the two troubled me.

Oh and one more thing. You can check out your mum's website at bubulamer.com and my team have finished working on her IMDB profile. It was quite a lot of work but they've done a sterling job. No one would know she wasn't a movie star if they searched online.

    Thanks, Dean. I'm sure she'll really appreciate that.

    I clicked the link to discover a website full of photos from my mother's glistening career as in imaginary actress. There were shots of her meeting Prince Charles at a variety performance, another of her on the stage in an all-female Macbeth, posters of her made up movies and a full filmography. I couldn't believe how much trouble they'd gone to.

By the time I got down to the dining room, another transformation had taken place. Ramesh and Kabir had put candles on every table and there was low lighting and a disco ball rotating on the ceiling above the early diners. Perhaps most surprisingly of all, as Ramesh served, Kabir was walking about with a microphone, crooning a Frank Sinatra hit. As I entered the room, he was bashing out a pretty faithful rendition of "Old Devil Moon".

"We thought we'd do something to help people relax and enjoy themselves," Ramesh explained as he greeted me at the door. "You look stunning, Miss Palmer."

I actually felt pretty nervous, like I was going to my end-of-school disco and I wasn't sure if my date would turn up – or, as had happened to me, he'd only said we were going together to get revenge for certain comments I might have made about him to every other girl in our year.

The ball's in our court, Gary Flint. You'd better watch your back!

"Thank you, Ramesh," I replied, curtsying like a weirdo. "You look like a waiter. But a very handsome one."

"Yeah, I know. I sent a selfie to Patricia and she said she can't wait for me to get home and serve her drinks." He raised his eyebrows suggestively. "That saucy minx."

I stood waiting for whatever came next and when it was clear he needed prompting, I said, "How about you show me to my table, Ra?"

He straightened up, grabbed a clean white tea towel from the concierge stand and escorted me across the room. "Of course, madam. And how many people will be dining this evening?"

"Oh…" I hadn't really thought about that until now. Three of my favourite people were in the building but I'd still be eating alone. "Just me, myself and Izzy."

"Wonderful, madam. Wonderful!" He rushed over to a table near the stage and drew back my seat in a suitably over the top manner.

I thought I'd get the drinks order in early. There was only one member of staff on duty and I didn't want to be forgotten in the dinner rush. "Madam would like a glass of white wine and a lemonade chaser."

"Exceptional, madam. Phenomenal!" All bows and twirling hands, he withdrew from the table and went over to the bar to fulfil every waiter's most sacred duty.

An unexpected hush fell between songs. Even the Dennison

kids were quiet as the Romanelli clan appeared at the entrance and, without prompting, Ramesh led them to their usual table. Gianna made a conciliatory wave across the room at me, perhaps feeling as embarrassed by our previous encounter as I was.

Sagrario and Celestino hadn't appeared yet, but Delilah Shaw was on her own with her first bottle of wine nearly emptied. She was singing along with Kabir's song and, when he passed her table, gave him an appreciative squeeze on the bum.

"Can I sit with you?" Heike asked when she turned up a few minutes later. "Lio hasn't come back from the station yet."

"Of course you can." I moved my bag off the free chair and she took its place.

She was the only person there who hadn't dressed for dinner and was still in her beach gear. I'd seen how few possessions she had in her room, so it was no surprise that she'd turned up without a ball gown.

"Thanks." She was different again. Not nervous, not sad, but more real somehow. Perhaps she felt she could be herself around me now that she'd shared her secret. "Are you feeling better after your fall?"

I did my *aren't-I-silly* laugh complete with a ditzy head movement. "Yeah, my own fault for not eating a proper lunch and pretending I like saunas. Happens all the time."

She laughed rather sweetly. "Yeah, I hear that's a common problem these days."

I raised my glass and then, perhaps a bit brusquely, said, "Actually, I have another question for you."

"Ufff, can I order a drink first?" She waved at Ramesh at the bar and, using the international signal for, *same as she's having, but let's make it a bottle,* sent her request across the room.

"You didn't seem very upset when the police took Lio away. Why don't you like her?"

Ramesh was on fine form that night and fast tracked a nice bottle of Verdejo with a pretty label over to us in no time. Like every good waiter, he had a corkscrew in his pocket and whipped the label off and the cork out before pouring Heike her drink. Not a drop was spilt.

"She's a bad person," she replied once we were alone. "It's not about her past or the things she's done. She's got a black soul and treats everyone she meets like they're disposable."

Lio would make a good fit for our culprit. No alibi, crazy past. What do you think? Perhaps Inspector Bielza worked it out before we did.

"Do you think she could be the killer then?"

She thought for a second, glancing around the room at the opulent dining room. "Well, she's capable of it and, since we spoke earlier, I've been thinking about whether she could have found a way to murder Álvaro and get back downstairs so quickly. But there's no way she would have killed the girl."

"How can you be so sure?"

She closed her eyes like she was suffering through a memory. "Lio's mother was killed when she was a kid. It's the only thing I know about her past because she talks about it all the time. She made a big deal about violence against women being the greatest sin, though she didn't have a problem with less physical forms of abuse. Short of physical pain, she did whatever she could think of to keep me in line."

I had the feeling again that, while I really wanted to believe this girl, I still had to be careful. "The way you acted around her, that was real wasn't it? You weren't acting, she really frightened you."

She gave me a curious look and I knew that she couldn't bring herself to answer the question directly. "Lio is a nutter, but she'd never hurt another woman. So, no, I don't think she's the killer."

I studied her pretty features again. There was such fierce intelligence burning behind her eyes and I had to wonder what her story was. She told me herself that she'd been living on the streets and more or less admitted she'd worked as a prostitute. I couldn't help wondering how she'd ended up like that and surprised myself by asking her straight out. "What about you? What brought you to the life you have?"

She answered in that same cool, aggressive tone she'd used in the sauna. "We didn't all grow up in cushy, middle-class West Wickham, Izzy. Some of us had crappy parents and crappy friends who made us do crappy things. Maybe if our situations were swapped, I'd be a bookworm and you'd be... me."

She was right and it put me in my place. "I'm sorry." I thought of what I could say next that wouldn't sound insensitive or smug. When nothing jumped out at me, I settled on, "Let's start again, shall we?"

Kabir's version of "It happened in Monterey" came to an end and a sparkling mirage appeared through the patio doors. "Ladies and gentleman, our special guest for the evening..." He allowed a few seconds of silence to build up the tension. "...Star of screen, stage and smaller screen, it's Miss Bu-Bu La Mer!"

Ramesh had popped over to the corner and was manning a spotlight that was directed straight at my mother. Her dress was so shiny that it was like staring at the sun. She made that *really, it's too much* hand gesture to the bemused audience as she went to collect her microphone.

How I was conceived from such a creature is beyond me. She was on stage, in a foreign country, pretending to be a celebrity like it was the most normal thing in the world. I, on the other hand, was glowing red with embarrassment even though it was dark, no one was looking at me and Ramesh was the only person there who knew Bu-Bu was my mother.

"This is a little tune I sang in the movie, 'Strangers on a Plane'. If you know the words, feel free to join in." She looked straight at the audience, and in her deep, breathy singing voice, started in on the song.

"The little things we do,

The little things we say.

I do them all for you...

In my way."

My mother is an incredible singer. She had the lead part in every staff musical that her school put on for the thirty years she worked there. Kids from Bromley High actually called round our house to get her autograph once – and she, just coincidentally, had a stack of 10x8" black and white headshots on hand for that very purpose.

Sadly, her performance at The Cova Negra was undermined by the fact that she didn't have any accompaniment and had to hum the jazzy instrumental parts between lines. To be honest I was a bit disappointed that, with all the effort everyone had gone to for her grand plan, they hadn't managed to pop into a studio and lay down a backing track.

As Ramesh's spotlight followed her, she stepped off the stage to walk between the tables and the second verse started up.

"The little things we try. (Ba da da da!)

The prices that we pay. (Di di di di!)

I'd pay them all for you... (Diddly diddly diddly di, ba!)

In my way."

By this point she was getting into her stride and I could see a few of her soon-to-be-adoring fans swaying in time with the beat of her clicking finger. The old Spanish couple had arrived and were instantly mesmerised.

Working up through a crescendo of *ba*s and *la*s, Mum got to the chorus and belted out the first line with all her might. Shirley Bassey wishes she could sing like Bu-Bu La Mer.

"I'm one hell of a woman,
So will you be my man? (Ba ba ba ba ba ba BA!)
I'll always love you, in my way,
So catch me if you can."

She had arrived at the Romanellis' table and grabbed Marco by the tie as she roared the finale of the chorus into the mic. She walked off again before Gianna could object and I thought for a moment she might jump onto the Dennisons' table to deliver the sax solo she'd started in on. Luckily, her long skirt would not allow it and, with a quick spin and some jazz hands, she started in on the final verse.

"The little words we speak, (Na na na.)
The little games we play. (Ski bi di ba ba di, bomb!)
I'll play them all with you… (WA WA WA WA!)
In my way!"

She repeated the chorus, holding the last note for an impressive twelve Mississippis before throwing her arms out at her sides and sending a wink in Marco's direction.

The room exploded. I've heard less noise at Wembley Stadium. Ian Dennison got up on his chair to wolf whistle, Delilah Shaw was clapping like a seal with her hands above her head and Marco hadn't taken his eyes off my mother since the song began.

Ramesh abandoned his post at the spotlight to present Bu-Bu with a bouquet of roses.

"Where on Earth did he get flowers from?" I asked, but Heike was overcome with emotion at the power of Mum's performance and didn't hear me.

"An old friend of The Cova Negra Hotel and Spa, Miss Bu-Bu La Mer!" Kabir explained once more, and I could tell that he'd been in on the ridiculous plan from the beginning.

You know what they say, "Like uncle, like nephew."

No one says that… but they should!

For a second, I forgot about judging the reactions of my assembled suspects and watched my mother receive her extended applause. The look of sheer bliss on her face was no act. Mum was born to be a performer and I was so happy for her to be there, soaking up the adulation.

But perhaps that wonderful, joyous moment, as she bowed, waved and mouthed thank-yous across the room, goes some way to explaining why I'm an awkward almost thirty-year-old woman who's still obsessed with the books I read when I was twelve and has never had a particularly stable relationship.

Every birthday party from my childhood became "Rosie's Royal Revue" every parent-and-child talent show was a chance for me to play the accordion while my mother wowed the school. Mum couldn't resist a chance to shine and I couldn't resist hiding in my bedroom for a week afterwards, recovering from my shame.

So… anyway. Good for Mum!

Chapter Twenty-Two

Marco went over to the star performer and escorted her to his table where his youngest daughter was waiting for her with a chair and a kiss on each cheek. The clapping finally died down and, after a "We love you, Bu-Bu!" from Ian Dennison, decorum was restored.

Heike started telling me the really quite heart-wrenching story of how she went from growing up in a small town in the country to sleeping rough in Hamburg, but I was distracted by the howls of laughter coming from the central table. Mum was clearly a hit with the Romanellis.

In all the excitement, I hadn't noticed Danny slink into the room under the cover of darkness to keep an eye on his fake client. I thought he might at least sit down and have dinner, but no. He remained on his feet throughout, hands behind his back, dark glasses still in place, and was perfectly positioned with a clear line of sight of the entrances, just in case he would be called upon to pull his toy gun from its holster. He was a natural bodyguard. Why he'd ever become a humanitarian medic was beyond me.

On the table next to ours, Ian Dennison was telling his family how long he'd been a Bu-Bu fan. "Of course, I remember seeing her on television before she was a big star. She was on some tacky cop show or one of those soap operas and I remember saying to myself, I said, 'Ian, that woman is going to be huge one day.'" He cast a jealous eye across the room to where Marco was enjoying the company of his celebrity guest. "I'm not one of these bandwagon jumpers who only likes her because she's here at the hotel."

"They're putty in her hands!" Ramesh whispered a variation of this each time he passed until I poked him in the ribs because it was getting too obvious.

"What do you think you'll do when this is over?" I asked Heike as soon as her tale was told.

She thought for a second, looking down at her empty plate. "I won't go back to Hamburg. I'd meet the same people and end up doing the same bad things." Her fingers went to the tops of her arms then self-consciously. "I've saved up a bit of money from this job. It should be enough to get a room somewhere. And then I'll have to find a normal job." She said this as if it was a grand ambition, the way other people talk about moving to the countryside or travelling around the world.

"Well, if you ever come to West Wickham…" I didn't finish the sentence but we both laughed and, just then, the second half of that night's entertainment started up.

Kabir had the microphone once more and got up on the stage to address us. "Ladies and gentlemen, I have a short announcement to make. Some of you may not know this but your waiter this evening is none other than my nephew, Ramesh."

"I spotted the resemblance," Delilah yelled out. "Same firm buttocks!"

"Well, I just wanted to tell him how much he's helped me this week and that, without him, I'd never have got through this difficult time. So…" He looked across the audience to where my friend was pouring Celestino a glass of red wine. "…Nephew, how about it? How'd you fancy coming up here and doing our party piece?"

Ramesh put the bottle down, reached under the free table beside him and pulled out a gold, sequined jacket to match Kabir's. "Uncle, I thought you'd never ask," he lied and ran up onto the stage.

The odd couple proceeded to sing a medley of songs with the words *nephew* and *uncle* crowbarred into them. We had Cat Stevens' classic "Nephew and Uncle" followed by the moving Paul Simon tribute, "Nephew and Uncle Reunion" and they finished things up with George Michael's always moving "Uncle Figure".

I can't say they could compete with Bu-Bu's performance, though their tap routine (complete with canes and top hats that Ramesh had stashed beneath the stage) was rather impressive and Delilah Shaw loved every minute. When it was over, Ramesh ran to our table to canvas opinion.

"You were great," Heike said. "You showed such… commitment to your performance."

"Do you really think so?"

"Of course," I reassured him. "It was excellent."

"Thank you, both. Thank you so much. Uncle and I haven't done that routine since Christmas 2002, so I was worried we'd forgotten it." It had been a while since I'd seen him so happy. Ramesh has different levels of joy but this was close to the time he thought he met Barbara

Streisand in a lift. "It went like clockwork!"

"Your uncle had a big influence on you growing up, didn't he, Ra?"

He didn't have time to reply because, just then, hell broke loose.

"Maaaaaaaaaaaaaaaarco!" Was the screech that broke the atmosphere in two and Lio came hurtling into the dining room. "I've kept your secrets, done your dirty little deeds and you didn't even come to the police station to see that I was okay?"

Jaime ran in to stop her but Danny was one step ahead and cut her off before she could get to the top table. Everyone there looked terrified as Lio started up another screeching protest.

"You just leave me there to rot, is that it? Were you hoping they'd blame me for the murders so that they don't have to look at you again?"

Marco was the only one who reacted. He stood up slowly as his family froze in place like dummies in a shop window. All Lio's perfectly presented composure had deserted her. I'd never seen so much as an eyelash out of place on her before but, after several hours with Bielza at the police station, she looked rough, raw and worn out.

"Come with me, Lio," Marco said, taking her arm to softly to lead her away.

"You can't shut me up. I told them I had nothing to do with the killings. I didn't say a word to help you or your sordid little organisation." She kept screaming even after they reached the foyer.

Gianna Romanelli ran out after her husband and their discussion continued though we could only hear Lio's part of it.

"It's your grave and you can lie in it."

There was a brief silence as we tried to catch what Marco mumbled in reply but nothing came back to us.

"Unlike the two of you, I know what loyalty means. I didn't tell them anything, but I can see your hands are all over this."

This time, I caught notes from Gianna's higher-pitched voice but nothing very clear.

"Let go of me," Lio responded. "And consider this my resignation. How could you not have thought to check on me? You're disgusting."

Lio loudly mounted the stairs and, when the Romanellis returned to the dining room, we all pretended to be deep in conversation and not the slightest bit interested in anything that had occurred.

"Wonderful paella this evening," I said unconvincingly and I thought

Ramesh might break into another song to cover the awkward moment.

Marco stopped halfway into the room and cast his fierce eyes about us. "I know what you're all thinking and it's not true. That girl is disturbed. She has a long history of problems and the only reason we employed her was to give her a second chance in life." His eyes rested on me for some reason as if I was the most judgemental person there.

Well, there's no way that's true. You're top three at worst!

Shut up and enjoy the paella.

"I didn't kill anybody. Whatever's been going on here had nothing to do with me. I didn't know the girl on the beach and I'd never have murdered the journalist just because he wrote bad lies about me. That's not my style." He waited to see if anyone would challenge him and, when we all stayed quiet, shouted, "I'm not a murderer," and stalked back to his table where he didn't say another word all night.

Chapter Twenty-Three

There was a peculiar atmosphere after that. Conversation never recovered, Kabir attempted to get through a few more hits but had lost his enthusiasm and sounded like Sinatra on anti-depressants, and even Bu-Bu's sparkling repartee at the central table couldn't bring the place back to life. I eventually went to the bathroom to have a break from the oddly stuffy air.

You can always tell the quality of a place by looking at their toilets and The Cova Negra's were top notch. In place of hand basins, there was a waterfall-wall complete with uniquely hewn boulders and subtle fairy lights. The soap was dispensed by a small sprinkler system and, there were no hand towels but, instead, you had to walk through a high-powered wind tunnel which whipped the water from you in seconds. It was all very impressive.

"I need to talk to you," a desperate voice said as I took a seat on my pre-heated toilet throne.

It wasn't the perfect moment to start in on a conversation. "Urmmmm, give me a sec."

Shame really as I was hoping you might try out the different music modes on this thing. There's nothing I like more than Japanese Toilet Muzak.

I ignored my inner monologue's love of tacky gadgets and hurried myself up. It was no great mystery who was waiting for me outside the cubicle. There was only one person at the hotel with the voice of an Italian teenager and, when I emerged, Valentina Romanelli was there waiting for me.

"You mustn't trust my father." She was hiding behind the rocky outcrop of the waterfall. "He's a liar and a cheat and I think he killed those people."

"Would you like to sit down and talk about this?" I asked but sadly we were in a bathroom and there was nowhere to-

No wait, there's a sofa over there.

We walked across to the plush chaise longue as she continued. "I only have a couple of minutes. My parents don't trust us to do anything on our own."

There was something I couldn't get my head around. "Why would you want to tell me anything bad about your father?"

Her expression hardened before she replied. "I hate him. Everything he does is poison."

"But he's your Dad!" I have three of them and, even my weird first stepfather Arthur still has a special place in my heart. The idea of such open hostility was difficult for me to process.

"He's a fascist. My mother too really, but she's not so open about it. He hates anyone just the slightest bit different to him. He doesn't let me have any friends unless they're from old Italian families. All this new-age peace and harmony he talks about is a lie. Inside, he's a monster and I despise him."

She was getting so worked up that I was worried the diners outside would hear us.

"Do you have any proof that he's involved in the killings?"

She paused and looked around the bathroom. "Not exactly, but I saw him the night before the conference."

She clearly needed me to prod her along. "And what was he doing?"

"He left our suite in the middle of the night so I followed him here." She pointed back out to the dining room. "I hung back and came down after him. There was a woman waiting for him on the terrace. She had dark hair. I didn't see her clearly but it has to be the girl who was killed, don't you think?"

I didn't know how to phrase my next question. "And what were they... doing?" It felt wrong to ask a fourteen-year-old girl something like this about her father.

"They were kissing at first and then my father pulled her round between the windows and I heard them having sex," she said very frankly and I remembered that she wasn't British, or ridiculously averse to naughty words like I am.

"Urrmmm. Good. That's good." My whole body had just blushed. "So this was the night before the conference? It doesn't resolve the fact your father wasn't in the hotel last night. There are photos of him on Twitter just before the girl was killed."

She started chewing the end of one thumb and I could see that, despite a glossy exterior, all her nails were bitten down. "My father would have found a way. Perhaps this girl wanted more from him and threatened to tell my mother about the affair. He could have picked her up in town, killed her on the beach, then gone back to Santander so no one would suspect him."

She'd clearly thought it through carefully. "What about your mother, do you think she knew he was having an affair?"

She slumped her shoulders and suddenly looked just what she was, a little girl trying to make sense of the horrible world around her. "Mum's different. She doesn't get worked up about things the way he does. She's too busy I guess. She has to look after us and she's always dealing with Next Phase. I don't think she worries about what Dad gets up to."

"And have you ever seen your father being violent? Has he hurt you or your mum for example?"

She didn't hesitate this time. "Not physically, but he's come close. There's this anger in him which boils over sometimes. When he screams at me, I see it in his eyes. He'd like to slap me. I know he would. And he's always telling us about what a bad kid he was. He used to get in trouble with the police for fighting and, I think he wishes he could go back to the way things were."

It was good to hear about the other side of Marco's personality. Until then, I'd only seen his public face, but Valentina gave me a peek behind the curtain.

There was something else I could ask her that no one else would tell me. "Valentina, your father had a gun in his room. Did you ever see it?"

She went all shy again. "Yes."

"Do you know where it came from and why he had it?"

Her pretty face perked up. Perhaps she'd been expecting a nastier question. "He's only had it a few months. Some horrible fascist group gave it to him. I was there that day. All those disgusting teen boys in military uniforms were idolising him and staring at me. The gun didn't have any bullets but he bought some in Prague when we were there."

"Has he ever fired it?"

She made a sad sort of laugh. "He gets drunk sometimes after the conferences. When we were in Paris he woke me up in the middle of the night and made me go onto the roof of the hotel to shoot bottles. I told him it scared me but he didn't care."

She folded her hands in her lap and then sat up straight like she thought her parents might be watching. "I have to go back to them now, but thank you for believing me."

I kind of wanted to adopt her right then. "Thank you, Valentina. It's very brave of you to speak to me like this."

She stood up to leave but held herself there for a moment. "You have to show people what he's really like. He says he's a pacifist but it's a lie. He didn't even think of that until we had an argument one day and I told him I didn't believe in violence. He just laughed and said it was a stupid idea and no one has ever won anything in this world without fighting." She swallowed hard and a look of ferocious anger shaped her face. "My dad is a killer."

I thought she might say something more but, happy with her delivery, she nodded, and swished from the room.

There were two things she'd said that stood out. The first was obviously the affair. If Maribel had started a relationship with Marco, it blew the case wide open. But that wasn't all. Valentina had witnessed he father's dark side first hand and someone had finally backed up my suspicions.

I'd caught a glimpse of it that first night in the bar. In the way he spoke and held himself, the force of his personality and the strength of his body; Marco was a loaded gun. I could see now that all it needed was for someone to pull his trigger and he would be deadly.

Careful, Izzy. We know he wasn't here when Maribel was killed. Why are you so fixated on him?

But I've considered all the other possibilities. Lio, Delilah and Ian were the only ones without an alibi for either murder and we've found nothing to suggest that one of them was involved. Marco has to be behind this somehow.

I went back to the dining room and a slight buzz had returned to the place. Ramesh was there to make sure the wine was still flowing and Kabir had invited Celestino up on the stage to sing a Flamenco style ballad as Sagrario performed a slow but complex routine in front of him.

Her hands clapped out a syncopated rhythm while her feet shuffled manically to express the passion running through her. She was a different woman up there, remembering the steps she and every

Andalusian girl would have learnt for the annual parties of her town. As her husband's impressive voice cried out, like a muezzin calling worshipers to prayer, she turned on the spot, gradually getting faster as the song concluded. I whistled and clapped with delight when they took their bow. I felt that they deserved just as much credit as my mother and was glad to see the other diners show their appreciation.

After dinner-

Wait! You didn't talk about dessert. You have to talk about dessert!

After a triple chocolate gateau with fresh whipped cream that I'd seen Cook making that afternoon, most of the diners filed off to bed. There would be no celebration that night. Lio's interruption had killed the party and brought the events of the previous twenty-four hours crashing sharply into focus.

Ian Dennison had his napkin signed by Bu-Bu and, fifteen minutes after Kabir's last song, the only people left were Mum, Danny and Ramesh.

"So, Mum?" I asked, as we moved out to the terrace together. "What did you find out from Marco?"

"Well, I can tell you with some certainty..." She dropped her voice to a whisper. "...Marco Romanelli is a very charming man." A girlish laugh broke free from her throat. "And what a hunk! I mean, have you seen his arms? If I was a few years younger and not married to Greg and he was a few years older and unencumbered by his family and we both happened to live in the same-"

"Mum!" I tried to get her back on topic. "Did you find out anything that would help me build a case against him?"

Her eyes were cast out to sea and she was clearly reliving her glamourous evening. "Not yet, darling. Not yet. But what I can tell you is that the Romanellis are one hundred per cent Bu-Bu-heads after this evening!"

"Wow, Mother. That's brilliant." With a sullen face, I showed her just how unimpressed I was.

She was immediately on the defensive. "Well, I was hardly going to ask him if he was a homicidal maniac right there in front of Carolina, Gabriella and Valentina."

"So then that whole song and dance routine was a waste of time."

"Not at all, Izzy. I was finessing him, darling, he needs to be finessed!" She spoke as if such information was absurdly obvious.

"I'll give it another go at breakfast! Now, Danny, my angel, you couldn't fetch old Bu-Bu a G&T?"

"I'll go, Miss La Mer," Ramesh jumped up from the table and ran to the bar, all excited.

It was Danny's turn to offer his angle on the case. Sitting on a chair with his bowtie loose, he appeared to finally be off duty. "I was watching this Marco fella all evening and I think you're right, Izzy. He's bad news."

"Thanks, Danny. I appreciate you doing your bit."

"There's definitely something off about him. Even before that mad woman came in, he looked nervous and uncomfortable. He kept shifting his eyes round the room like he was waiting for something to happen."

"He's been like that since this morning," I said. "He's no longer the Zen master he claims to be."

"I wouldn't mind him mastering my Zen!" my mother replied, once again ignoring the issue and focussing on which male subject had the biggest pecs.

Now I see where we get it from!

As if fate was determined to prove me a hypocrite, at that very moment, Jaime came in.

"Good evening, everyone," he said in his warm Spanish accent. "I've finished my shift and I thought I might have a word with you, Izzy. If that's alright."

Danny instantly stood up, back in bodyguard mode. He walked over to Jaime and looked him in the eyes. There was a weird moment of recognition between them and they both slunk back a little as if to say, *Oh, it's you; my intercontinental twin.*

"Guys, will you give us a minute?" I asked and Mum relinquished her chair for the officer to sit down.

Ramesh reappeared at that moment with a jug of gin and tonic and glasses for everyone. I would have asked for some lemonade to put in it but didn't want to look like a baby in front of Jaime so sipped at my disgustingly bitter drink as if it was no big deal whatsoever.

"There's been rumours all afternoon," Jaime told me, once the others were across the other side of the terrace laughing and dancing together. "I found out what Bielza has been hiding and, I guess it's not so bad like we thought." He wrapped his hands around the icy glass to cool them down.

"The reason she did the interview on her own, you mean?"

"That's right." He took his time over the answer. "Marco admitted that he's having an affair."

I thought for a moment, considering what this could mean to his innocence or otherwise. "Funny. His daughter just told me the same thing."

"His daughter?" Jaime sounded faintly impressed by this. "What a guy."

"Did he say who his mistress is?"

"Only Bielza knows and I can't access the tape without her permission."

I decided to try out a theory on him. "Marco could be using the affair as an alibi. The best lie is one with a hint of truth to it."

"It's possible. But that still wouldn't explain how he could have been in a club in Santander with fifty witnesses at the time that Maribel was killed."

"But are we so sure that he was there all night? I looked at the photos on Twitter and there's a gap where he could have come back here. Have you spoken to anyone who saw him?"

He let out a weary sigh. It had been a long day for him and I didn't blame him for switching to Spanish. Concentrating in a second language is exhausting. "We're looking into it. To be honest, it's not typical to deal with a double murder around here. The odd domestic situation but that's normally an open and shut case. Our resources have been stretched pretty thin today."

I felt sorry for the guy, I didn't want to push him, but I couldn't let up. "Marco's daughter, Valentina, saw him kissing someone here at the hotel on the night before the conference. She thought it must be Maribel. But perhaps Marco was stringing more than one woman along. Perhaps that's the key to this." A shout of joy came up from Ramesh as he and Danny took turns twirling Mum around and I half wished we were over with them. "What if Marco killed Álvaro himself but he got his girlfriend to deal with Maribel?"

The pro-policeman was quick to break down this argument. "For what reason? Even if Maribel had met Marco this week and started a relationship. Why would Marco want to kill her?"

"Because she was helping Álvaro. That must be it. Unless…" Another brick wall, another dead end, so I tried a different route. "What about the photos you found in Álvaro's room? Did you discover anything useful in them?"

Jaime bit down gently on one lip before replying. "Nothing. We know of no connection between him and Santa Maria del Mar. And all those photos from his youth in Italy showed were that he hung around with rough kids and priests."

"Perhaps it's what's not in the photos that's most significant. The killer wouldn't have left anything incriminating. We have to work out what's missing to understand why Álvaro was killed."

"Or, on the other hand, the photos might have nothing to do with the murder and that's why they weren't taken."

I didn't like his answer but it made sense. A giant question mark was floating above The Cova Negra Hotel. My mind was overflowing with theories but, even if I could work out who the killer was, I wasn't entirely sure I could prove it.

"Do you think Bielza would really cover for Marco if he was guilty?" I took another sip and regretted it. It tasted like kitchen cleaner.

Jaime let out a sigh. "It's hard to know. She's a tough woman, which doesn't make her a dirty cop. But something about the way she acted today made me doubt her." He glanced up at the building we were sitting beside. His eyes traced a path from window to window, up to the third floor. "I don't know if it's just because Marco's famous. I mean, how deep does her connection to Next Phase go? I have no idea why she went to their conference in the first place. I've worked with her for several years but she's an incredibly private person."

"If we can work out what happened ourselves, there would be nothing she could do to stop us. We'd bring Marco to justice somehow. So, let's concentrate on the facts, not who might be trying to cover them up."

He smiled at me then and jingled the ice in his glass. "Okay. What are you thinking?"

"No, you first. I want to hear every hypothesis you can come up with. No matter how crazy or unlikely. Maybe by ruling out all the impossible ideas, we'll come across something that makes sense."

He raised his glass to that and we spent the next hour bouncing theories off one another. Danny looked on jealously throughout and Ramesh occasionally came by to persuade us to dance. But when the drink had run dry and it was time for Jaime to go home, I felt we'd moved a tiny bit closer to understanding why Maribel and Álvaro were in the Santander morgue.

Chapter Twenty-Four

I woke the next morning with the dawn and, unable to sleep, decided to hunt around the hotel for Kiki Dee. She was much more independent than I could ever be and poor Elton was clearly pining for her. He'd hardly touched the ham sandwich that Ramesh had prepared for him.

Though they all had rooms of their own, Danny, Mum and Ramesh had ended up passing out in my suite. I guess the drinking had continued after I'd slipped off to bed, as the mini-bar was empty and the lounge was a mess. Still, it was Ramesh who'd have to clean it up, and at least he'd got to enjoy himself first.

When my search for the missing cat proved fruitless – which was yet another mystery I was struggling with – I returned to my room to work on the three lists in my head. My suspects were clear, but the list of clues didn't get me far. The photos, gun, diamonds and other stolen goods were on there, but as I couldn't be sure who'd taken them, this didn't get me very far. What I needed was one of those perfect Christie-esque objects found at the scene. A left-handed pair of scissors perhaps or a single, size-sixteen shoe. Or even something which would at first seem insignificant but ultimately lead me to the killer.

Perhaps there'll be another body and you'll get your wish.
Would you stop that!?

I sat by the window listening to the sounds of the hotel waking up. Kabir was surely downstairs already, getting the place in order for the breakfast rush. He would be busy without Ramesh on hand.

At least he won't have as much work to do with Álvaro checked out.
I told you to stop it!

I thought about David. He'd be waking up, in a cell without a view. He'd have a day of accusations and nasty evidence to get through and I felt a bit closer to him in that moment. Even spending time with Danny again couldn't make me forget about David and my sadness and regret were running wild.

Alright, enough of this. Pick yourself up, brush yourself off and let's go and have that full English breakfast we've been planning.
Ahhh, I like your thinking. Something we can finally agree on.

"Izzy, Izzy! It's terrible!" Kabir rushed to talk to me as soon as I reached the ground floor. "Ramesh hasn't slept in his room. I think he must have been... murdered!" The poor man's face was wracked with fear.

"Naahhh," I said in a silly voice for some reason. "He just got drunk with Mum and Danny. He's sleeping it off in my room."

He looked even more appalled at this news than the idea his nephew was dead. "That lazy little so and so. I'll see that he gets down here, you mark my words."

The normally cheerful man rolled over to the lift and punched the button.

"Urmmm... what about breakfast?" I asked a second too late and the door closed behind him.

As there was no one on duty, I popped into the kitchen to order up the greasy treat for myself. Cook seemed less scared of me than she previously had. Perhaps Ramesh had put in a good word.

I requested my "beicon con huevos" and she nodded and got frying. I was the first one to breakfast and helped myself to some cereal while I waited for the real food to begin.

Izzy, I know I give you a hard time, but I just want to say, thank you. Paella last night and a slap-up breakfast this morning. That's brain food that is.

When Ramesh made it downstairs, he looked like he had neither been to sleep yet nor woken up. He shuffled about like a mummy in a Hammer Horror film and could only fulfil requests which did not require him to think. He was the human equivalent of a wheelbarrow and carted plates back and forth to the kitchen on command.

I was determined to make the most of my morning. Not only did I plan to sample every last delicious ingredient on the breakfast menu, I would observe each guest who came down. This would be the day I cracked the case wide-

I thought you hated that expression. I thought you said it was cheesy.

Nope, not anymore. I'm re-appropriating it. From this day forth, it's okay to say.

This would be the day I cracked the case wide open! I just knew it. My confidence was at an all-time high, I could see the wood for the trees and everything was falling into place.

Lio was the first down to breakfast and sat at the far side of the dining room from me, staring over aggressively. I stared back as I spooned cornflakes into my mouth. But then there was a half hour wait for anyone else to arrive and my plan to play mind games with my suspects had to be put on hold.

Finally, when Sagrario and Celestino took the table next to mine, I whispered across to them, "I'm on to you!" except I didn't know how to say that in Spanish and all I could think of was, "I know you!" So they looked back blankly and whispered to one another like they were worried about me.

They needn't have been concerned. I knew what I was doing; I was stirring the pot. Delilah was the next down and I worked the same magic on her, only in English, so she understood exactly what I was talking about. She looked a little flustered and went to a table out of my line of sight. The Romanellis were the next to receive my, *I know what you're up to,* treatment. I glared at them and it seemed to do the trick. Marco bustled his three girls past me, meaning Valentina didn't even have time to throw a co-conspiratorial smile my way.

There was no sign of Her Royal Highness, Inspector Bielza, but her sleepy underling at the front door popped by at ten o'clock to tell everyone that his boss would soon be along to make an announcement.

I waved good morning to Heike and the two Dennison kids came down to breakfast on their own. I thought it was a bit weird but they seemed happy enough, piling their plates with nothing but cakes and then indulging in a food fight. I didn't blame them. Though clearly not the best-behaved children, I'd have enjoyed doing that when I was their age.

It was another half hour before we discovered what was holding their parents up. Sharon Dennison came downstairs shaking her head and rubbing her hands together like she was trying to get them clean. "Ian!" was all she managed to get out and no one paid her much attention so I went over to speak to her.

"Are you okay, Mrs Dennison?"

Her eyes were fully panicked and it occurred to me that she'd come down in her pyjamas, though I'd only ever seen her dressed for breakfast before.

"Ian didn't come back," was all she could get out to begin with and she took a deep breath and tried again. "He went out first thing this morning and was supposed to be here by now. I've been waiting for him for the best part of an hour." Her voice was high and streaked with fear.

"I'm sure he'll be around here somewhere," I tried to reassure her. "Perhaps he got a phone call." I turned to the other guests. "Did anyone see where Ian went?"

The room fell quiet as everyone considered the same possibility that had instantly jumped into my head.

"Not since last night," Heike replied and no one else said a word.

"Come on, Sharon." I steered her through the dining room by the arm. "Let's take a look outside." I shouted to Ramesh to keep an eye on her children, though up against those two he wouldn't stand a chance.

The sky was overcast that morning and spits of rain had started to fall. The air was still humid and the heat had not dispersed.

"He said he was coming down here to meet someone. I was still half asleep when he left and didn't ask who it was." It was the clearest she'd spoken all week, but then the emotion got too much and her voice broke. "What if something's happened to him?"

I tried my best to comfort her but there was no sign of her husband in the garden, tennis court or the outdoor swimming pool and so, without discussion, we found ourselves drawn to the beach. Yet again, as I stepped onto those creamy-golden sands, my mood changed entirely. But this time, it was not joy or wonder I felt, but relief. There was no one there. No Ian, no body.

The only sign of life was Kiki Dee. She was padding along the water line towards the cliffs nearest the hotel. I had to wonder if she'd spent her whole holiday down there, chasing seagulls or trying to catch fish when the tide came in. I kept walking as she jumped up onto the low rocks at the base of the cliffs and sat atop of them like she was proud of herself. Sharon Dennison had stayed behind where the path met the sand but I pressed on. That magnetic pull tugged me forward as I got to the rock pools and boulders and started to climb.

There was a series of natural stone steps up to where Kiki was sitting. I scrambled on my hands and knees and had to pull myself up by my fingertips to get to the highest level. When I reached the top, I peeked over the edge of the rock to confirm my fears. Kiki was gently licking Ian Dennison's battered face. He was looking straight at me, but the life was gone from him. He was just a shell now and nothing we could do would bring him back.

There was no doubt about it, he'd come down from the ledge high above us and been killed on impact. Spurts of blood decorated the rock where his body had landed with a calamitous splat. There were bits of loose stone and turf lying about the place and, if his death wasn't enough of a mystery, there on the ground beside him was the missing gun.

My relief was replaced by sadness for the family who would mourn him. He'd either fallen, jumped or been pushed and, after the events of the last two days, I knew which was most likely.

Chapter Twenty-Five

It was my first time dealing with broken-hearted relatives. I was more used to corpses who no one liked. Not that Ian Dennison was everybody's cup of tea, but his wife was clearly distraught when I broke the news.

"I'm sorry," was all I had to say and she fell to her knees on the sand, tears already present on her cheeks.

I'd picked up Kiki to make sure she didn't contaminate the crime scene and she meowed very respectfully in poor Sharon's direction. I called Ramesh at the hotel who sent the skinny officer down from the lobby and, within minutes, the whole circus had returned.

Jaime was there with his tubby partner to take care of the grieving widow. There was more of the same for Santander's forensic detection unit that morning. Bielza arrived just after them and then it was my job again to lead her to the body.

"This is the last thing I need," she said, as if she was the one who was lying there with her brains dashed out. She looked at me with her critical glare. "Weren't you supposed to stop this from happening?"

I thought that was a bit rich coming from her. "I told you who the killer was. This isn't my fault."

She rolled her eyes as her officers got to work. "Don't start with that again. Real life's not like an Agatha Christie novel. More often than not, killers don't manage to be in two places at once or even make it look like they were." Her voice fell lower. "Marco Romanelli was with his mistress on the night of Maribel Ruiz's death. We've spoken to her and she has confirmed it. There's no way he could be the killer."

"Hardly sounds like an impartial witness," I snapped back, tired of having my ideas ignored. "Have you considered that she's lying?"

"And how do you explain the witnesses who saw him in town that night? Or the fact he wouldn't have been able to get in the hotel without showing up on a video camera?" Her casual disregard for my ideas was beginning to get to me.

"Honestly, Bielza. Marco's the only one who benefits from any of this. There's more to say that he was involved than that he wasn't. The rest is just details."

A smug look crossed her face then. "And the gun? Is that just a detail?"

I tried to think of a comeback and failed.

"It's very clear to me now what happened." She nodded to herself as she looked down at the carnage before us. "This Dennison was behind the whole thing. He killed Maribel, then killed the journalist and, when he couldn't take the pressure, jumped from the cliff to end his life. Yes, that all makes perfect sense."

Her arrogance was overwhelming and I couldn't take it anymore. "It makes zero sense. Why would he have wanted them dead? How did he get the gun? And why would Maribel have come here in the first place?"

She was quick with her reply, though I could see her reasoning was only clicking into place as she went. "Maribel sneaked onto the beach late at night for a bit of fun, Dennison saw her and decided to take a chance on a pretty girl. When she turned him down, he killed her. Álvaro found out about it and so Dennison stole the gun and killed again."

She paused to slot more evidence into place. "Dennison's room was just along the hall from Álvaro's and it would have been no trouble to pretend to be asleep when my officers got there. Of course, the thing he hadn't counted on was the guilt that comes with any murder. He couldn't live with it so he got up this morning to end things. By bringing the gun with him, he confessed to his crimes."

"Hey, you're pretty good at this," I said in a sarcastic tone that she couldn't fail to catch. "Have you ever thought of becoming a detective?"

She turned to look at me, her gaze as hard and judgemental as ever. "You are a bad loser, Miss Palmer. You don't want it getting out that you've failed in your one great talent, so you're making up stories."

"I'm making up stories?" It's not often I get really angry with someone, but all my pent up aggression was spewing out. "Your whole scenario is based on the fact he has the gun. But why would it have landed so far from his body? It could just as easily have been thrown down after his killer pushed him over the edge."

"Oh, please, it probably fell from his pocket when he jumped." She smiled then, like I was a foolish child and she had so much to explain to me. "Listen, Izzy. I know you'd like to believe that Marco Romanelli was, involved but there's absolutely no evidence to suggest that's true."

"We'll see about that. We'll..." I was out of words, out of ideas and out of breath. I knew there was no getting through to her. She'd made her mind up from the beginning and nothing I could say would convince her otherwise.

I took one last look at the scene before leaving. There was poor Ian, splayed out across the brackish pools of water that had turned rusty red. The shiny silver gun was several metres away along the rocks with its silencer still attached but there were no killer clues, no all-revealing objects to serve up the murderer to me. Except for–

"The gun," I screamed at the inspector and if she hadn't already thought I was crazy, she would now. "It has a silencer!"

"What on earth is wrong with you, girl?"

I didn't answer her, but climbed down the rocks and raced up the beach as fast as I could. My long, gangly limbs have never been great on sand and it felt like I went slower the more effort I made. It definitely wasn't the best encouragement for my new-found determination.

Izzy, you're annoyed at Bielza because she's set out to prove that Marco isn't the killer. Has it crossed your mind that you've made a similar mistake? The only idea you've entertained is that he's our culprit. What if your obsession with him has made us overlook other evidence?

You're probably right but shut up and let me think.

I kept motoring my legs across the sand because, even if I was getting nowhere, it felt good to try. When I finally got back to the hotel, it was my mother who was looking after Sharon Dennison on the terrace. The new widow was still bawling out tears.

"Ian was such a fan of yours. He was so thrilled to meet you last night." It was no surprise that my mother was the focus of attention even now.

"You poor thing." To be fair to Mum, she had her arms around the woman and, with the police once more busy interviewing suspects, was the only one there to provide sympathy.

"Sorry, Mum," I interrupted. "I need to talk to Mrs Dennison."

"She's your mother?" Sharon replied and Bu-Bu looked nervous.

"That's ridiculous, I've never met this person before. But being the gracious person I am, I will allow Izzy to talk to you." With a guilty expression, she stood up and shuffled off to have breakfast.

There was no time for messing around. I got straight to it. "I know there's a connection between your husband and Marco Romanelli. What did you come here for? Why all the secrecy?"

Sharon had one of Mum's handkerchiefs and was dabbing her eyes and nose. "We're broke!" She said and another string of tears jumped out into the world. "Ian's business is a disaster. People aren't importing classic cars the way they used to and we've taken a big hit."

"But what's that got to do with Marco?"

Another loud sob, another runny nose. "Ian thought that, if he could come here and get close to Marco, that… Well, he wanted to change the business and become the official agent for Romanelli cars in the UK. He thought, if he didn't make a big deal about it, if he did it all subtle like, he could convince Marco that he was the man for the job."

Her words knocked the wind out of me. "Is that it?" I asked, unable to believe that I'd pinned all my hopes on some killer link between Maribel, Álvaro and Ian and only ended up with a potential deal between car salesmen.

She put her head in her hands so that her usually mumbly voice was almost indecipherable. "Marco wasn't interested. He wouldn't give Ian the time of day."

I remembered who I was talking to and, instead of pressing her for more information, tried to be sympathetic. "Oh, Sharon. I'm really so sorry for what's happened."

Looking up at me, she opened her arms and brought me in for a hug. It seemed like the least I could do. A snotty shoulder from her crying was no price to pay if it made her feel a little better.

She eventually pulled back. "You don't think that's what did it, do you? He was always so hard on himself, never felt like he achieved enough, but I told him we loved him no matter what. If he killed himself, just because of money… I… I don't know what I'd do."

The man I'd seen dancing with his idol Bu-Bu La Mer after dinner the night before really didn't look like he was about to commit suicide, but I didn't want to tell her my theory and get her hopes up.

"I'm sorry, but I have one more question for you. Whatever you tell me, I won't mention it to a living soul." She dried her eyes one last time before I spoke. "Is there any way that Ian could have been involved with the burglaries in the hotel?"

Her face grew serious and, just for a few seconds, she stopped crying like the distraction had helped. "Ian a thief? That's impossible. He's the straightest man I've ever met. He's never got so much as a parking fine in all the years we've been married. And besides, if he'd nicked the kids' computer games and they'd found out, they'd have murdered him for it." The words she'd just used must have clicked in and she let out a shrieking cry.

I gave her another hug. I needed it almost as much as she did. The killer blow that I hoped she would be able to deliver had turned out to be a feint and I was back to square one.

Chapter Twenty-Six

When the team of officers returned from the beach, Bielza made the announcement I'd been expecting.

"I'm sad to inform you that another body has been found. However, I can confirm that we will no longer require you for the investigation. I'm confident of what went on here and, once you've given your statements to one of my officers, you'll be free to go." She offered her inhuman smile and went off to write up the fantasy she'd concocted for herself.

It was hard to know what was driving her. Was it the lazy desire to avoid an unsolved triple-murder on her territory or something more sinister? Was she really so set on helping Romanelli that she'd pin the blame on poor dead Ian? I added these to the list of questions I still had no answers to.

Suddenly possessing as much energy as Ramesh, as he lethargically distributed the cooked breakfasts, I decided to speak to Valentina at the buffet counter.

"Did you see your dad leave first thing this morning?" I asked in as subtle a voice as possible as I piled an unhealthy amount of sliced cheese on a piece of toast.

"Sorry, Izzy. I can't help you." Even her frown was youthful and attractive. "I woke up late. By the time I came down, everyone had heard about the dead man. But I don't believe Dad really knew him, if that's what you were thinking."

"Thanks," I replied truly unenthusiastically and she clearly felt sorry for me as, no longer worried who might see, she put her hand on my arm and I stopped hogging all the cheese.

"I wish there was something I could tell you to help, but I simply don't know."

I nodded and she walked back to her family with a very reasonable portion of bread and meat. I know I was behaving like a spoilt teen right then but the whole morning had left me feeling empty. I sat back down at my table, where my cooked breakfast had turned cold, and stuffed slice after slice of cheese down my gullet.

This time, when people looked at me, it wasn't with fear, it was

183

with pity. *Look there's that girl who thinks she can solve murders stuffing her face with cheese. I heard she's a rubbish detective and will soon be really fat,* they all no doubt thought.

Come on, Izzy. Stop being so defeatist. Poirot never gives up!

And Poirot never pigs out on Manchego. So that's two ways we're different.

Even as I was suffocating my sorrows with those neat cheesy triangles, the facts of the case were still dancing around my head. The unresolved threads were tying themselves around me. They were getting tighter and tighter until I could hardly breathe. I had no idea what Maribel had been doing at the hotel.

Only we do, because of those photos in Álvaro's room.

Or why the killer weighed her down with stones.

Surely, that's obvious. It was their first kill. They knocked the girl out but couldn't bring themselves to finish the job, so they weighed her down and watched the tide come in.

Well, I can't say who robbed the other hotel guests.

Come on, you worked that out even before anything was taken.

And I certainly couldn't tell you how someone could be in two places at the same time.

No maybe not, but that doesn't mean you can't see a way to explaining it. Don't forget the silencer.

Would you stop contradicting me?

No.

Fine, then answer me this. What evidence do we have that could possibly prove Marco was responsible for the killings?

There isn't any. And that tells us all we need to know.

Well, you could have pointed all this out earlier.

Sorry, I thought you'd get there on your own.

I let out a sigh and considered what to do next. I still hadn't begun to process Ian Dennison's death. I was looking at the case as if two people had been murdered when, in all likelihood it was three. With each murder I'd been able to narrow down my list of suspects, so perhaps there were more people I could dismiss.

I went to see Jaime to find out what the police knew. He was at the front of the hotel chatting with his colleagues.

"I need to talk to you," I said to get him away from them. The female officer beside him laughed and one of the others punched him on the arm so I had to follow up with, "I don't fancy him, if that's what you're thinking!" which not only made me look like an idiot, but totally made it sound like I fancied him.

Which you do.

"What have you found out this morning?" I asked when we were alone in the hotel games room.

He was stiffer and less open than he'd been the night before. "The Inspector is fairly certain that we've found the killer. The pathologist thinks the time of death was around eight o'clock. Most people were still in their rooms at that time but Heike was up with the Romanellis getting her last pay cheque."

"So Marco's got an alibi then?"

He shook his head miserably. "It looks that way, yes."

I plonked myself down on the pool table. "I still don't buy it. There's absolutely no reason for Dennison to have acted that way. Killing some random girl, it doesn't make sense."

Something changed in Jaime right then and I could tell that Inspector Bielza's reasoning had begun to work on him. "You know in all those mysteries you read where the only possible solution is so complicated and contradictory that you'd need a PhD in mathematics to understand it? Well in real life, that never happens. In real life, the simplest solution is usually the right one."

"Oh, come on, Jaime. That's not what's happening here. Are you really going to give up and tell Maribel's mum it was just some madman? Do you think that will give her any kind of peace?"

His soulful brown eyes looked more conflicted than they had all weekend. "I don't know what to tell you, Izzy. It's the only explanation I can see."

I waited for a new argument to spring to mind that would convince him, but nothing came.

"We've done our best, but it's over. Not every tragic case like this can have a satisfying ending." He turned to leave and I thought I'd lost him for good.

Come on, brain. Give me something.

I already told you. The photos! What was it that you couldn't see in the photos? Or rather who.

185

"Her mum…" I shouted with far too much enthusiasm and my good old brain went into overdrive. "Jaime, I need you to do one more thing for me and, if it doesn't work out, I'll accept that Dennison was the maniac responsible for everything. I need you to go to Maribel's mum and ask her two questions. First, and this is unlikely but it's better to check, I need you to find out whether Maribel could have come here to the hotel on Thursday night, the day before she was killed, and secondly, ask the mother if she'd ever met Marco herself."

He hesitated but I knew he'd give in. "Okay, Izzy. I'll go. But that's the last of it. I'll only be messing with the poor woman's head if I keep visiting her."

I gave him my phone number and he promised to contact me as soon as he heard anything. He walked off with a perplexed expression on his face and left me alone with the ping-pong table, the pool cues and a rather worn looking table football. I wasn't giving up just yet. As long as I had that glimmer of a chance to work out what had happened, I would never give up.

The photos weren't the only thing my subconscious mind had dredged up. Though I hadn't given it nearly enough thought, it was true that I already knew who the thief was. Well there were two of them actually and at that very moment, they were sipping orange juice on the terrace.

"What did you do with the gun?" I asked and they stared back at me with an identical guilty look. "I don't care about anything else you stole but you have to tell me what happened to the gun."

For once, it was Sagrario who was the first to reply. "That's crazy. Why would you think it was us?"

"You were the only ones bumbling about the hotel on the day everything was taken. Now tell me what you did with the gun."

Celestino suddenly looked younger, there was a snappiness about him as he answered. "What we told you about the recession was true. After the bank took our shop and our home – that we'd been living in for forty years – we had no other option. We try to steal from people we don't like. We focus on conferences and posh hotels because no one ever suspects us. Who would imagine that such a sweet pair of grandparents could be professional thieves?"

"How did you get into the rooms then?"

"With the right equipment, it's easy enough to clone the key cards at these places." Celestino sounded rather proud of himself.

"That's right," Sagrario added. "We rob from the rich to give to ourselves. It's their own fault for assuming that we're past it."

I let out a frustrated moan. I didn't have time for any of this. The Romanellis would be leaving at any moment. "I don't care why you do it. I don't care about the phones or the cameras or even the diamonds. What did you do with the gun?"

"We didn't take any gun," Sagrario responded like I was accusing her of something terrible. "We only steal what we can sell easily. We wouldn't be so stupid to take a weapon."

Fair enough. That's vindication if ever I heard it.

"Thank you for your honesty. And here's a little tip for you, if you want to keep up the frail little old couple act, I'd give up on the tennis sessions." I moved to leave, then another thought occurred to me. "Wait, what about the Bluetooth speaker from the Romanellis' room. What happened to that?"

They looked at one another in a cartoon double take. "What's a Bluetooth?"

This was more like it. I'd stored up all my good luck till the final moments of the investigation and I was on a roll.

Time to stick your evidence right in Marco's face!

Not yet.

The Inspector then? Shove what we've found out right in her smug mouth.

Nope, there's still work to be done. And until we hear from Jaime, we've got nothing.

I went back to the foyer where bags were already lining up for departing guests. It looked like Heike and Lio would be the first to go. It made me a little sad to see. I'd come to like Heike – the real person I'd got to know over the last day, not the act she'd put on before that.

"I'm sorry we started off so badly," she told me as I walked over to see her. "It's been nice spending time with you."

I don't like farewells. Never have. When my mum and dad broke up, I cried for a month. "Yeah, you too." Considering what I already knew about her, I wasn't just sad to say goodbye, I was worried where she'd end up. "What do you think you'll do now?"

A gigantic grin stretched both cheeks on her perfectly bronzed face. "I'll be alright. It turns out I've got a benefactor of my own. I'll get a flat somewhere like I've always wanted. It's time to settle down."

I thought we would just wave goodbye and never talk again but she stepped forward and wrapped me up in an extra tight hug. "Thank you, Izzy. You've helped me more than you could know."

She picked her bags up, passed through the police officers at the entrance and went out through the rotating door to the taxi. The girls got in and I watched the car pull away through the window. For some reason, nothing she'd said struck me as strange until the car was out of sight.

"Wait!" It was a silly thing to shout, they were never going to hear me.

I was still tired from my trek up the beach but managed to get my arms and legs moving once more to propel me from the hotel and down the path.

"Heike," I shouted, wishing I had asked for her phone number so that I could have simply rung her and not got all tired and sweaty again. I made it past the fountain, I made it all the way down the gravel drive and, just as I got to the gate, the taxi pulled into the road.

I bent over, my lungs on fire, my every muscle cramping.

We should probably do more exercise.

Chapter Twenty-Seven

How could I have been so stupid? I couldn't even blame a hangover or a late night for my slow reactions. Heike had practically confessed her secret and I'd been too dumb to cotton on. It didn't matter though. I'd got her meaning and in a few minutes time, everything would be in place.

Sadly, the hotel was at the top of a slope and the walk back up was even more exhausting than the run down had been.

We should probably do more exercise.
You already said that.
I know, but I wanted to make sure you'd heard.

By the time I got back inside, Danny had appeared. He was looking rather sore-headed in his crumpled bodyguard costume. I guess that my mum had given up on her celebrity act too as she was yet to break out in a song or spin some unlikely narrative and, when not comforting Sharon, had spent most of the morning reading the paper. Ramesh had ground to a halt and, slumped down on either side of the artist formerly known as Bu-Bu La Mer, both he and Danny were practically comatose.

"Ra, when you were cleaning the empty rooms yesterday, didn't you come across a portable speaker?"

He looked like he'd just gone ten seconds with Mike Tyson. His head wobbled dozily and his eyes were only half open. "Urmmm… maybe?"

"Come on, it's important. It would have been somewhere near where Álvaro was murdered. Did you find one?"

"A speaker? Yeah. There was a black one with a cross on it and a phone too. They were in one of the rooms on the first floor. I handed them into Kabir in case someone calls for them. It's amazing the things people leave behind. I found a set of false teeth yesterday. Can you imagine-?"

"Thank you, Ramesh," I cut him off as there were slightly more important things to think about than the contents of The Cova Negra lost property box.

I had a quick check about to see where everyone had got to. The remaining Dennisons were in the foyer with the police. I could see that

Bielza had revealed her suspicions as the two kids and their mother were in fits of tears. As if it wasn't bad enough that Ian was dead, now they had to get used to the idea that he was actually a sleazy, murderous thief. Well, it wouldn't be for long if I had my way.

I caught sight of the Romanellis taking one last walk around the grounds before their departure, Delilah was yet again tucking into an all-day breakfast, the Spaniards must have gone off to pack and, just then, I received the text I'd been waiting for.

No and yes.

...was all it said and so I replied with my final question for Maribel's mum and then grabbed the toy gun from Danny's shoulder holster.

"Izzy, what are you doing?" he asked and I put a finger to my lips to keep him quiet. "Don't worry about me, but, when Jaime gets here, tell him this is only a toy gun and I'll need his help outside."

Mum was looking worried about me, which was nothing new, so I put the gun in my pocket to calm them both down. "Everything's fine," I told them. "Mum read your paper, Danny have some coffee."

With their fears subdued, and Ramesh fast asleep, I was free to roll the dice for the final time. I casually strolled across the room to where Delilah Shaw was pigging out.

"Urmmm, Delilah," I said, showing her a flash of the gun. "You're going to have to come with me."

She let out that squawking parrot laugh of hers and, when she realised I wasn't joking, the amusement on her face faded away. "What on earth are you thinking?"

I put my hand on the grip of the pistol and motioned for her to head outside.

"I'm not messing around. Move."

I know this is somewhat out of character for me. I'm not really a taking-hostages-by-gunpoint kind of person. If I ever have to use a real gun, I'll probably end up shooting myself. But bear with me, because I had a good reason for it and this was the only way that crossed my mind to get things done.

Hey, don't blame me for this.

With her hands displayed above her waist to appease me, Delilah flicked her legs out from under the table and stood up. I couldn't risk attracting the attention of the police as they would probably shoot me so, as casually as possible, I walked Delilah across the terrace. She kept checking on me over her shoulder as we cut through the garden to the path which led to the cliffs. In the distance, Marco and Gianna Romanelli had their arms around one another and were gazing out to sea.

"Marco," Delilah shouted before we got there and I figured we were far enough from the hotel to pull the gun out and hold it against her.

"Quiet," I said but the Romanellis had already spotted us and were trying to work out why Delilah was walking along awkwardly with her hands in the air.

"Izzy, what's this about?" Marco said and even then I couldn't help remarking how charming his accent was. "Your obsession has to stop. The police has founded the killer. It's time to forget."

Gianna searched about for help in vain. There was no one down on the rocks beneath us. No one within earshot. I'd never seen her look so scared.

"You know what this is about, Marco." I wasn't happy with how that came out. I sounded like the villain instead of the detective and I considered trying the line over again. "It's about the truth. It's about the real reason Maribel came here to the hotel and Álvaro was murdered for the secrets he'd discovered. It's about the affair you've been having with the woman whose head I'm holding a gun to."

Marco took a step forward to reason with me and so I pulled the hammer thingy back. (Sorry, I'm not great with guns. I'm not entirely sure that's what you're supposed to do with them but it looked pretty cool.)

"Don't come any closer, or I will shoot her." I'm afraid my acting just wasn't up to scratch. I was trying to sound all serious and intense but it came out sounding like Keanu Reeves when he's trying to sound all serious and intense and it makes you go, *Ahhh, poor Keanu. So pretty, but such a bad actor.*

"It's all in your mind, Izzy," Delilah tried. "I'd never met Marco before this week."

"Not true. You were on a panel together in London three years ago." What pleasure it gave me to deliver that nugget of truth! Though I couldn't see her face, I could feel Shaw reel back against me as the words sunk in. "I imagine that the two of you have been meeting up in secret ever since. The only reason Marco booked a conference in

Santander was because this is where you take your holiday every year. You thought you could get away with it, even with his wife here."

I watched for Gianna's reaction. Though I'd strung together most of the story, there were plenty of holes that I still needed to fill in and this was the first. I hadn't been sure whether Gianna had known about Marco's relationship with Delilah. From the way she'd spoken to me on the beach, I knew she had her suspicions, but, as her eyes jumped over to look at him right then, it was clear she hadn't suspected the nasty British woman I'd just brought to the party.

"Marco?" Her voice was scratchy, her throat dry, and she smiled incredulously. "This isn't possible."

I began to lay out the evidence. "I'm not lying, Gianna. You have to believe me. Think about it; who chose this place? I'm going to guess it was Marco and that you were in charge of planning the other venues."

I could see from her reaction that I was on the right track. "What did he tell you? That it would be a nice break for you and the girls? You said yourself that you're the one who does all the work for Next Phase so why was he so keen to come here?"

Gianna was like a spectator at a tennis match, looking back and forth between her husband and his lover. Keeping my gun trained on Delilah, I moved to the side to see her reaction. To my surprise, she had the same impervious look as always and I could see that even the dramatic finale I'd planned would struggle to move her.

"Of course it's not true," Marco attempted to save himself. "I barely know this woman… I mean, we met that one time, but you've seen, I had nothing to do with her this week."

Gianna's previous calm was extinguished and she let out a torrent of abuse in Italian, which was punctuated by her two tiny fists as they slammed against her husband's broad chest.

"Oh, give it up, Marco," Delilah said, rolling her eyes as if this was all such a bore. "It's not going to do any good now, is it?"

I felt my phone buzz in my pocket again and pulled it out whilst they were bickering.

The answer is yes. Her mother broke down and confessed what happened. I'm on my way back to the hotel, I'll tell Bielza everything.

As I read Jaime's message, Marco saw his chance and stepped forward to grab the pistol. I pulled up just in time and pointed the weapon at my favourite extreme-right lifestyle guru.

"I'm not finished yet."

Chapter Twenty-Eight

I shifted the gun to two hands and took a couple of steps backwards to avoid any further challenges. "Actually, all three of you, move away from the edge of the cliff."

"That isn't a real gun, is it Izzy?" Marco was so smooth and self-assured. It was almost upsetting that anyone could have a gun pointed at them and still sound like that. I'm less confident ordering in KFC or deciding which socks to wear.

I turned it on its side to look at the barrel and read the name stamped there. "Glock 17. That's standard Spanish police issue, or don't you know anything about guns?" Luckily for me, he clearly didn't. "I managed to borrow it this morning, but you had a weapon of your own, didn't you, Marco?"

Taking his wife by the shoulder, he slowly moved away from the precipice. "Do we have to go through this again? I know you're upset at what happened, Izzy, but it's not my fault. The gun was stolen. I never even fired it."

"Another lie, your daughter told me you shot bottles on a Paris rooftop. In fact you bought bullets especially, isn't that right?"

"Listen, Izzy, calm down. We can talk about this. There's no need for anyone to get hurt here."

"Nice try, but it won't work." I was loosening up by now, getting my mind into the role.

That's right, Izzy. You're wild! You're a loose cannon and no one knows when you'll go off. Run with that.

I turned my attention to the wronged party. "You know, Gianna, I feel sorry for you. To live with a man like Marco who doesn't know how to tell the truth. I bet whenever you confronted him about your suspicions he'd use that voice of his."

"Izzy, this is ridiculous," he began, but I cut him straight off.

"That's exactly it, Marco. Thanks for the demonstration. It's a voice I've heard before. The voice of a man who thinks he knows better than a woman, who wants to convince her that she's crazy to think so poorly of him." I turned back to her husband, pointing the gun straight at his head now. "It won't work anymore, Marco. Those days are over."

He raised his hands for the first time, more in appeasement than surrender. "Okay, Izzy. Okay. Just take it easy and tell me what you want."

I'd got a bit distracted with all the emotion and drama and the fact I was having to improvise as I went along. I kind of wished Ramesh had been there to help me, though I'm pretty sure he'd have turned the scene into a musical number.

"Urmmm… I want to go back to my previous topic. You said you'd never shot the gun before and that it was stolen from your bedroom, but that wasn't true. I could tell that whoever had robbed the rooms were professionals. They used hacked key cards to get inside and there were only a few people who had the opportunity while you were at the conference or later that evening during dinner. The Austrians and Brits couldn't have done it which only left the old Spanish couple. They've been poking about ever since I got here and, in the end, their innocent act didn't wash with me."

My voice had gone a bit too gangster so I reined it back in. "I just discovered that they weren't so foolish as to steal the gun. It was too conspicuous. They were after valuables and a gun would only bring them trouble. You have no alibi for where you were when Álvaro was killed…"

"Izzy," Delilah began before I could shut her down. "I was with Marco when-"

"Quiet!" At some point, my nervous act had become real and the pistol was shaking in my hand.

Eat your heart out, Ramesh. Now this is method acting.

"When your room was robbed, it gave you the perfect opportunity to sort out your problem with the press. You told the police that the gun had been stolen so that they couldn't pin Álvaro's murder on you. What had he found out that frightened you so much? That the old woman who claimed to be your long-lost great aunt was really the lover whose will you'd wormed your way into?"

I gave him a moment to reply, but he was suddenly speechless. "Your supporters wouldn't be happy if they discovered you'd been a full-on conman. A rough and ready street kid come good? Sure, that's a narrative they could get behind. But if Álvaro had revealed the truth, that would have spelt the end for Marco Romanelli and Next Phase."

The tension was really getting to me. My palms were sweating, the muscles in my arms were dancing and my legs were weak from standing still for so long. "No. Álvaro Linares had to be dealt with."

"You've jumped ahead of yourself." Any nerves that had been peeking out of Marco were buried away again and he was back to his confident best. "Sure, I had no alibi when Álvaro was killed and maybe I had every reason to want him out of the way, but Maribel was different. I had no connection to her. At the time the police say she was murdered, I was in Santander. How can you explain that?"

"It's a good point, Marco. And it had me stumped for a long time. I could only come up with one way you could have killed her in fact and it would have required incredible timing, precision and stamina. But then, you're Marco Romanelli, the high priest of order and exactness, it surely wouldn't be a problem for you."

I spread my feet out wider to steady myself. "I saw the tweets that were sent that night and it's true that people spotted you at a tapas bar in the marina just after one o'clock and then, a few hours later at a club. That gap in the middle would have given you just enough time to drive to the next bay on from here and swim round the headland to meet Maribel as you'd planned. You realised that she was working with Álvaro and couldn't risk any more scandal so you knocked her out. But killing someone isn't as easy it seems and, rather than finish the job yourself, you buried her in the sand by the water's edge then waited for the tide to come in."

"This is ridiculous." His voice rose up to a high note of astonishment. The way his wife was looking at him right then told me it was not entirely impossible.

"No, it's not ridiculous, Marco. Unlikely perhaps, but not ridiculous. You're an incredibly strong swimmer. I saw it on my first day here. You have … let's say… an athletic physique. Most people would struggle to swim a few kilometres late at night after already consuming a few drinks, but not you. You could have killed Maribel, swum back to your car and driven into Santander once more. I've considered the time frame and it's certainly possible. But perhaps there was an easier way to go about it."

I paused for a few seconds before delivering my second explanation. "Your lover Delilah."

She let out a laugh before speaking. "I finally get a look in, do I?"

She sounded pleased about it. "As I tried to tell you before, I was with Marco in Santander when Maribel was killed and we were in my room together when we heard the shots from Álvaro's bedroom. No hard feelings, eh Gianna?"

Gianna was as still as a statue. She hadn't made a sound since her outburst and it felt good to get some revenge on her behalf.

I held Delilah's gaze and pointed the gun at her chest. "Yes, I imagine that's what you told the police. Inspector Bielza never took either of you seriously as suspects so I had to assume you'd come up with a pretty tight alibi. What I failed to consider was that you could have both been involved in the killings."

"Oh, come on, now. This is all getting silly," Delilah responded with that wonderful British habit of making dramatic situations sound like no big deal.

"Is it? Or did you take charge of murdering Maribel so that your boyfriend would have an alibi? I suppose he did his share of the work when he killed Álvaro. And perhaps you got rid of Ian together, after all, it's nice to do things as a couple once in a while. By dumping the gun on his body, you thought you'd deflected any lingering suspicion. Well, think again!"

The sun had burnt a hole through the clouds and beams of light shot down to us as Marco once more tried to reason with the crazy girl with the gun.

"Izzy, I understand you're upset and I understand why you might think these things. But you still haven't explained why I would have wanted Maribel dead. Why would I kill a girl I'd never met?"

I answered his question with one of my own. "This isn't your first trip to Spain, is it, Marco?"

He looked confused and peered between the two women in his life before answering. "No, I've been here many times. Why do you ask?"

"But when was the first time? I mean the very first time you were here?"

His words came even slower this time. "I was young. In my twenties. I came with a youth group at my local church. They took us to another church over here to give kids from poor backgrounds a chance to travel."

"And when you say, 'over here' it was very close, wasn't it? Just a few miles from where we're standing in fact, in a village called Santa Maria del Mar. It wasn't all mass and bible studies, was it, Marco? You were there in the summer. You went to the beach and the village parties. You had a good time and got to know the local girls. Tell me, Marco, what year was that?"

"1992," he replied, more decisively than I might have expected.

"That's right, twenty-eight years ago. The summer before Maribel Ruiz was born." I didn't feel like joining the dots for him. I relaxed my shoulders and took a deep breath because the worst of the revelations were over with.

"Bloody hell, Marco." Delilah was quicker than I'd given her credit for. "The dead girl was your daughter."

Chapter Twenty-Nine

"Wait, this isn't possible." Unlike Keanu and me, Marco was a pretty good actor when it was required. "I mean... I never knew."

Just then a white and grey gull popped up at the top of the cliffs, eyed the four of us and veered off with a screech. The others didn't notice it because they were all staring at me, waiting for the next part of the story.

"You met a girl called Susana, she was younger than you and had a boyfriend, but that was no barrier for Marco Romanelli. When you left and Susana discovered she was pregnant, she married her boyfriend and they raised Maribel as their own. Susana didn't tell anyone about you and, even when she discovered that her daughter had died at the hotel you were staying at, she kept her secret safe."

This was another grey area in my thinking and I could only hope that Álvaro's laptop would be recovered to fill in the gaps. "I don't know how Álvaro discovered the truth. Perhaps it was Maribel herself who told him. She was a brave girl and did not believe in your jaded world view, so I can only think that she came to the journalist offering to help. She gave him photos from the Santa Maria parties in 1992 – yet another reason why Álvaro had to die. After all, Next Phase believe in order and your life was starting to get messy."

Even over the sounds of the sea and the swirling wind, I could hear Gianna breathe out loudly as she processed what I was saying. This was harder for her to listen to than anyone and I wasn't done yet.

"You made a mistake, Marco. You removed every last photo of Susana and, with time, I realised what that meant; you were in those photos with her. It struck me as strange that she wouldn't have appeared in a single shot given that Spanish people never miss their summer fiestas. It's practically a law here. There were photos of the man who raised Maribel – a man who looked nothing like her – but not one of her mother."

That high, fluted tone of Marco's peaked once more. "You can say I killed the journalist, and if I was capable of that it would only make sense for me to pin the blame on Dennison. So fine, you can believe I am a murderer if that's what you want. But I'm not a monster. I would never have killed my own child."

The way he looked at me then, the way that he spoke, was almost enough for me to believe he was a true innocent. For one brief moment, I bought into the myth of Marco Romanelli and I needed to pause before I could guide them on through the final pieces of evidence.

"So who did, Marco?" I gave him the chance to answer. I wanted him to prove me wrong. "Who else stood to gain from this string of deaths other than you? Is your wife responsible, even though she was in the same room as me when Álvaro was shot and has an alibi for the time of Ian's death? Or did your mistress do the deed for you?" Another pause, another silence. "I can just see talk radio's own Cruella de Vil lending a blood-stained hand. Is that what you saw in her in the first place? Did she offer to snuff out your enemies in return for your love?"

I didn't need the gun to create tension. I could see how nervous he was becoming and it was time to deliver the final blow. Rather disappointingly, Delilah had other ideas.

"Gianna!" She clicked her fingers triumphantly as she said it. "Gianna must be behind all this. I know I didn't kill anyone and, though you may not believe it, neither did Marco."

She's skipping ahead. How is that fair? No one butts in when Poirot is laying out his conclusions.

Yeah, but to be honest, I always found that a bit unrealistic.

Delilah's stab in the dark was missing something so I set her straight. "Weren't you listening? Gianna has an alibi for two of the murders. How could she have been with me in the dining room at the same time as the shots were fired?"

A wind kicked up over the cliff and pulled at my long, white summer skirt, but it was the only answer I got. Delilah couldn't come up with an explanation and I bet some part of her was wondering if Marco really had found a way to get rid of Maribel and Álvaro.

"Tell them, Gianna." Without really meaning to, I pointed the gun at her and my gentle prompt was transformed into a deadly ultimatum. Whoops. "It's just like Marco said, there's no way you could have been in two places at once."

She hadn't spoken since I'd revealed her husband's guilty secret. Even for Gianna, who was cold and controlled at the best of times, she was oddly distant.

"That's right," she finally conceded.

I turned back to Delilah. "There were at least ten witnesses to say where she was when we heard the shots. Gianna had come down for lunch and was looking for her family. The only way she could be the killer is if she'd made it seem as if Álvaro was murdered at that moment when, in actual fact, he was already dead. But that would have been rather difficult to achieve." From the look on Marco's face he was struggling to keep up. Perhaps I should have spoken more slowly. "Gianna, tell them how difficult it was to achieve."

I turned back to her and she still wore that faraway look, like she was only half listening to what was being said. Her skirt flapped noisily like a flag on a pole and she was so slight and petite that I thought the wind might carry her off at any moment.

"Go on, Gianna. Tell them how you would've had to set up your kids' Bluetooth speaker and a cheap phone with a gunshot ringtone in an empty room next to Álvaro's. Tell them how you shot him with the silencer on and took your time looking through his possessions before you came downstairs for lunch. And, in case they haven't quite figured it out, you should probably explain how you called the phone connected to the speaker at full volume so that we heard the shots at a time when there was no way you could have been involved."

The wind was really howling now. It was whipping around us like we were in the eye of a tornado. Gianna was swaying as it rippled past her but she remained as silent as the three people she'd murdered.

"Marco never knew about Maribel because he doesn't involve himself with the business you created. He just likes getting up on stage and being adored. When his daughter reached out to meet him, it was you she spoke to. But you couldn't have your husband's dirty little secret destroying your hard work."

Normally people scoff and get angry when I accuse them of murder but not Gianna.

"Did you set out to kill her or did you think you could just pay her off the way you paid Heike to be your alibi this morning? Perhaps Maribel wasn't satisfied with money. She wanted to meet her real father so, when she turned you down, you pulled the gun. You couldn't bring yourself to shoot her so you smashed the handle into her skull then buried her in the sand to watch her die. Have you cleaned it with bleach or will the police find traces of her blood on the weapon which was in your possession at the time Maribel was murdered? That in itself is enough to send you to prison."

Marco had the major advantage from the beginning of knowing he and Delilah weren't the killers. If he'd had more than stuffing in his head, he would have worked this out long before I did. Clearly, Gianna was the brains behind his whole organisation.

He took a step towards his wife before speaking. "This isn't true, Giovanna. Please tell me it can't be true."

She replied in Italian and the words hit her husband like a spray of bullets.

"What about Ian?" I wouldn't let her off so easily. She deserved to face up to the agony she'd caused. "You killed him to cover your trail and now two kids don't have a father. Imagine I shot Marco right here and now, think about how your daughters would feel. Think how they'll feel when they find out what you did."

Her eyes locked onto mine. "That ridiculous man heard the shots from Álvaro's bedroom and saw me leave. He was trying to blackmail me so I had to deal with him too." It was hard to believe how little emotion she showed as she confessed these things. "The saddest part about it was that all he wanted was a meeting with Marco for his pathetic car company. But I couldn't risk any loose ends so I arranged the meeting here this morning and, when I pulled the gun, he slipped over the edge without me having to do anything. It was perfect."

Delilah clucked like a surprised hen, Marco was still struggling with this new reality and a thought came to my head.

I trained my gun on Gianna once more. "Why are you telling us this?"

She sighed like she was glad it was over. "You're very clever, Izzy Palmer. I'm so happy I got to see you at work. But my father was in the army and, unlike my husband, I can tell the difference between a real gun and a toy."

That was when she ran for the edge. The pistol in my hand was suddenly useless. I screamed for Marco to grab her but he was too slow. She slipped right past him and the wind pushed her towards the cliff like a bad spirit. I launched myself forward to stop her. I willed myself on. My gangly legs and lolloping arms did what they were told to for once and I got to the edge just as she went over.

How I caught her is beyond my comprehension. She must have thought she'd made it. Her mind had embraced death but I snatched her legs up in an awkward bear hug and held onto her by the feet. The rest of her body dangled down the cliff face as Marco arrived to help pull her up.

"Stuff me, Izzy!" That awful woman Delilah was finally impressed by something. "You were like Keanu Reeves in the Matrix."

Chapter Thirty

My previous murder enquiries had all ended on a sombre note, but this one was oddly celebratory. The Spanish police officers wanted to shake my hand. Kabir and lovely Jaime both gave me hugs. Sharon was still in tears, but managed to find her voice to thank me for clearing her husband, Danny was all smiles and Ramesh looked happy as he had slept through the whole thing.

The only person who was less than ecstatic was my dear old mum. "What were you doing with that gun, you silly girl?"

With a villainous glare, Gianna had been carted off to the local station and we were sitting on the terrace with lemonades all round.

"Well, there was always the risk she would jump over the cliff to escape imprisonment so I thought I'd get her away from danger."

Mum was quick with her answer. "Clearly not far enough away. And why didn't you just wait for them to come in off the cliffs instead of charging over there with a fake gun?"

"Well... urmmm... that's a good point actually. I didn't think about that." Just because I'm good at detective work, it doesn't mean I have any common sense. "I suppose I got caught up in the moment. And besides, I needed Delilah to go with me and there was no way she'd have agreed to a quiet stroll otherwise."

People normally had a bunch of questions when I solved a murder. I must have got better at summing up the case as they were oddly content with my explanation. It was a bit disappointing to be honest. I was hoping to show off just a little.

Inevitably, it was my faithful friend Danny who came to the rescue. "But it could still have been Marco and Delilah working together. What told you it was really Gianna?"

Hurray! A chance to really milk it.

I sipped my sweet and delicious lemonade and made them wait. "It took me a while to realise that it wasn't just Marco who benefitted from the killings, it was Next Phase. Gianna was the one who cared about the movement the most. It'll all come out in the trial but I'm certain that Marco was supposed to be with his daughters on the tennis court when Álvaro was killed. She wouldn't have done it then if she thought her husband could be blamed. Unluckily for her, he was off with Delilah instead of attending to his parental duties."

"Interesting!" Kabir intoned and the others looked suitably impressed so I continued.

"Gianna's trick with the gunshots that we all heard was almost too clever. It provided her with an alibi but, when I saw the gun again and remembered it had a silencer, it didn't make sense that the killer had removed it to kill Álvaro. I knew that Marco wouldn't have gone to such lengths for something that couldn't provide him with an alibi and that was when I finally accepted he wasn't to blame."

"That's brilliant, Izzy." Jaime beamed across the table at me. Danny clearly wasn't happy to have him there and had been sitting in poses that best showed off his muscly arms since we sat down together. "Bielza must be jealous."

I wasn't so confident. "I still feel bad for the Dennisons. If I hadn't got so hung up on Marco being the killer, I might have been able to stop Gianna before Ian was killed. If I'd realised earlier that the Spaniards were the likely thieves it might have crossed my mind that the gun was never really stolen."

"They got away before we could arrest them," Jaime explained. "But they won't be able to run that scam now they've been found out."

I wasn't sure how I felt about this. I don't approve of criminals, but they were just so cute, I didn't want to see them go to jail. "Their scam, and the fact Delilah was all over Ramesh whenever Marco was around, were two obvious things I should have picked up on. I thought that Marco's reaction to the news of Maribel's death was a sign that he was involved, but he was just worried about the affair coming out. I'm so angry at myself for being short-sighted."

Agente Caliente frowned a little. "You can't think like this. You have to remember the good you've done. Think of Maribel's family. It might be a small thing but they won't have to question themselves anymore about why she died." I have to admit his odd phrasing and Castilian accent were still pretty sexy.

"Yeah, Izzy," Danny added, reaching his hand across the table to stroke my arm. "Think how happy you've made everybody." He smiled his lovely smile then shot Jaime a hostile look.

"A word please, Miss Palmer." I hadn't heard Inspector Bielza approaching and she did not sound happy. "Torres, your break's over. Back to work."

Jaime jumped off and ran into the hotel and I rose to accompany the inspector to wherever she wanted to take me.

"Obviously I'm happy that the case is adequately closed," she told me as she led us through the restaurant and into the lift. "Obviously I wouldn't say this in front of my officers, but I was wrong and you were…" she paused to find the right words. "…less wrong."

"Urmmm… Thank you, Inspector."

"Quiet now, I haven't finished." She poked the button for the third floor and the antique lift jerked into life. "The right person is in custody and you should be proud of yourself for that. There's no doubt about it. I jumped to conclusions thinking that Ian Dennison was the killer and, I admit, I was happy to believe the case was closed when it certainly wasn't."

When we arrived at my floor, she motioned for me to open my suite and then confidently walked inside and over to the balcony as if she'd been there a hundred times before. Once we were both outside again, she continued.

"You might think that I was protecting Marco Romanelli but that's not quite true." She paused to look along the coast towards the city and I could tell how difficult it was for her to say this. "He had confided his secret to me and, I might not like the man, but I wasn't going to let unnecessary gossip come out of my station."

"You don't like him?" I'd had a number of surprises since she started her explanation but this was the biggest. "Then why go to his conference? Why didn't you even consider that he was involved?"

She was the one who looked shocked now. "He had a solid alibi. There were photos on Delilah's phone of the two of them together in the marina at the time of Maribel's death. And I went to the conference because I wanted to know what we were dealing with."

She fell quiet and gazed across the cloudy horizon. I thought I'd have to prod her along but she soon started up again. "Santander was the last stand of the northern Republican army in the Spanish civil war. My grandfather was captured and immediately executed by the fascists." She breathed in deep like this fact still stung to think about.

"Terrible things happen on both sides in any war but this was the story I grew up with. It left me with a great fear that history could repeat itself, that my country could be ripped apart once more. And so, whenever a new movement like Next Phase appears, I feel I owe it to my grandfather to find out what they want. A smooth-tongued, handsome leader like Marco Romanelli is even more frightening to me than some military thug."

The English civil war happened in the seventeenth century so it was impossible for me to imagine how such an event had shaped her country. Whatever hangover had been felt from our revolution had dissipated over three and a half centuries of British history.

Her usual, serious tone was even graver than before. "I hope that, with Gianna's arrest, their organisation will die, but that might be wishful thinking."

"If wishes were horses, beggars would ride," I replied and, when she clearly didn't understand what I was talking about, I explained. "It's an English proverb. It means that wishing doesn't generally do us much good."

"I see. Well we have a similar expression in Spanish, but my family gave up wishing long ago."

Inspector Bielza was not the kind of person I could imagine going out drinking with on a Friday night. Everything she did was coated with weight and seriousness. It felt bad to end our relationship on discussions of death, war and massacres so I changed the topic.

"Why did you choose to bring me up here?"

"I'd heard the view was pretty." She finally smiled and it made me feel a bit lighter. "And it is… it really is."

We stood there for a while longer to make the most of it. I could hear my mother entertaining everyone on the terrace beneath us. Ramesh was fully awake and was thrilled by every fake celebrity anecdote she dished up, even though he knew they weren't true.

The vista before us stretched all the way to the Basque Country in the east and Asturias in the west. The sea was fierce and broke in high, white peaks as it entered the cove. Each wave seemed to pause in the air before the sound crashed over to us. Far out at sea there was a beam of sunlight penetrating the cloud – like a tiny spotlight shining on no one – and the wind sang a howling song.

Chapter Thirty-One

We stayed one more day to enjoy the beach and have the hotel to ourselves. Delilah was the only guest who was scheduled to still be there but she went off with Marco when the police were done with them. He had a lot of explaining to do to his kids and I can't say he looked overjoyed to be leaving with the woman who had previously been his secret lover. He surprised me by waving across the foyer when they finally departed. I couldn't decide whether it was a sign of thanks, or just his ingrained charm that was hard to let go of.

That day was rather sad and beautiful. We couldn't be happy after everything that had gone on and Kabir occasionally looked heartbroken that his retirement project was tainted with death.

Still, it was good to spend the time together without odious guests around. Mum and my old next door neighbour, my best friend and his uncle; a weirdo family unit with three luxury suites, two swimming pools, a tennis court and our own private beach.

Kabir invited the remaining police officers to lunch and we all sat down together as Cook knocked up a paella in a huge black pan on a stove on the terrace.

I love paella!

I know you do.

My Jaime obsession had waned a little. I was getting used to being around gorgeous men by now and had found two who were just perfect for me. What did I need a third for?

I've got some ideas!

SHHHH!

In the afternoon, Ramesh and I took the cleaning trolleys outside and raced Mum and Danny across the patio. We lost every time. After that we played a highly unprofessional game of doubles on the tennis court and I discovered that Ramesh had no concept of the rules.

"You know I'm allergic to sport, Izzy," he tried as a defence. "It's like TV for stupid people."

Dinner was a more intimate affair. Cook had gone home early and so it was just the five of us in the dining room and Kabir told us all about his plans for the place. "I hope you come back in the spring when we re-open, Izzy. You did a wonderful job making up the rooms."

Somehow, this compliment made me blush more than anything he'd said about my detective skills.

"And, Ramu... Well, I'm sorry to say, but I don't think you're cut out for cleaning."

"Thanks very much, Uncle," he sincerely replied. "I'll take the head barman job instead."

After dinner, it didn't take much persuading to get Mum up on the stage for another rendition of the song that Ramesh had written for her. In fact he joined in for the chorus. His delivery of the line "I'm one hell of a woman," was almost as convincing as Mum's. He was finally allowed to sleep in a suite of his own that night, and I made sure that Danny understood his place was on one of the sofas.

Leaving The Cova Negra meant facing up to another sad reality. David's parents had been texting me updates since I'd called them and they predicted it would only be a few days before the verdict was announced. Now that my investigation was over, there was little else to think about and my troubles once more invaded my mind.

I was sad to be leaving our beautiful home for the week, but London was calling to me and I knew it was time to go back.

"Mother, why didn't you buy return flights like a normal person?" I asked as the four of us attempted to squeeze into Ramesh's car the next morning.

"They were far too expensive, darling. And Ramesh said that it wouldn't be a problem."

Our driver grinned guiltily over the roof of the car. "Sorry, Iz! I thought you wouldn't mind."

After Danny and I had repacked the car three times, ditched several piles from Ramesh's magazine collection and Mum's gigantic seashell and pebble haul, we just about squeezed inside.

"It was so great having you all here," Kabir told us through the window. "And thank you again, Izzy. I don't know what I'd have done if you hadn't solved the case."

Ramesh was all smiles. "No, Uncle. Thank *you*."

"Ah, before you go, Ramu. I have something for you." The kindly hotelier took a plain white envelope from his pocket.

"Oh, Uncle. You shouldn't have." I thought my friend was going to get teary as he opened it.

"It's the minibar bill."

All trace of joy had left Ramesh's face and he was staring in horror at the sheet of paper. "But, Uncle, this is more than the cost of the rooms."

"You should have been more careful." The hotelier's voice was sober and stern. "Those things are very expensive. I would let you off, but I think it's better that you learn your lesson so that it doesn't happen again."

Shocked into silence, Ramesh wound up his window and we rolled off down the drive.

Kabir quickly dashed after us and banged on the roof. He opened the driver's door and pulled the envelope from the dashboard. "I got you there, my boy!" He tore the bill up and threw the pieces into the air so they rained down like confetti. "Never forget that 'An Uncle and nephew reunion…"

"…is only…'" Ramesh didn't manage to get the line of the song out as he had burst into tears of joy and jumped from the car to give Kabir one last hug.

When we left for the second time, Kiki and Elton both settled on Danny's lap, where they slept for most of the long journey home. Even Mum joining in with an extended version of "Bonjour Croissant Fromage" didn't wake them up.

And when we got back to Britain, the sky looked greyer than I could ever remember. Frost-covered England appeared to have skipped autumn and gone straight to winter and the Spanish sunshine already felt like an impossible dream.

Two days later, I was back in a black skirt and white blouse, waiting outside the Old Bailey for my support crew. Along with David's parents, aunt and niece, I'd asked Dean to go with me as he'd got alarmingly good at moral support over the last couple of months. It was no joyful reunion. David's relatives were bleak and forlorn. The trial had not gone well and they could only foresee one outcome.

Inside court that day, my only relief was that I would not have to take the stand again myself. David was brought out by the clerk and the judge asked the jury whether they'd reached a verdict. I'll spare you all the formalities, the slow ratcheting up of tension like they do on TV talent shows before they announce the winner. In fact, I'll cut straight to…

213

"Guilty."

My boyfriend looked over at me and my whole body exploded with sorrow. I'd never seen a person look so sad in all my life. For the sake of my sanity, I tried to remember that he really had killed somebody and it only made sense that the jury considered him a murderer, but it didn't make me feel any better. The judge delivered his final comment and I didn't hear one word of it.

As they led him away, his eyes remained on mine until the very last second. His mum and dad cried and Auntie Val tried to cheer us all up but there was nothing that the friendly old woman could say to make it better. The nicest man I'd ever met was on his way to serve a lengthy sentence and I couldn't help thinking that it wasn't a question of right or wrong but which of the two lawyers had schmoozed the jury most successfully.

On the day he received his sentence, David asked that not even his family were in attendance. He rang me that afternoon from prison and I knew from the first word that it wasn't good news.

"Hi Izzy." His voice was entirely emotionless. He was a poorly programmed robot. "I wanted you to hear it from me." That was as far as he got before I started crying. "Hey, it's not so bad. Ten years, isn't a lifetime at least."

His words made the tears come faster. "Ten whole years of your life? How is that fair, David? How is that right after everything Bob did?"

I don't know if it was for his sake or mine, but he managed to put on a cheerful voice. "Oh, come on now. We can't have murderers walking free across our fair nation. It's my own fault for killing the man." He made it sound like it was a silly mistake, like losing his keys or breaking the screen on his phone. "I think it's probably for the best."

My nose was feeling left out so it started to run. "How can it be for the best?" Even my voice sounded snotty and wet. "The lesson of every revenge thriller, and at least one Christie novel is that, by ridding the world of rapists and murderers, people like you are acting for the greater good. I can't just sit around waiting for you for a decade."

There was a momentary hush, like the phone signal had died and when he spoke again he was calm and confident. "That's right, my love."

Some part of me must have already understood his meaning because I suddenly got louder, angrier and more determined. "That's not what

I meant. I'll wait for you, you know I will."

I closed my eyes and pictured him standing there on the phone just like in any prison movie. Grim-faced crims in tracksuits walked past behind him and he sheltered within the cabin of the telephone to speak to me. "No you won't, Izzy. I wouldn't do that to you."

"David…" The tears burst out of me again. I was a toddler having a full-on tantrum by this point. "You don't mean that. You don't. I love you and I know you love me."

He had to be crying, but he didn't let it show. "Of course I do and I always will. Which is why I'm doing this." The slower and more compassionately he spoke, the more his accent emerged. I don't think I'd ever loved anyone as much as I did in that moment. My true and unwavering adoration was a firework that was about to explode.

"Please, David. Please don't do this." I doubt he understood a word I was saying by this point.

He cleared his throat and was serious and controlled once more. "This is for your own good, Izzy. You won't see me again. If you try to visit, I'll turn down the request. It might sound cruel, but in the long term, it's the right thing to do."

"It's not fair. Just take your time to think about it."

"I've been thinking for months. This is the way it has to be."

"No, David." My phone was soaking wet by now, my hands shaking. "You're wrong. It doesn't have to be like this."

Ten seconds passed – one for every year of his sentence – before he spoke again. "I'm sorry, my angel. I'm sorry for everything. I hope you can forgive me."

The phone went dead and I let out a scream they must have heard up in London. I fell on my bedroom floor and lay there as my body jerked with every sob and tear. It would be days before I felt human again, a week before I re-engaged with the world and a month before I was sure what I wanted to do next.

Chapter Thirty-Two

Dean was the one who found me the office. I rented it from a friend of his who apparently didn't like money as he charged me about one fifth of normal London prices. I couldn't have imagined a better location. Right on Leicester Square, overlooking the cinemas that I'd visited so often as an artsy teenager with my only mate Simon.

Whenever there was a film premiere, I could sit at my new desk and look out the window to see Tom Cruise or Jennifer Lawrence or whoever was entertaining the crowds of tourists and artsy teenagers. The Empire Cinema was shining in all its glitzy glamour and, in the centre of the square, a funfair was being set up for the winter, covered in colourful lights.

Everyone was there for the big unveiling. Danny was standing beside me behind the desk, smiling enthusiastically as ever. He'd just got back from a trip to Eritrea and was acting like we hadn't seen one another in decades. Ramesh was pouring champagne (well, Cava, but it's the same thing, right?) as if to show off what a capable barman he was.

"What are we waiting for, Izzy?" Mum asked as I still hadn't made the announcement fifteen minutes after everyone had arrived. She was annoyed because Greg already knew what I was going to say, but had been sworn to secrecy.

She'd brought her usual crew with her of course. Fernando and his wife had come along with the Dominski clan, Brian from the supermarket, several of our neighbours, a couple of Dean's tech nerds and two of my fathers.

"Come on, Izzy," Dad cheered me on. "We're awfully excited."

I stood by the window where one of Greg's easels was positioned with a red velvet blanket over it that Mum had bought especially for the occasion.

"Fine, fine!" I tried to sound reluctant but it was a pretty poor performance. "So, most of you know what we're doing here. Thanks to Dean ..." I pointed over and he did a far too theatrical bow.

"It was nothing, everybody. It was nothing." Every time I saw him, his transformation shocked me. He straightened back up and put his arm round his pretty red-haired girlfriend. With a little help from my dad, they'd met at a bar a few weeks earlier and seemed to be made for one another.

Anyway, back to me. "Yes, thanks to my kind friend, we are standing in my new office. Before I unveil the name and logo that Greg and I have been working on, I wanted to say a few words."

Apparently Dean wasn't the only one who'd grown more comfortable in front of an audience. "It's been a very strange year. I've had my highs and lows but something wonderful has happened. I've gone from being a murder mystery fan to a full-time detective and that's thanks to all of you here. Every single person in this room has helped investigate one of my cases and I wouldn't be here today without you."

"Get on with it, Izzy!" Mum was frantic with curiosity. I'm pretty sure she thought that I'd chosen her name after all.

"Oh, alright then. I'd like to ask my wonderful stepdad Greg to come forward to reveal his design for the logo of my brand new detective agency."

There was some applause and, as modestly as he does everything, he came up to whisk the veil away. "Ladies and gentlemen…" Looking over at me, he waited for a few seconds to get the crowd worked up. "I give you… 'The Private I Detective Agency'."

Beneath the velvet covering was a large board with the name of my new business. For Mum's sake, there were bullet holes in place of dots and the whole thing was in the shape of an eye. Initial reactions seemed positive. My assembled friends, loved ones and the random people my mum had picked up along the way all cheered.

"Oh, Izzy," she began then had to stop as she was choking up with emotion. "Oh, Izzy. It's wonderful, I'm so proud of you."

It's not often I see my mother lost for words, but this was such an occasion. Her voice faded out and she began to make some low squeaking noises of appreciation. Ramesh soon joined in with this quiet gushing and the two ended up with their arms around one another, reminiscing over stories from my past.

I decided to leave them to it and mingle. Mingling at a party is high on my list of least favourite things, but it's not quite so bad when I know everyone there. I'd got halfway around the small, sparsely furnished room when Danny saw his opportunity and leapt towards me.

"Izzy, can I have a word?"

It had been more than six months since he'd declared his love for me and, considering just how much he had in common with a springer spaniel, he'd been waiting surprisingly patiently for the follow-up conversation.

As subtly as possible, I slipped out of the main office into the even more compact reception area. Once we were there, our disposable plastic champagne flutes in hand-

Despicable! Wasting the planet's resources just to save you a bit of washing up. You should be ashamed of yourself.

Oh, do shut up! This isn't the moment.

Once we were out there alone, neither of us quite knew what to say.

Tell me something. Have you ever been in one of those situations where you've been in love with a man your whole life only to finally give up on him after you find the kindest, most affectionate boyfriend imaginable, the news of which forces your childhood sweetheart to admit he's in love with you too, except, by that point you've already pinned your heart to the new guy, who then turns out to be a murderer?

And if you have, did that second bloke get sent to prison for his really quite understandable crime and tell you that you shouldn't wait for him, despite the fact you were crazy about one another? And if you're still with me on this and the original crush wouldn't give up on you, I'd really like to know, how long did you decide was an appropriate amount of time to wait before starting in on the new relationship?

"So, here we are," Danny tried and I think we both realised how cheesy it sounded.

"Here we are," I repeated in the hope it would smooth everything over. It didn't. It really didn't.

Kiss him, Izzy! Put your sexy lips on his sexy lips and smoosh them about.

As tempting as that sounded, I contained myself and waited for him to say something else.

"Maybe it's too soon," he finally came out with.

"Yeah, probably."

There was a sudden burst of laughter from inside The Private I Detective Agency's London headquarters. I heard shouts of "bath", "pigeon" and "totally naked" and it was enough to reveal that Mum was telling stories about me from when I was little. The joy everyone was having in the next room only served to make our conversation more awkward.

"I mean…" I'd never seen Danny look so sweaty, though it was only about seven degrees outside. "David and you only just broke up and, after everything you've been through this year, it probably isn't the time to be starting anything new." I was pretty sure that the voice in his own head would have been furious with him right then.

"Totally. I mean…" It was my turn to get all nervous. "I mean, the timing really isn't great and you're going to be travelling again soon, so maybe…"

"Yeah." He let out a relieved sigh. "Maybe it's best if we just leave it for now and think about trying again next year sometime. I'm going to be busy and you're just about to start this place up so that's probably for the best."

I nodded my head in a big over-the-top manner like I was talking to a small child or perhaps a Labrador. "Exactly. We should schedule it for next year sometime, that's definitely the best option."

With the decision made, we pretended to be happy about it and turned to head back into the party without another word. The space was so poky that I ended up smacking the door straight into him and we had to do this awkward shuffle around one another to be able to open it again by which time I'd come to my senses.

"Wait," I said and closed the door again. "No. That's not what I want."

Go on, Izzy. Smoosh him!

"What I want is to spend time with one of my favourite people. What I want is to take things slowly and see where it might lead us, because, I have to be honest, I think about David just about every minute of the day, but I think about you too."

The sad puppy expression had disappeared from Danny's face to be replaced by his happy puppy one. "I understand that, Izzy, I honestly do."

I filtered out the laughter and the clinking plastic glasses, I just about managed to ignore my mother's loud voice saying "Izzy called it her 'teeny weeny'!" I tried my absolute hardest not to think of my ex-boyfriend for a minute and focus on the lovely man standing in front of me.

"I want to go on a completely normal, no expectations whatsoever day out with you, Danny. Would that be okay?"

His smile grew three sizes bigger and I'm pretty sure he'd have leaned in to smoosh me right then if it hadn't been for the outside door opening and a man who looked like a Victorian convict walking in.

"Sorry," he said in a thick east-end accent. "I'm looking for Izzy Palmer."

I cleared my throat to sound a bit professional. When that didn't work I tried one more time then gave up. "I'm Izzy Palmer, of The Private I Detective Agency. How can I help you?"

"Right…" he seemed quite uncertain on the issue. "Yeah… I read about you online. My name's Stanton. A friend of mine went missing and I reckon you might be able to help."

I tried to wipe the smile off my face, it was completely unprofessional and I deeply regretted it but… Woooooooooooooo! My first real client!

I put my most serious face on and opened the door. "Step into my office, Mr Stanton. Would you like a glass of champagne?"

Get your **Free** Izzy Palmer Novellas...

If you'd like to hear about forthcoming releases and download my free novellas, sign up to the Izzy Palmer readers' club via my website. I'll never spam you or inundate you with stuff you're not interested in, but I'd love to keep in contact. There will be one free novella for every novel I release, so sign up at...

www.benedictbrown.net

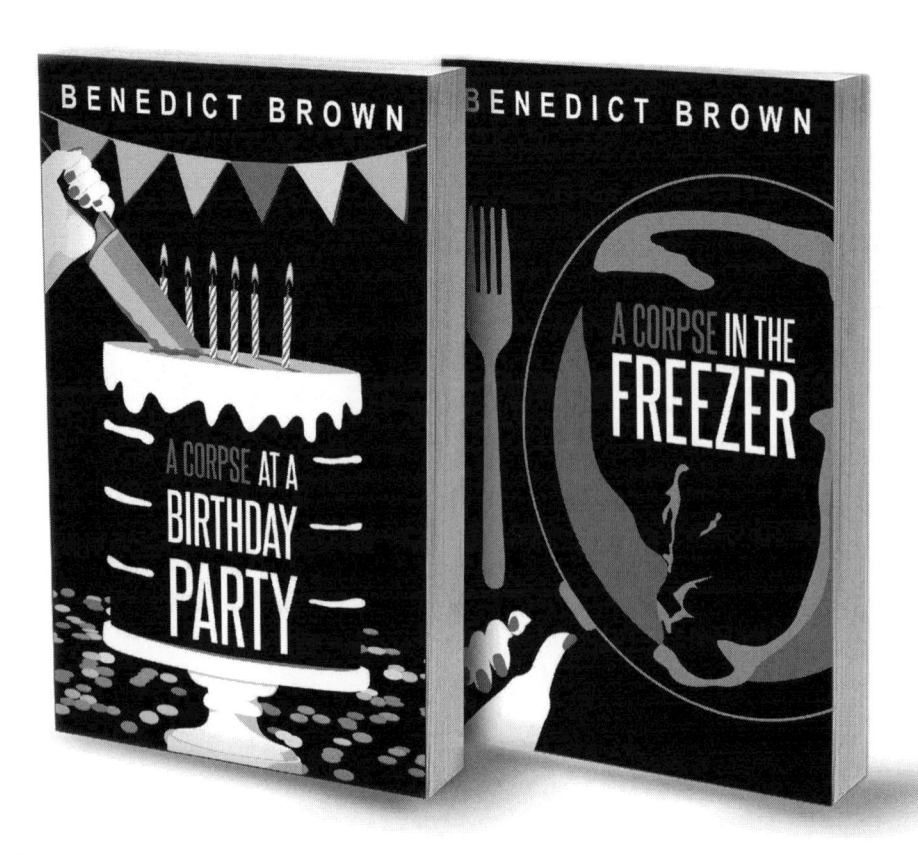

Get the next **Izzy Palmer Mystery** from September 20th at **amazon**

BENEDICT BROWN

A CORPSE IN LONDON

One dead body, nine millon suspects.

About This Book

Some of my favourite mysteries are the ones that take me away to exciting foreign climes. My family tended to go for rainy walking holidays in Wales and the north of England when I was a kid, so even Christie's tales set on the south coast seemed sunny and exotic to me. Izzy references a couple of the more famous titles in this book and, in **"A Corpse on the Beach",** I have tried to create an escapist holiday mystery of my own. It was largely written during the eight-week lockdown in which I barely left my house, and I think that escape is something we all need right now.

I've been living in Spain for fourteen years and it was inevitable that Izzy would make the trip to my adopted home in one of her adventures. This book is set on the coast a couple of hours north of us. Cantabria is a beautiful region. It's green and hilly and has a stunning, sandy coastline which reminds me of South Wales, but with slightly warmer summers.

The Cova Negra hotel is fictional but based on the huge, Balneario spa hotels which are common in the north and sprung up to cater for rich travellers during the nineteenth century. They are grand, mansion-like buildings which are just perfect if you're looking to bump someone off in a luxurious setting. One tip I have for potential murderers, try not to plan your crime with Izzy around, you'll only get caught.

Izzy's next adventure will be called **"A Corpse in London".** After her holiday in the sun, Izzy returns home for the winter but is soon caught up in another investigation when a famous actor drops dead in Piccadilly Circus and his family enlist her help to find the killer. I'm afraid you'll have to wait until September to read it but there'll be one more book in time for Christmas so I don't think I'm too much of a slacker.

Make sure you sign up to the **readers' club** on my website where you'll be able to access the free novellas and stay up to date with new releases.

Acknowledgements

My favourite part of the back bit of the book, here are my sorrys... Sorry to Austrians Germans and especially my real-life friends Lio and Heike – you are not the people pretending to be you. Sorry to Spanish people for attempting to reflect the way you speak English. In my defence, I've taught my language in your country for many years and there are certain mistakes I have heard a million times. For anyone feeling insecure about their English, just remember that the vast majority of British people can't construct a sentence in any other language and you should be proud of your ability – especially if you've just read this whole book!

Oh, and sorry to Keanu Reeves; Izzy and I actually really like you. Parenthood, Bill & Ted, Point Break and Speed are, if anything, underrated movies and you were great in them and many others (but perhaps steer clear of any more Shakespeare).

Thank you as always to my wife and daughter for being inspirationally wonderful and accepting of me as I locked myself in the office and wrote this, to my family for reading my books and my crack team of experts – the Hoggs and the Donovans (**fiction**), Paul Bickley (**policing**), Karen and Jonathan Baugh (**marketing**) and Mar Pérez (**dead people**) for knowing lots of stuff when I don't. Thanks to all the fellow writers who have helped with this one too, especially Pete and Rose.

I will never stop being grateful to my friend Lucy Middlemass. You're still with me through everything I write. And if there is any bright side, Lucy, at least you don't have to keep reading my silly stories.

And finally, thank you so much to all of you who keep reading. In the last six months, I've had such a warm response to the books and I've really started to believe I can transform this passion that I have worked at for twenty years into a career that can sustain my family. If you loved the story and have the time, please write a review on Amazon. Most books get one review per thousand readers so I would be infinitely appreciative if you could help me out.

About Me

Writing has always been my passion. It was my favourite half-an-hour a week at primary school, and I started on my first, truly abysmal book as a teenager. So it wasn't a difficult decision to study literature at university which led to a masters in Creative Writing.

I'm a Welsh-Irish-Englishman originally from **South London** but now living with my French/Spanish wife and presumably quite confused infant daughter in **Burgos**, a beautiful medieval city in the north of Spain. I write overlooking the Castilian countryside, trying not to be distracted by the vultures, hawks and red kites that fly past my window each day.

I previously spent years focussing on kids' books and wrote everything from fairy tales to environmental dystopian fantasies right through to issue-based teen fiction. My book The Princess and The Peach was long-listed for the Chicken House prize in The Times and an American producer even talked about adapting it into a film. I'll be slowly publishing those books over the next year on Amazon.

"A Corpse on the Beach" is the third Izzy Palmer novel in what I'm confident will be a long series. If you feel like telling me what you think about Izzy, my writing or the world at large, I'd love to hear from you, so feel free to get in touch via...

www.benedictbrown.net

List of Spanish References

Having compiled this list, I now realise that most of these things are food.

FOOD

Ensaimadas are explained in the text, but let me reiterate how tasty they are. They're fluffy and sweet and delicious. Possibly the best cake in Spain (as long as we're counting Torrijas as a desert).

Jamón – Iberian ham is surely Spain's greatest gift to the world (sorry, flamenco, Paella and Pablo Picasso). It's worth flying there as soon as you can just to taste.

Pincho (de tortilla) A pincho is generally a bit of bread with something delicious on it that is sold in bars in the north of Spain. A typical night out for people in my town will be going from bar to bar eating and drinking at an incredibly slow pace that normally leaves me both hungry and sober. I don't know where they get the patience from. A pincho literally refers to the toothpick or skewer that holds it together, it can have anything on it but is particularly good with jamon, tortilla (potato omelette), seafood or even…

Croquetas – I will probably never leave Spain as I have an addiction to these small fried crispy tubes of breadcrumb-coated béchamel. All the best ones I've eaten were made by someone's grandmother but that doesn't stop me from ordering them in every tapas bar I go to.

Pimientos de padron – Small, green fried peppers about one in ten of which is surprisingly spicy.

Chorizo – chorizo (come on, Ramesh, that one was obvious.)

Crema Catalana – very similar to crème brulée. Often comes with cinnamon or a Marie biscuit on top.

Verdejo – a variety of delicious white wine common in the Rueda region not far from where I live.

Beicon con huevos – bacon and eggs

Perdona, Señora. Sabes hacer Lemon Meringue Pie? – Excuse me, madam, do you know how to make lemon meringe pie?

Menú del día – menu of the day. A typically three-course menu available in Spanish restaurants which is affordable and almost invariably delicious.

OTHER THINGS

Buenos días, Buenos días, queso… croissant (to the tune of Bonnie Tyler's "Total Eclipse of the Heart") – Good morning, good morning, cheese… croissant.

Agente – Officer – The common term for a normal police officer in Spain.

Hay una chica muerte en la playa – There's a dead girl on the beach.

Perdona, donde está la catedral? – Excuse me, where's the cathedral?

Mi gato es blanco – My cat is white.

Policia Nacional – National Police – there are different kinds of police in Spain but as my fictitious hotel is located near a big town, they would deal with it instead of local or Guardia Civil.

Belén Esteban – I don't feel you have to know who she is as Izzy certainly doesn't. I included her as a joke for any of my Spanish friends who end up reading the book. She's a really terrible TV personality on an incredibly trashy reality show called "Save Me" which aims to turn the suffering and mental breakdowns of over-exposed celebrities into entertainment. I'm not a fan.

Fascistas - fascists

El agente del amor – the agent of love (not a typical saying, as far as I know!)

El agente del amor – the agent of love (not a typical saying, as far as I know!)

Prostituta – I'll leave you to work that one out.

Escoba – A typical card game played by old people in bars every afternoon across Spain.